Paris Before the Deluge

BY THE SAME AUTHOR

The Year 5865

Paris Before the Deluge

by
Hippolyte Mettais

translated, annotated and introduced by
Brian Stableford

A Black Coat Press Book

Edited by Peter Gabbani

English adaptation and introduction Copyright © 2014 by Brian Stableford.
Cover illustration Copyright © 2014 Jean-Félix Lyon.

Visit our website at www.blackcoatpress.com

Introduction

Paris avant le Déluge, here translated as *Paris before the Deluge*, was initially published under the signature "Dr. H. Mettais" in 1866 by the Librairie Centrale. It was the author's fourth publication from the publisher in question, directly following *L'An 5865, ou Paris dans quatre mille ans* (1865; tr. as *The Year 5865*),[1] to which it is a companion-piece. Whereas its predecessor had offered a broad description of the world four thousand years in the future, paying particular attention to the fate of the city of Paris—by then in ruins and the subject of strange legends to which the civilized inhabitants of the new world lend little credence— *Paris avant le Déluge* offers an image of the world more than four thousand years in the past, paying particular attention to a city once located where modern Paris stands, but of which nothing survives, following its catastrophic destruction, save for a few fragments of legend whose significance is no longer understood. The two speculative novels also form a trilogy of sorts with the naturalistic quasi-autobiographical novel *Souvenirs d'un Médecin de Paris* [memoirs of a Parisian physician] (1863), which deals with the Paris of the present day.

Although *Paris avant le Déluge* closes the trilogy in question in terms of the order of publication, at least

---

[1] The introduction to the Black Coat Press edition of *The Year 5865* (ISBN 9781612271002) contains a summary of what is currently known about Mettais' life and career, which there is no need to repeat in full here.

5

some of its text might have existed prior to its finalization with that intent. There had been an earlier phase to Mettais' literary career in the early 1840s, when he published two melodramas of his own and a third in collaboration with a once-popular writer of works of that sort, Georges Touchard-Lafosse. A long gap of more than twenty years separated that set of three from the later set, although Mettais did published one non-fiction work—a political pamphlet—in the interim. The latter group is far more ambitious in literary and philosophical terms, and by that time, Mettais probably regarded his earlier ventures as juvenilia. The formulae of the conventional melodrama in which they dabbled are, however, not entirely absent either from *L'An 5865* or, more particularly, *Paris avant le Déluge*.

The third and longest of the three parts into which the narrative of *Paris avant le Déluge* is divided deliberately recasts the substance of conventional early-19th century French melodrama within the pseudohistorical framework established in the first two parts. It reads as if it might be an adaptation of an earlier manuscript telling a story set in the familiar city of Paris before and during the 1789 Revolution, which was belatedly adapted to its new framework in order to transform it into something markedly different. Whether or not that is the case, the adaptation does indeed achieve such a transformation, offering an exceedingly odd admixture of the exotic and the familiar—in terms of its plot, the very familiar, given that it toys with one of the standard clichés of contemporary melodrama.

The cliché in question was dubbed by Paul Féval in *Les Habits Noirs* (1863; tr. as *The Parisian Jungle*)[2],

---

[2] Black Coat Press, ISBN 9781934543030.

who was perfectly willing to employ it even while treating it sarcastically, as the "cardboard baby," because dramatic versions of it tended to introduce the character in Act One as a babe in arms—usually played, therefore, by a doll—mislaid by a mother, sometimes stolen, but often simply lost or given away by virtue of social inconveniences surrounding the birth. The character then reappears in Act Two as a young adult whose birth is surrounded by a mystery, which is ultimately to be solved in the denouement by courtesy of what Féval calls "his mother's cross": some trinket lost along with the baby whose eventual recognition, usually by the mother, leads to the revelation of the character's true identity, on which some kind of inheritance usually depends.

Sanctified by the doyen of all Romantic writers, Victor Hugo, who employed it with regard to Esmeralda in *Notre-Dame de Paris* (1831; often known in translation as *The Hunchback of Notre Dame*), the melodramatic potential of the formula was mined so assiduously by the *feuilletonistes* who began to flourish in the 1840s that by the 1860s, when Féval satirized it while still making the most of it, it had become rather difficult to refresh or recomplicate. Versions involving two "cardboard babies" had become commonplace, and Mettais' move in increasing the number to three might have smacked of desperation had the story told in the third part of *Paris avant le Déluge* been presented as an account of tribulations suffered in the year 1789 rather than the third millennium B.C. Shifting the cardboard baby formula more than four thousand years in the past, however, was an unprecedented imaginative flourish of considerable boldness and even more considerable eccentricity.

It is also possible that the frame into which the cardboard baby narrative was shifted, if that is really how the story was put together, was not built specifically for that purpose, but began as a separate work of pseudohistory that petered out because the narrative ran out of steam and stood in dire need of refreshment itself. Whether the subsequent combination, however it came about, eventually leads to a fruitful synthesis of the thesis and antithesis is open to doubt, but the alchemical fusion is certainly not without interest. The juxtaposition transforms the significance of the Biblical Deluge as well as the significance of the 1789 Revolution, adding a flamboyant ironic twist in the process to Madame de Pompadour's oft-quoted flippant prophecy, "*Après nous, le Déluge*," which seemed to many later writers an apt summary of the decadence and fate of the *ancien régime*.

Although it certainly does not constitute an example of "decadent style," as defined by Théophile Gautier, *Paris avant le Déluge* is very preoccupied with the idea of historical decadence, which was an important topic of discussion in nineteenth-century France. Historical theories promoting the idea that civilizations had a natural life-cycle analogous to that of individuals, in which grandeur and power were inevitably transitory, leading to decline and decay—first popularized in France by the Baron de Montesquieu in the 18th century—were reinforced and revitalized by archeological investigations, particularly those carried out in Egypt in the wake of Napoléon Bonaparte's campaign there. They were also combatively counterweighted by the development of another 18th century idea, the theory of progress: the idea that the advancement of science, and the consequent development of new technologies, was the principal dynamo of social change, facilitating a process of incessant improvement, or "perfectibility."

The stark opposition between the hypothesis that contemporary French civilization was doomed, after a long period of growth and increasing magnificence, to decline and destruction, and the hypothesis that, unlike all the failed experiments that had preceded it, but from which it had learned, might endure until it obtained a kind of perfection was thrown into much sharper relief by the 1789 Revolution and its aftermath. The Revolution had been represented by its proponents as an inherently progressive process, and also as a cleansing process reacting against and providing a solution to the alleged decadence of the *ancien régime*. When it was followed by the Empire and the Restoration, however, and even more so when the Restoration was followed by the July Revolution of 1830, the revolution of 1848, and the *coup d'état* of 1851 that established the Second Empire, the picture became very confused.

Supporters of revolutionary politics still insisted on representing their ideas and their efforts as progressive, and as an antidote to symptoms of decadence, while their opponents stigmatized them as a hindrance to progress and as symptoms of decadence in themselves. That was the ideological battlefield on which Mettais pitched his philosophical tent, in *L'An 5865*, *Paris avant le Déluge* and their naturalistic predecessor, extending Montesquieu's hypothesis regarding the life-cycle of civilizations onto a far broader temporal stage, where it almost becomes a myth of eternal recurrence.

One of the major themes of *L'An 5865* is the unreliability of history, especially at the interface where oral tradition is translated into documentary form, when a confused conglomerate of memory, folklore, legend and myth is initially concretized by writing. In *L'An 5865* the reader is invited to appreciate many of the misconceptions that the historians of the hypothetical future have about our era, hence cultivating an understanding of how such misconceptions come about, assisted by the ravages of time, and perhaps also geological upheavals, which routinely obliterate all but a few vestiges of a dead civilization's writings and monuments. In *Paris avant le Déluge* the perspective is inverted, as the reader is invited to wonder how the vestiges of long-past civilizations that have survived earlier geological upheavals might have been misinterpreted to form our mythology of prehistory.

Writing in the 1860s, Mettais had little idea of the geological chronology that we have now refined with the aid of radioactive dating methods. He was aware of the work of geologists, archeologists and paleontologists like Charles Lyell, Jacques Boucher de Perthes and Georges Cuvier, whose work had cast severe doubts on the chronology of Biblical scholars like James Ussher, famous for dating the creation of the world to 4004 B.C., but the question of how far that chronology might have to be extended was still very much open to question. Although the geologist Benoît de Maillet had suggested a figure of two billion years, most estimates were much more restricted, only dealing in hundreds of thousands, or even tens of thousands, of years. Much depended, of course, on the notion of how the geological changes whose evidence remained in the strata had occurred, and debate was still fierce in the 1860s between "uniformitarians" like Benoît de Maillet and James Hutton, who thought that slow processes like erosion and sedimentation were primarily responsible, and "catastrophists" who put the primary responsibility on violent volcanic activity and inundation. The latter had the upper hand, because they not only had the Biblical Deluge on their side, but also the esthetic appeal of melodrama; although science, as time went by, came down very firmly on the other side, the literary dice were always loaded in favor of fire and flood.

The catastrophists not only had the Biblical Deluge as a trump card, but also the Deluges featured in various other mythological sources, most notably the Epic of Gilgamesh and Greek myths featuring Deucalion, both of which were known to Mettais, although the former, discovered in 1853, had not yet been translated. Catastrophists also had a similar, if somewhat more problematic, trump card in Plato's accounts of the island of Atlantis, briefly mentioned in his *Timaeus* and more elaborately described in the fragmentary *Critias*, the latter being all the more intriguing because no one has any idea whether a longer version ever existed. Plato, the great pioneer of exemplary fiction designed to illustrate and dramatize philosophical notions—what Voltaire called, when he repopularized the method, *contes philosophiques*—had, of course, invented the idea of Atlantis himself, as a potentially useful means of dramatizing a design for an ideal society, and represented it as an item of secret history by way of a strategic literary device. From one point of view, the device in question has been fabulously successful in generating plausibility, although it is probable that Plato would have been horrified by that "success," considering that it was causing his readers to miss the point entirely (which, if, in fact, he never completed the *Critias*, might be why he abandoned it).

It is not entirely clear from a superficial reading of the main text of *Paris avant le Déluge* how seriously

Mettais took the story of Atlantis, although the lengths to which he goes in pretending to take it seriously—especially in his pseudoscholarly footnotes—are strongly suggestive of a sarcastic literary device; it is, of course, the most blatant liars and practitioners of tongue-in-cheek sarcasm who strive most ostentatiously to pose as truth-tellers. There is, however, a highly significant clue in the introduction he provided to his novel, even though it does not address the question of Atlantis directly, presenting instead an argument related to the Biblical myth of the Deluge, attacking the issue of how seriously the account given in *Genesis* should be taken. The conclusion of the argument, unsurprisingly, is that it ought not to be taken too seriously, and that the chronology it contains needs to be extended if it is to be made compatible with modern geological evidence, but what is more interesting is the form of the argument supporting that contention.

Having dismissed as patently ridiculous the idea that *Genesis* is the word of God, for whom Moses merely served as an amanuensis, Mettais asks us to consider Moses' motive for writing the book. Given Moses' objectives and problems in leading the Children of Israel out of Egypt, Mettais asks, what was his purpose in writing *Genesis* for them? He then goes on to offer a logical account of what that purpose must have been, and how, in consequence, the story of *Genesis* ought to be regarded—essentially, as propaganda rather than history. He does not ask the same question about Plato's invention of Atlantis, but one is entitled to assume that he would have answered it in a similar fashion. Nor does he raise the question in respect of his own book, although he is surely inviting the reader to do so. The vital question to be asked in respect of *Paris avant le Déluge*, therefore—

in the author's own estimation—is not the question of whether it is rationally plausible as a conceivable account of prehistory, but what the author's purpose was in writing it, and what the philosophical objectives are of his invention.

Part of that purpose was, of course, to expand Mettais' ongoing fictional consideration of Paris as a key example of "civilization," and the fact that, in order to do so, he blithely invented a second Atlantis to partner Plato's, is perhaps equally significant in assisting the measurement of how far his tongue was in his cheek. If three cardboard babies are to be reckoned better than two, two Atlantises are surely better than one, especially for an author whose literary ambitions stretched over thousands of years while everybody else was dealing in mere hundreds, if they were bold enough to attempt any expansion at all.

In fact, Mettais was rather restrained in his invention of a colony of Plato's Atlantis; several previous scholarly fantasists, apparently writing in all earnestness, had moved the "actual" site of Plato's Atlantis all over the globe in an attempt to reconcile it with various items of historical and geographical data and their own ideological concerns. The Swede Olof Rudbeck, for instance, had written a treatise in 1675 "proving" that Atlantis was really Sweden. The Comte de Buffon, whose monumental *Histoire Naturelle* (1749-88) was one of the key French works challenging Biblical chronology, suggested in 1746 that the "real" Atlantis was probably in the vicinity of Sicily in an era when the Mediterranean was dry land.

The most important of these innovators by far, however, from Mettais' point of view—the only one he cites in his footnotes—was the French astronomer Jean-

Sylvain Bailly. Bailly's *Histoire de l'astronomie ancienne* (1775) supplied Mettais with an argument that he uses in his introduction, to the effect that astronomical records conserved in China and India provide convincing proof of the fact that astronomers, and hence the world, must have existed long before 4004 B.C. Bailly does not stop there, however; he went on in subsequent works to develop an extensive theory of racial emigrations occasioned by climatic shifts, developing an elaborate argument in *Lettres sur l'Atlantide de Platon et sur l'ancienne histoire de l'Asie* (1779) to "prove" that Atlantis was actually Spitzbergen in the Arctic Ocean—a notion that Mettais wisely ignores, as it does not suit his purpose, although he is obviously not unsympathetic to the underlying argumentative method.

An inveterate reprocessor of myths, attempting to find the "underlying truth" beneath the supernatural icing, Bailly also credited Spitzbergen/Atlantis with an inventive astronomer-king named Atlas, the supposed inventor of the terrestrial globe. Mettais also introduces an Atlas into his story, but in a much more modest role. Bailly was one of Voltaire's many correspondents, but never contrived to convince the great skeptic of the accuracy of his deductions. More pertinently, with regard to Mettais' novel, Bailly was also one of the prime movers of the 1789 Revolution, presiding over the instigating Tennis Court Oath, and serving as Maire of Paris from 1789 to 1791, when he fell from favor, ultimately losing his head during the Terror. Again, Mettais is more restrained in his invention, refusing to allow his great scientist Chephren to participate in the Revolution in the Parisian Atlantis, in spite of his democratic sympathies, but making him a reclusive ark-builder instead.

Given this historical context, it is easy to appreciate that while Mettais' particular recycling of the myth of Atlantis was boldly innovative in literary terms, it was conscientiously moderate by comparison with contemporary scholarly fantasy, the latter typically being far more reckless and intellectually irresponsible than literary endeavor. This is because, like Moses in Mettais' representation, writers of fiction often have a clearer idea of their purpose, and hence of their rhetorical strategy, than scholars, who are more likely to be blind to their own ideological prejudices and perversions. Mettais' novel is exactly contemporary with Charles-Étienne Brasseur de Bourbourg's *Monuments anciens du Mexique* [ancient monuments of Mexico] (1866), whose interpretation of the relics in question waxed lyrical about the "proof" they provided of the role of Atlantis in providing links between the cultures of Central and South America and the civilization of classical Greece and Rome, and thus helped to inspire such classic scholarly fantasies as Ignatius Donnelly's *Atlantis: The Antediluvian World* (1882) and the Atlantean component of Madame Blavatsky's Theosophical doctrine. Although it remains a matter of opinion as to whether Mettais or Brasseur was the more ingenious inventor, Mettais, if one analyzes his rhetoric correctly, was surely the more clear-sighted.

Although Mettais was far from famous in his own day and was largely forgotten thereafter, *Paris avant le Déluge* does stand, whether by virtue of influence or pure coincidence, at the head of a significant tradition of French Atlantean fantasy, rich in adventure stories and melodramas, which often have a significant philosophical edge. Mettais' speculative fiction was contemporary with the early works of Jules Verne, who also imported the Atlantis myth, albeit peripherally, into *Vingt mille lieues sous les mers* (1870; tr. as *Twenty Thousand Leagues Under the Sea*). Verne's example was undoubtedly more crucial in stimulating the production of such works as *Atlantis* (1895; tr. as *The Crystal City under the Sea*) by his sometime collaborator "André Laurie" (Paschal Grousset) and *L'Atlantide* (1919; tr. as *The Queen of Atlantis*) by Pierre Benoît, but *Les Atlantes* [The Atlanteans] (1903) by P.-B. Gheusi and Charles Lomond, and *Les Pacifiques* (1913; tr. as *The Pacifists*) by Han Ryner[3], are closer in spirit to the modified Platonic tradition of Mettais' novel.

Although the coincidence in timing between Mettais' contributions to the tradition of speculative fiction and Verne's is primarily striking as a study in contrasts, in which Verne emerges as by far the more fluent and elegant story-teller, it is worth noting that *Paris avant le Déluge* appeared between the two editions of *Voyage au Centre de la Terre* (1864; revised 1867; second version tr. as *Journey to the Center of the Earth*), in which Verne addressed the question of the true age of the Earth as suggested by the evidence of geology. Although it is now largely forgotten that Verne's novel existed in two versions, because the earlier one was never reprinted and never translated, it is significant that the first version accepted a explanation of the "creationist" account of the origin of humankind, while the second offered a more elaborate evolutionist account, reflecting a change of mind by the novel's principal scientific source, Louis Figuier, between the two editions of his *La*

---

[3] Included in *The Human Ant*, Black Coat Press, ISBN 9781612273235.

Terre avant le Déluge [1863; revised 1867; second version tr. as *The World before the Deluge*).

If Mettais had read Figuier and Verne, as he probably had, he could only have seen the first versions of both their books, which makes his own dabbling with the theory of "transformism" all the more original and interesting. The project of accelerating the hypothetical evolutionary process in order to produce a human being by metamorphic means, credited by Mettais to Chephren, was recapitulated in several later works of French speculative fiction, including Louis Boussenard's *Les Secrets de Monsieur Synthèse* (1888; tr. as *Monsieur Synthesis*)[4] and André Couvreur's "Le Valseur Phosphorescent" (1923; tr. as "The Phosphorescent Waltzer")[5]. The fact that Chephren is, in Mettais' fictitious prehistory, the prototype of the Biblical Noah contrives an intriguing transfiguration of the notion of the ark that anticipates much later accounts of biotechnological "arks."

In sum, although *Paris avant le Déluge* is primarily interesting now as a historical curiosity, it is of some historical significance, as well as being monumentally curious. It does not have the imaginative scope of *L'An 5865*, being more narrowly confined by its notional framework, but it does have a similarly endearing quirkiness in its notions of antediluvian architecture, geography and transport. Its hypothetical exercises in the sociology of religion and the politics of revolution are undoubtedly primitive, but they are not without a certain dash and daring in the context of their time—when, it ought to be remembered, the censors of the Second Empire had not entirely relaxed their once-vicelike grip on

[4] Black Coat Press, ISBN 9781612271613.
[5] Black Coat Press, ISBN 9781612272801.

literary expression, and advocacy of democracy and freethought were still subject to manifest diplomatic hazards. The novel remains an important document in the history of French speculative fiction and the modern development of the Atlantis myth.

This translation was made from the copy of the first (and only) edition of the text, as reproduced on the Bibliothèque Nationale's *gallica* website. All of the author's footnotes are clearly labeled as such, and I have placed his notes in quotation marks, except in one instance where an unusually long note is appended to a chapter. Where an addendum follows one of the author's notes outside the quotations marks, it is my additional observation. The other footnotes are mine.

Brian Stableford

INTRODUCTION

Today, according to the oldest interpretation of *Genesis*, it is five thousand eight hundred and ten years since our world was created.[6]

The earth existed long before then, according to the scientists—at least sixty-six thousand years, says the illustrious and pious Buffon, who proves it. That earth was not inhabited by humans, because it was uninhabitable for our species, but it contained animals and fish. Whether there were vegetables, Buffon does not say.

Humans finally arrived, but in what epoch, how and in what conditions? That is what it is very important for us to know.

Moses, one of the oldest and most respectable writers who remains to us, says that the first man, Adam, was created sixteen hundred and fifty-six years before the deluge.

Sixteen hundred and fifty-six years! That is a very long time, I admit, but it is insufficient if I want to have any confidence in general history and scientific facts, which reveal to us a very advanced civilization in that epoch. I know that it takes a people less time than that to pass from infancy to maturity, and from maturity to old

---

[6] 5810 – 1866 = 3944. This differs from James Ussher's 1650 calculation by sixty years, but that discrepancy has a Biblical basis in the textual ambiguity of the date of Abraham's birth, so some alternative calculations do offer 3944 B.C. as the likely date of Adam's creation, alongside numerous other figures based on different estimates and interpretations.

age—or, to put it better, from barbarity and ignorance to civilization and from civilization to decadence, but the people still require they be founded. And the antediluvian people of Moses were not rapid in development; they were slow—very slow—in being born. That is easily understandable, in fact; they only had one man for a father. One single man to supply numerous and civilized peoples in a period of sixteen hundred and fifty-six years!

It is true that Moses shows us that period occupied by only a few generations of patriarchs and a few petty princes almost as powerful as them. The earth was almost deserted then, only a few parts of it being inhabited, and none civilized. Everyone lived as he liked, doing good if his instinct inclined him that way and evil if he was evil. And it appears that people were more often evil than good, since God repented of having created the world and resolved to punish and annihilate it beneath the waters of a universal deluge.

Thus recounts Moses, who was writing more than two thousand five hundred years after the creation of the world, eight hundred and fifty years after the deluge.

I will admit right away that other historians, also very commendable, give our history a very different chronology.

To write as accurate a history as possible with our very feeble means of investigation, it is evidently necessary to consult inscriptions, commemorative monuments, testimonies—any authority, in sum, that might guide the writer. Good faith is not sufficient.

Do we know what authorities Moses consulted in order to discover the truth about a period as long as the one covered by his book, and to learn about events that had happened two thousand five hundred years before him, and often had no witnesses?

The sacred writer does not inform us. On the other hand, we do not see in the most ancient and reliable histories, other people recounting what he recounts, or that they furnished him with materials to compose his book.

One might ask oneself, in consequence, whether Moses really had the intention of writing an exact history of his time and the times that had preceded him, and if he also wanted to talk about times to come. In any case, we only ever see him occupied with his brethren, their education, their beliefs and their conduct. It appears very evident, therefore, that he was only writing for them, for the people of his blood—I do not say his nation, because his nation did not exist prior to him.

Moses was, therefore, a legislator, not a historian. We ought not to be surprised, therefore, if the historian continually gives way to the legislator, and if his history is sometimes faulty.

I say that Moses' history is sometimes faulty, and I shall explain myself, although everyone knows it, because I would be desolate were anyone to think that I do not have all the respect for his accounts that they deserve. I believe in them, and I confess without difficulty—but I also believe in philosophical and reasoned history; I believe in science.

When Moses represents to me the fathers of his nation, his ancestors, living before the deluge in all the simplicity of the family and nature, I believe him. But history tells me that not all of the universe was there, any more than France and present-day Europe are in the Kabyle.

If he talks to me about his fathers after the deluge, and shows them to me as pastors living in the midst of their flocks, as patriarchs rich in the number of slaves they have acquired to serve them and fight battles, if necessary—nomads like the Arabs of our own day, seeking everywhere for the best pastures and installing themselves temporarily where nature smiled upon their needs and desires—I believe him.

I believe him, and I say in consequence that it is not imprudent to suppose that those families of patriarchs and pastors, who had the same way of life and some relationship between them, also had the same belief, the belief in God—as, moreover, almost all the peoples did then, in spite of the variations that each one added to it, according to the views of its legislator, and in accordance with climatic influences, which it is necessary never to forget in order to understand the theology of a nation.[7]

It can also be presumed that the belief in question was revealed in religious worship that was indubitably very simple, and that the tradition was very similar in all the primitive families.

Since I have mentioned tradition, I do not think that I will be thought very bold in saying that from the moment that there is belief in God, religious worship established by tradition, there is also a tradition relating to the origin of the world, its creation—the past, in sum, and the future. It is difficult to imagine a thinking man without presuming him to be occupied with those grave questions.

---

[7] The insistence that climate was an important factor in determining theological beliefs was promoted by several 19th-century French writers, but is particularly evident in the works of the positivist Auguste Comte (1798-1857).

But was there a written belief? Were there durable monuments of the past? Were there books and inscriptions in that era among the families of the patriarchs?

Why bother? The father instructed his sons and his slaves; he told them what his father had told him, adding to it what he thought useful to his designs. The life of herdsmen is scarcely suited to written sermons; they have enough to do attending to the needs of the day...

Moses was therefore the first Hebrew writer, and *Genesis* the first book that was composed for that nation.

That ought not to astonish us, in any case, if we have not forgotten the calm and regular life of the patriarchs, devoid of ambition, and if we remember, on the other hand, the important and multiple roles, replete with perils, that Moses had to fulfill in the midst of his brethren.

Dispersed in different countries and slaves of the Egyptians, who treated them harshly, the Hebrews had at that time no national bond. They were isolated, devoid of any strength, demoralized and brutalized under the whips of their masters, but, in spite of that, feared by the government that did all it could to oppress them. All their desires, therefore, were for a better future. But if they groaned, if the cursed their persecutors, no one made a move, until Moses formed the incredible project of liberating them and taking them far away in order to found a nation.

"It is the will of God," that strong, profound and energetic man, full of the enthusiasm with which history credits him, said to them one day.

It is the will of God! With that mystical, superhuman cry, he soon gathers six hundred thousand Hebrews, removes them from Egypt and walks with them for forty years through an immense and arid desert to reach the land of his fathers and conquer it.

But the difficulties were great! Moses does not dissimulate them. He was a poor pastor, pursued for a murder, in the service of foreigners for many years, obscure, unknown to anyone and devoid of all influence in consequence. It was not difficult for him to persuade his brethren, who were as unhappy as he was, to flee oppression—but how can he guide that multitude, how can he govern them, and, in sum, submit them to his views?

How does he know that among those six hundred thousand people, whom he must reduce to passive obedience in order to arrive at the noble goal of which he has dreamed, there will not be envious, mutinous and treacherous individuals? How does he know that he will always be able to feed that considerable host, with whom he wants to traverse a vast and desiccated region, and that the hunger he anticipated will not make those coarse men regret the onions[8] and the golden gods of Egypt? How does he know that there will not be plots against his life, rebellions against his authority?

That is precisely what happened, as we know, and yet, Moses accomplished his prodigious task. He surely accomplished it, in the main, with the admirable narration of *Genesis*.

Today's history has no expression sufficiently vivid to praise Julius Caesar in antiquity and a few others in

---

[8] In English versions of the scriptures it is the "fleshpots" of Egypt that the Children of Israel regret, not, as in French versions, the onions, but in translating from French to English rather than from Hebrew, it seems more appropriate to reflect the French priority.

24

modern times, including Charlemagne and Napoléon. How far above them, in my estimation, Moses was!

Like Caesar, he wielded both the pen and the sword; he was a conqueror like him, and more than him. But Caesar was rich, powerful and also ambitious, while Moses...

With nothing, Moses created something; alone, he gathered his scattered people, as a shepherd gathers a flock lost in a dense wood; alone, with no money, no power, no credit and without any strength—and, moreover, without ambition to sustain him—he extracted a human multitude from the chains of a powerful nation, a civilized nation; he led them, not by caressing them, but with a severity that was sometimes cruel, through a thousand perils into the country that he wanted to occupy, and made them into a people.

Who else has ever done that?

Flatterers have said that a religious man turns everything he touches into gold. It would be truer to say that he spoils everything he touches.

Instead of seeing Moses as he is, and his work as it presents itself to the free thinker, that great man has been made into an instrument and his book the inspiration of another. Admittedly, that other is God.

That is too bold an assertion.

But that does not astonish me; I recognize the tree by its fruit, and the man by his voice.

A caste that cannot reign by the sword has wanted to reign by means of belief. With that aim, it has taken possession of our monuments, our inscriptions and our ancient documents, and declared itself their sovereign and infallible interpreter.

It is a fine entitlement.

It is the caste in question that represented God to the warrior barons of the Middle Ages wearing armor and a helmet, with a sword in his hand, fighting for the noble and powerful lords who will endow his elect most magnificently.

If that caste had lived in the time of the patriarchs, it would have shown them God with a crook in his hand, guiding the flocks of the faithful into lush pastures, and those of infidels into meager and desolate fields.

In our day, God is merely, for them, a magnificent king seated on a golden throne, with a crown on His head and a scepter in His hand, listening graciously to the prayers of His intimates. In front of Him are scales to weigh the virtues of Levites and the petty merits and crimes of "men of the world." For some He prepares resplendent thrones, for others a few sufficiently habitable corners in the empyrean or the fires of Hell.

Well, it is that caste which, having taken possession of *Genesis*, tells us: "This is the work of God, and we order you to believe it."

The work of God! Does one see Kings delivering the works of their intelligence to the criticism of the reader?

People can experience other needs than that to command—the need to persuade, for example—but what need has God, who commands and persuades as He wishes, to write books, and books full of scientific errors into the bargain?

The work of God! That is a very serious assertion, it seems to me, if it means that God had a different relationship with Moses than with other men who attempt great things, for every one of the sacred writer's pages easily allows glimpses of the ignorance and prejudice of the human mind, as each of his actions easily reveals the man: a man who wants to reach his goal no matter what, even by means of rigor, even by means of cruelty, always obedient to the maxims of conquest, which are almost never the maxims of right and justice.

Would God have written that book? Would God have inspired that conqueror? Was God, then, guilty of ignorance and cruelty? Did the Perfect Being not have all the perfections? Did He not know, in dictating to His prophet, the scientific truths that are familiar to us? Did He not care to educate him with regard to justice and forbearance?

That cannot be.

Oh, I know full well that those errors and that martial conduct do not frighten our zeal. They are explained; they are annotated. God did not want to eclipse the writer completely; God did not want to make use of exact science in the midst of a primitive and ignorant people with its own prejudices, superstitions and beliefs...

The entire earth belongs to God; God could have given Moses the idea of taking possession of the land of Canaan, of expelling the inhabitants he could not kill and passing the blade of his sword through all those he could reach, without distinction...

It is a crime worthy of death, people still say, like the men of the Inquisition, to forget God. Moses therefore acted in accordance with the spirit of God in ordering the massacre of twenty-three thousand of his brethren who, in his absence, had thought about the gods of Egypt...

A strange morality, in truth! Where, then, does it come from? Who, then, has revealed to these philosophical dictators that what is bad today was once good, for one man alone? Into what privy council have they entered in order to know more about that than anyone else?

Let them give us the key to their science, then, in order that we can judge it for ourselves. Yes, for ourselves— and why not? Are we other men than them, so that we cannot understand? Why do they want to make this book, which is ours as well as theirs, which we admire no less than they do, a sealed treasure of which they alone have the key?

No! They are mistaken. There is no mysticism to explain in the book of Moses.

The book is simple and simply written; not everything in it is perfect, but the idea is profoundly unusual; it is the sublime idea of a man of genius.

What, in fact, did Moses want? We have said it: to make a free people of his scattered and enslaved brethren.

What did he have to do to accomplish that great task, worthy of a veritably inspired man?

Well, my God, there was nothing to do except what he did.

The God of Moses was Jehovah, the God of the patriarchs and the antediluvian pastors as well as the Israelites who came after the deluge.

But had the Israelites conserved their belief intact in the midst of their various peregrinations and during the long sojourn they spent among the polytheistic Egyptians? Had not many of them renounced their mores to embrace those of their masters, and their religious aspirations in order only to live with those they saw elevated around them every day?

How, then, could a people be made with elements so disparate, badly seated, to say the least. A people is a society with the same views, the same desires and the same perspective; it is a union of common interests. All the efforts of the great liberator had to be directed to unifying the views of the Hebrews, exciting the same desires, presenting the same perspective to them all.

We can, in fact, see him completely occupied in making his belief the belief of all, in raising up in the minds of people imbued with prejudices and little versed in the mysticism necessary to religion, the God that he worships and wants everyone to worship, the God that has chosen him for His support, his King and his Legislator, the great, omnipotent God who created the universe with a single Word, the terrible God who punishes those who do not obey Him and who laughs at His prophets with a universal deluge.

That is why Moses wrote his book; and his book was perfect, because it was the belief that bound those people together; it was the same religion, the same worship, the same laws; it was the same memories of the past, the same hopes for the future. In sum, that book created a people.

Moses' goal was thus attained. What need was there, in consequence, to look any further for irrefutable monuments and reliable guides, to establish a history such as we understand history today? What did the chronology of times past and other peoples matter to him? What did the rest of the world matter to him? Did he worry about it? Did he not have his own belief, his own chronology and his own history, which served his objective well? Did he want to pass himself off as a scholar, to discuss the dates, the opinions, the religions and mores of others? Did he want to acquire the merit of a historian, who desires to instruct posterity as well as and more than the present, by leaving it his science, the science of a scrupulous man who only writes what he has seen or checked against irrefutable monuments?

No! His aim was greater; he wanted to save his brethren and create a people.

Oh, that goal might well make one forget a few chronological exactitudes; that goal might well absolve a writer of a few hazarded assertions that science and history do not sanction; that goal might well cause one to pardon a excessive severity—which was, after all, only the severity of a leader who sees his institutions imperiled, or a conqueror who is drawing in his wake nearly a million human beings in need of shelter and bread.

That goal might well also relieve him of the accusation of frivolity of belief in recounting, without reliable testimony, the great event of the universal deluge. Do not all the ancient peoples speak of it?

They do not mean a universal deluge such as we understand it, but a deluge that seemed so to them, so frightening, immense and devastating was it. All religions have consigned it to their records, and Moses, who was brought up in Pharaoh's court, who had lived for many years among a numerous, educated, largely civilized people—the people of Egypt—had a perfect right to repeat what he had heard said.

We would be wrong to ask of *Genesis* more than it wishes to give us; we would be wrong to weigh those words as misers weigh gold, torturing them in order to reconcile them with the verities of modern civilization. We ought to take that book, that admirable book, for what it is, for what it really is, while blessing it for the good it has produced.

It will still remain to us as a precious monument, if not of the true history of the antediluvian peoples, at least to the popular traditions of the epoch and to the savant and energetic skill of a great man.

As for the exact history of other peoples of the time—the general, philosophical and scientific history of the worlds as it was then—we must seek it elsewhere; for Moses was not the only person to write in those days, and his ancestors and his nation were far from being the most civilized in antiquity.

What he does not tell us, the Atlanteans, the Hindus, the Egyptians and even the Greeks tell us in showing us the genealogy of their kings, the eras and chronological dates of their peoples, inscribed in their ancient documents, in writings of every sort, on their monuments and in the memories of their traditions.

Now, the history of those peoples reveals to us that before the Hebraic deluge the earth was very populous. They tell us that in those times there were simple and primitive peoples, that there were semi-civilized peoples and others that were savage and barbaric. There were also civilized peoples, and even a very advanced civilization, for one sees them already practicing the sciences the most difficult for the human mind, devoting themselves to the longest and most complicated calculations of the most advanced astronomy.

Well before the deluge, astronomical problems had been resolved that we have only resolved after long centuries of civilization, in spite of all the scientific baggage that reached us from various directions and which served to elevate our knowledge greatly. I shall only report one example, which seems to me to be utterly conclusive.

The solar years and the lunar months are, as everyone knows, in a perfect and exact relationship thanks to the sagacity of our astronomers. But our astronomers were only able to arrive at that perfection of calculation by recording with scholarly attention the astronomical events of a period of six hundred years. That was our

Julian period; scholars call it the lunisolar period, or period of six hundred years.[9]

Now, according to the historian Josephus, whose word is well-founded, that lunisolar period, one of the most beautiful conquests of our modern astronomy, was known before the deluge, and by even the patriarchs.

Thus, science and civilization existed on the earth in those days!

Thus, I shall add, seizing that fact, which has fallen into my hands to furnish me with a proof for which I was no longer searching of the facility with which Moses treated the chronology of early times, the period of sixteen hundred and fifty-six years that *Genesis* caused to elapse between the creation of the world and the deluge, is impossible, for, as Buffon says: "in order to suspect the lunisolar period of six hundred years, [antediluvian peoples] would have required at least twelve hundred years of observations; in order to ensure themselves that it was a certain fact it would have required more than double that, which already makes, therefore, three thousand years of astronomical study…and must not those three thousand years of astronomical observations have been preceded necessarily by a few centuries in which science was as yet unborn?"

It is evident, in consequence, once more that the book of Moses ought not to be taken literally everywhere and forever.

---

[9] The lunisolar period is actually 532 years in the Julian calendar, but it was often mistakenly reckoned as 600 years, including a much-publicized assertion by the astronomer Giovanni Cassini (1625-1712), allegedly based on Josephus, which was cited by Buffon and Bailly, among others.

It is evident, as well, that if I show the earth inhabited and civilized before the deluge, and I have competent authorities familiar to everyone for it, and that if I say that the deluge was not universal, I can be worthy of trust in spite of *Genesis*—or, to put it a better way, to make it clearer, in spite of the interpretation that a few people give to the story of *Genesis* when they take it too literally.

And in fact, I conclude definitively and frankly that the deluge was not universal, and I shall interpret what *Genesis* says logically and scientifically.

General history, moreover, will still be here for us.

I know full well, and I admit once again,[10] that in history, it is necessary to know when to stop.

However, although I do not have a complete confidence in the stories it tells us, and which it is often as well only to accept subject to verification, it is necessary to recognize that there are points that one cannot call into question, certain reference-points that we ought not to forget if we want to know the truth.

Those reference-points are chronological dates.

If, therefore, the deluge occurred sixteen hundred and fifty-six years after the creation of the world, two thousand three hundred and forty-eight before our era, and if it was universal, what became of the peoples who inhabited the world at that time?

They were buried beneath the waters, Moses says; they all perished, except for Noah and his children.

That assertion is very strange, because it is in precisely that epoch that the history of various peoples

---

[10] Author's note: "If my book *L'An 5865* is read attentively, it will be seen that I have not wanted to say about history anything other than what I say here."

33

emerges from uncertainty and darkness to enter into the ways of the known.

The history of China presents us with a few shreds of the marvelous a further three thousand five hundred and sixty-eight years before our era, but in the year two thousand six hundred and thirty-seven it establishes its dates with certainty and continues to the present day without interruption.

The history of Egypt is certain two thousand four hundred and fifty years before our era.

India, Greece and, above all, Atlantis, were known before the deluge. We have the genealogy of their kings, we have authentic monuments of them, and we have the chronology of their peoples. Now, their peoples appear to us to have been so numerous and so civilized in the days that followed the epoch indicated for the deluge that it is impossible to admit that they only had Noah and his sons for forefathers.

At any rate, it is not my intention, believe me, to issue an indictment here against Moses and his book.

Moses was a great man, one of the greatest geniuses that antiquity produced.

His book is a book above all praise. I admit that with conviction.

The errors that he advances are the errors of the time. The truth of one epoch is often the error of another; one ought to rectify it, not criticize it; that is, in any case, in the designs of God, who does not enable human intelligence to march with giant strides.

I only want to say one thing, and I repeat it: that the Hebraic deluge was not complete and universal. That is sufficient for my objective, for it cannot only be via that glimpse of ancient times that the historical episode has reached us that I want to recount, regarding the two Atlantises, that of Africa and that of the Pah-ri-ziz.

PART ONE
THE AFRICAN ATLANTIS

I. A Bird's-Eye View of the Island

Atlantis was an island of great celebrity in remote antiquity; its origin and even its life are lost in the night of time. The ancients say that it was the most anciently inhabited land.[11]

It was situated on the west coast of Africa, in the midst of the waters that, presumably taking their name from it, were called the Atlantic Sea.

It was, the ancient historians say, three thousand stades long by two thousand wide—which is to say, about a hundred leagues by fifty, approximately the size of France.

Its population was immense, swelled by that of small islands that surrounded it in great number, over which it reigned and which linked it to the neighboring continent.[12]

Atlantis extracted from its own soil almost everything necessary to life: wheat, wine, fruits, the most

---

[11] Author's note: "The Atlanteans, says Solon and Plato with him, were already a great people nine thousand years before the voyage of the former to Said in Egypt—which is to say, about 600 B.C."

[12] Author's citation: "'They [the kings of Atlantis] also reigned over the entire region from Libya to Egypt, and over the coast of Europe as far as Tyrrhenia.' Plato, Dialogues of *Timaeus* and *Critias*."

sought-after perfumes, fabrics, precious kinds of wood for construction of luxury and furniture. All minerals were abundant there, including gold, silver, iron and orichalcum, a precious metal of which only the name is any longer known.

Thus, its commerce was immense, but it was praised above all for all its beauty and the mildness of its climate as well as its admirable fertility. The earth produced two crops a year there, watered as it was in winter by benevolent rains and in summer by canals that refreshed all the fields.

The cities were splendid. They had magnificent temples filled with golden statues, and decorations of the same metal and of orichalcum, magical palaces, expertly constructed ports and numerous harbors for vessels.

Its metropolis, most of all, was indescribably beautiful and wealthy. It was surrounded by profound ditches filled with water, over which a large number of bold bridges had been projected. Broad canals departed from there to extend throughout the island, greatly facilitating communications. Those that opened to the sea were broad enough to allow access to triremes. A host of other smaller canals served for the transportation of people and merchandise.

Atlantean warriors were reputedly heroic; their boldness and good fortune were universally feared.

The civilization of Atlantis arrived in due course at a height that astonished the world of that time, all of which was warmed by its benevolent radiation, which expanded everywhere.

What science there was in Egypt, Phoenicia, Chaldea, India and China—among all the oldest peoples, in sum, whose surprising knowledge we still admire today—came from Atlantis.

Like all peoples, the Atlanteans had their period of infancy, their period of growth, that of degeneration and their end.

The period of infancy was undoubtedly simple; a people is not born in splendor and opulence, like the son of a great lord. But it was wise, apparently, and eminently wise, for it imposed its beliefs and their worship on others.

The theogony of the Atlanteans even had the rare good fortune to become almost universal, to survive its authors for many centuries after their disappearance and to make polytheism the religion of all civilized peoples even in recent times. The greatest gods of ancient Greece and Italy came from Atlantis. It was in Atlantis that Uranus, Neptune and Atlas—all the familiar gods and heroes of mythology, in fact—reigned successively, and of whom we have been taught to consider as myths, although a serious history says otherwise.

Whatever the first theology of Atlantis was, however, it was not the last; at least, it was not the only one prior to the catastrophe that carried them away.

Like many peoples, the Atlanteans experienced over time the need to modify and even change their beliefs, rendering them more subtle and more worthy of the philosophy of scholars making progress.

We should not criticize them for that, for those days were not the least glorious of their life. The debates were lively, even bitter, it is true; but from their collision a higher expression of religious philosophy eventually emerged: Brahmanism, which lent its dogmas and its doctrine to more than one religion, and gradually spread through almost all the peoples of the Orient, into China and India, where it still endures, even though it appears to have been annihilated for centuries.

If the debuts of the Atlantean people were happy steps and giant strides, history does not leave us unaware of the fact that its period of growth also shone with an unprecedented gleam, and that its power eventually became immense.

But was it happy in those days? Were there political revolutions in that beautiful country?

One cannot doubt it—and that should not surprise us on the part of people who had achieved such a great civilization, for the power of their kings cannot have been in harmony with the rights of the citizen. The power of kings over men was absolute and unbridled, for it was also absolute over laws. The law was nothing other than the will of the god Neptune speaking in his temple, and therefore theirs, the god always speaking, undoubtedly, as they wished.

What is astonishing, in consequence, in the fact that the people eventually thought that it would be better to have fixed laws than arbitrary ones, and to make a *tabula rasa* of their government?

We do not know anything about these revolutions, however, except that they occurred. That is unfortunate for the philosophy and science of today—an irreparable misfortune, for the little we know about the island causes us keenly to regret what we have lost.[13]

---

[13] Author's citation: "'There is a misfortune common to noble and ancient families. The testimony of historians has been effaced, the thread of tradition has been broken in the deserts formed by war and the centuries of ignorance that are the deserts of time. But a confused notion remains, a few facts engraved in memory, the duration of which advertises the importance of the truth. A long memory, the memory of humans, is something else entirely: I give great weight to ancient tradi-

The African Atlantis had, therefore, all the best-founded entitlements to the credence and renown of history, our study and our admiration, or at least to our curiosity.

But where is it? What became of it?

"Atlantis disappeared in the space of a single day and night, under floods and earthquakes. It is buried at the bottom of the sea."[14]

In what time?

History does not say. But it must have been in a very distant era, since no other monuments, documents or reports of Atlantis existed other than a few volumes mysteriously buried in a library in Said in Egypt, where only a few scholars, of whom Solon was the first, discovered them, and which have not survived to our era.

Fortunately, their civilization and their sciences were not extinguished with them. They had spread them far and wide before dying. There was also their name…but so many centuries have passed over it, so many upheavals followed in their empire, so many barbarian feet trampled it that it was lost in the desert. As Citizen Bailly puts it, no more than an indistinct echo of it was any longer heard; it was no longer understood as anything but the memory of a dream.

That, I repeat, was a great misfortune!

Then again, perhaps the Atlanteans were, after all, like our noble and ancient families of the Middle Ages, who did not know how to write. Fully occupied with living as great lords, with fighting and conquests, and of finally settling here or there, according to the needs of

---

tions preciously conserved by a sequence of generations.' Bailly, *Lettres sur l'Atlantide*."

[14] Author's citation: "Plato, *Dialogue of Timaeus*."

their population, perhaps capriciously and perhaps also in accordance with points of honor, such as they were reckoned in the mores of antiquity, perhaps the Atlanteans could not write.

II. The War of the Gods

About three thousand five hundred years before our era—which is to say, more than a thousand years before the deluge—the Atlanteans were in the full flower of their growth. Their feats of arms, which had been numerous and brilliant before, were immense in those times, permitting them to consolidate the large-scale conquests that they had made in all parts of the world.

Thus, they had tributaries everywhere; they had founded substantial colonies everywhere, establishing the supremacy of their tactics, their courage and their civilization.

They would have been able to rest on their laurels, which were adequate for men of war, but their active and restless spirit could not rest in peace. No longer battling externally they were gripped by the need to argue with one another. They did so with all the vivacity of their enthusiasm, which was sometimes devoted to the sciences, and sometimes to religious philosophy, which is exactly what gives the greatest purchase to acrimony and dissent.

It must also be admitted that the worship of Uranus and company was already old and that its origin did not date from the times of high civilization—perhaps reasons strong enough to render it suspect to the generous and free thinkers who eventually took it into their heads to weigh everything in the balance of their logic, without listening to the arguments of the believers who thought it good to worship Uranus because he was the god of their ancestors, without wondering whether he was really the god of the world.

At any rate, the ancient theogony—which is to say, pantheism—was fiercely attacked in those days, and, if it did not crumble away entirely, it could not prevent the triumph of a rival and powerful deity: the divinity of the monotheists, the divinity of progressives and scholars— in sum, the divinity of Brahma.

Between polytheism and monotheism these was an immense difference. The former was the religion of materialists, the second the religion of spiritualists.

The old believers were either simple people who made gods of men who were reputed to have done good, or flatterers and sots who raised altars to the powerful individuals who governed them.

If they placed a god on high, nothing said so.

It was precisely this God that the new believers wanted to reveal, leaving to human beings that which was only human, and seeking beyond for the Creator of the world.

Brahma was the name they gave to that Supreme Being, whom they called unique, eternal, omnipotent, perfect, existing by Himself, containing everything within Himself, the Creator and moderator of all things.

Thus far, everything went well and could be agreed upon by all, but humans never stop in time. If reason and conviction give them a good idea, it is very rare that their innate imperfection—which is to say their prejudice, their pride, their love of the marvelous and the incomprehensible, and their immoderate desire for pedantry—does not push them beyond the good and the true.

Brahma was not only the God of all, invisible and incomprehensible; they wanted to characterize Him, to give Him attributes, to specialize His being, His constitution, His essence, His various transformations and His mystic trinity; they wanted to reveal how He had created humans, His ministers, His court, how He reigned, how He administered the heavens and the earth. They made Him a father, a master, a king—in sum, they spoiled the idea of God; they created dreams, but those dreams were very scholarly, full of grandiose, sentimental and, above all, incomprehensible hallucinations.

But a religious system, no more than any other political and social system, cannot be born without subsequently exciting around it an upsurge of different opinions. The minds of all thinkers awaken then, possessing some with the desire to arrive at the truth by discussing the new system seriously and conscientiously, and others with the passion of contradiction, and in yet others with sentiments perhaps narrower still.

Once the impetus was given to theological discussion among the Atlanteans, it did not stop at the new religion of Brahma. Scarcely was it established than it was obliged to submit to the reproaches of a dogma that claimed to be more perfect and which we would, in fact, regard as such, because it is singularly similar to our own, to the point of sometimes being confused with it.

The dogma in question was that of Buddhism.

In that epoch lived a pure young man of high intelligence, a friend of the good and the true, which he sought in peace and meditation in the bosom of a retreat for which he was not made, for he belonged to the military and royal caste, and in that capacity, should have been destined for the agitation of politics and war. His name was Sylax.

Sylax was, above all, a philosopher and an ascetic. So far as he was concerned, Brahmanism had not yet forgotten enough of the religion of the old believers in Uranus. He even reproached it for worshipping the material that was forbidden to it. But the Buddha Sylax had a faith that he had scrupulously purified in retreat, and with inescapable logic he proved to his adversaries that God was as immaterial as a principle, without a beginning or an end, like a principle, and that although Brahma was all of that, the Brahmins had forgotten the immaterial principle and no longer saw anything but the forms and idols they adored.

His own dogmas were based uniquely in spiritualism, rejecting any appearance of materialism with the most scrupulous care. As in Brahmanism, unfortunately, there was no shortage of mysticism in it: mysticism pushed as far as dreams of the uncomprehended and doubtless the incomprehensible.

We shall not charge him with a crime on that basis, because the Buddha, like all men living voluntarily in retreat, given to absorbing meditations on the future life, annihilated in the profound and unfathomable mystery of the generating and moderating principle of the world, thought with his heart, his desires and his illusions, not with his mind and his reason.

His morality was severe, even more so than the destination of the man that his strength of mind required. Having renounced all the pleasures of the world, he thought it good to make a virtue of absolute silence, the abnegation of society, the celibate monastic life of study and the contemplation of divine perfection.

That life was hard, but minds were inclined to theological discussion and it began to be fashionable for scholars to live like that.

[Author's note: However little is known about the history of present-day Buddhism, it can easily be seen that although it was born later than the man of whom I speak, its dogmas and doctrine are nevertheless those of the Buddha Sylax, the dogmas and doctrine of Christianity, with a few variations. Even its liturgy and hierarchical organization have an extraordinary resemblance to those of Christianity, sometimes so perfect that one cannot doubt that one served as a model for the other.

That resemblance goes so far as confusion on one very unusual point, which is none other than the narration of the death of Christ. That legend is recounted in its entirety in *Obervations sur les Doctrines Samanéenes* by Dr. Abel Rémusat,[15] a scholarly Orientalist—as everyone knows—who found it in a very old Chinese book.

Here it is:

"The nations of the Far East say that 97 lis from China lie the borders of Si-Kiang. In that land there was once a virgin named Ma-li-a. She lived in the reign of Youen-Tchi, of the Han dynasty. A celestial God appeared to her, saying: The Lord of Heaven has chosen you to be his mother. After these words, she conceived and gave birth to a son. Full of joy and veneration, she wrapped him up and placed him in a crib. A company of celestial gods sang and rejoiced in the void. Forty days later, his mother presented him to the holy instructor and named him Ye-sou. He was not yet twelve when he went with his mother, who was going to make her devotions, to the temple, but on the way back they became separated. After searching for her son for three days, Ma-li-a found him again in the temple, sitting on a seat of honor

---

[15] Jean-Pierre Abel-Rémusat (1788-1832) was the most important sinologist of the 19th century; the chair of Sinology at the Collège de France was created for him. His "Observations sur le religion samaneene" is contained in *Mélanges Posthumes d'Histoire et de Literature* (1843) and might be apocryphal, as the cited document obviously is.

conversing with old men and scholars about the works and doctrines of the Lord of Heaven. He was delighted to see his mother again, returned home with her, and lived with her as a respectful son. At the age of thirty he left his mother and his teacher and traveled the land of Yu-Te-a, instructing people as to what is good. The miracles he worked were very numerous. The principal families and those who occupied employment in the region were proud and excessively wicked, which led them to envy him because of the multitude of people who joined him; they therefore planned to have him killed.

"Among the twelve disciples of Ye-Sou there was an avaricious man named Yu-Ta-ssé. In return for a sum of money, he guided a troop of men by night who captured Ye-sou, tied him up and dragged him before Anassé in the courtyard of the house of Pi-la-to. There they took off his clothes, attached him to a stake and inflicted five thousand four hundred blows on him, so that his entire body was torn to shreds. Nevertheless, he still maintained silence, and like a lamb, did not murmur. The cruel populace, taking a bonnet made of thorns, forced it down over his temples, threw a wretched red cloak over his shoulders, and prostrated themselves hypocritically before him as if he were a king. His persecutors then constructed a wooden machine, very large and heavy, resembling the character Ten (a cross) and obliged him to carry it himself. It was so heavy that he fell down several times on the way. Finally, his hands and feet were nailed to the wood; then, as he was thirsty, he was given a bitter and acidic beverage.

"On the day of his death, Ye-sou was thirty-three years old."

If the author of the Atlantean religion, the Buddha Sylax, probably the forefather of present-day Buddhism, is little known, no one, by contract, is ignorant of the name of the creator of the Buddhism of our days, Siddhartha.

Well, Siddhartha was an Indian prince who lived eleven hundred years before Jesus Christ according to come, only seven hundred years according to others.[16]

I hasten to say, in order to be completely honest, that few people suppose the legend of Ye-Sou to be found among the primitive dogmas of Siddhartha, but that it was introduced at a later date—no one knows by whom or in what era.

That supposition is probably true, but it is difficult to believe that a religion admitted by a considerable number of adherents—Buddhism counts about two hundred million—could be corrected and augmented surreptitiously, accepting important beliefs extraneous to the views of its author.]

---

[16] Modern estimates prefer death dates in the fifth century B.C.

III. A Voyage Around the World

The adepts of Buddhism multiplied in a prodigious manner in a short time in the heart of Atlantis, but Sylax took no pride in that. A zealous servant of conviction, he saw nothing but his God, heard no voice but His, and did his utmost to reveal them to the minds of all.

That mission was fine and great, but it was also difficult, for the Buddha had to contend with a host of adversaries and the struggle was fierce. He sustained it energetically, and, it must be said, with a benevolence that might have won him more disciples than his arguments. But what does it matter? The success was colossal. Sylax was delighted; he thanked Heaven with all the simplicity of a generous man who has saved his brethren from a shipwreck.

He could have rested on his triumph, to enjoy in peace the laurels with which his disciples covered him. He did not do that; his task was unfinished. So long as he could see an unbeliever, he did not think he had the right to sleep, and there were still many of them, even among his friends, and even among the admirers of his knowledge of his philanthropy.

That was precisely where the difficulty lay, for there were men who were strong logicians, as learned as him and as benevolent as him, but deaf to any voice other than their reason, and hence not at all inclined to submit to the dogmatic beliefs of a religion, whether it called itself pantheism, Brahmanism or Buddhism, for they saw nothing therein but human hands, the will and the teaching of their peers, when they only wanted to obey the voice of a superior being, God himself.

Among those men, the Buddha had an intimate friend, a childhood friend, a friend for whom he would have shed blood with devotion and pleasure, the savant philosopher Me-nu-tche.

Me-nu-tche's resistance was neither systematic nor ill-intentioned; it appeared to be based on a profound personal conviction, a conviction formed in childhood under the reasoning of his father.

Me-nu-tche's father was a distinguished philosopher in Atlantis. He had nourished his son on the belief in a God, a creative God, but he had informed him simultaneously that God was a father, a good father, and that it was sufficient to the recognition of a son to love and worship him in his own fashion, without worrying about rituals or fanatical beliefs inscribing a more-or-less ridiculous ceremony that diminished the God he wanted to worship.

To convince such a man was, therefore, a very difficult enterprise. Sylax was learned, profound in all the sciences; he had studied the great book of nature seriously, turned the most arduous metaphysical questions over and over, but Me-nu-tche was also knowledgeable, and, although as young as his friend, he had similarly sounded all the depths of metaphysics.

The Buddha was, however, not deterred. He was convinced that he had taken the right path, the road to Heaven, but he did not want to walk it alone, without his friend. He swore that he would bring him along it at his side.

He was wrong to swear, for an event he had not foreseen threatened to take his friend away from him forever.

The religious question was not the only order of the day in Atlantis at that time. The progressive civilization of that eminently savant people was continually searching the unknown. Politics, social economy, history, geography, astronomy—all the sciences, in sum, destined to add to human well-being or ornament human intelligence—were being seriously studied. Scientists were working ardently therein, and the government actively stimulated the zeal of the scientists.

All those lofty questions, however, could not be elucidated from the fireside. A few bold scientists therefore formed the project of a voyage around the world. That project seduced the ardent soul of Me-nu-tche, who made his friend Sylax party to his resolution, pressing him enthusiastically to accompany him. Sylax had but one aim, however, which was to convert people to his religion. Nothing else mattered to him.

The day of the departure arrived. Me-nu-tche said his farewells to his friend, and then embarked. His vessel had only moved a short distanced from the port when he perceived another ship emerge from the harbor. That ship carried numerous passengers, including the Buddha Sylax.

Sylax had reflected; he could not bear the idea of being separated from his friend, whom he had not yet converted, perhaps forever. Heaven had suggested an idea to him that seduced the Buddha.

Too ascetic to forget his mission, too good and generous to forget his friend on the road to perdition, Sylax had found a means of reconciling the duties of friendship with those of the apostle.

He departed in Me-nu-tche's wake, but he left in order to preach his dogmas and his morality: to preach them everywhere that his friend went, and to found religious establishments everywhere.

To that effect also, he did not depart on his own; he had zealous disciples with him, of both sexes, in order to provide all the needs of his instruction and the institutions that he wanted to establish.

There is no need to forewarn suspicious minds regarding the purity of these various missionaries; celibacy and chastity were, among the ancient Buddhists as among the new ones, a fundamental article of their religion. Very meritorious in anyone, those virtues were in addition a sacred bond for those who lived the monastic life, like Sylax and his apostles, and we have no more reason to suspect their vows than the vows of monks who live in the faith of other religions.

Sylax and Me-nu-tche, although imbued with different opinions that kept them constantly on the terrain of discussion, were glad to be reunited for a voyage that promised to be long, and which was bound to be menaced by many perils.

The seas of that epoch were doubtless well-known to Atlanteans who had traveled them often—the greater part of them at least—but they were numerous, much more numerous than today, and there were no men who had traveled them all.

Those seas, moreover, along with lakes and rivers that were then of a breadth and depth of which we have no suspicion, made irruptions inland so frequently that they ate into them everywhere and established themselves everywhere, with a suddenness that drives populations and navigators to despair.

Ships were very nearly the only means of transport for long-distance journeys, but the dangers that sprang up before them are easily understandable.

The pilots guiding the vessels that carried Sylax and Me-nu-tche were fortunately among the best, so their voyage began amid the best possible auguries. So long as they were in known waters their skill was not found wanting, and they went through the most dangerous passes with an ease that won the admiration of everyone.

Those mariners were guiding scientists, however, and those scientists had not given themselves the mission of studying what everyone knew. They wanted to launch forth into the unknown, to navigate the least well-known seas, to see people of whom little more was known than their names, and finally to establish certainty with regard to countries whose history and geography were entirely uncertain.

The danger would commence here, but the anticipation of danger could not frighten the Atlantean scientists. Science has its fanatics just as religious belief does; it also has its martyrs.

The first five months of the voyage were fortunate for everyone—for the mariners who had directed their vessels very skillfully, and for the scientists who had already been able to correct a few scientific errors and acquire some new truths—but the beginning of the sixth month was exceedingly menacing.

Having left the little Atlantean port of Tehpuec, which faced the cost of Africa, the scholarly voyagers had headed for that coast. Their initial aim was to visit their various establishments in Libya, those that they had in the confines of Egypt, and from there to head for the more northerly countries of Europe, which were almost unknown to them, passing via their colonies in Greece, perhaps to advance thereafter into the very heart of Europe, where no one had any memory of ever having penetrated.

The northern regions of Africa did not offer then, as they do today, seas of sand and deserts, but a liquid surface strewn with island and islets of various dimensions. It was that sea that the two Atlantean vessels traversed, traveling everywhere with the security of men accustomed to the crossing, in order finally to arrive in the vicinity of Egypt, which they perceived to their right, but which they saluted from afar like a good friend, because it was not their objective.

The direction they had taken at first had seemed to indicate an intention not to reach the countries of Europe immediately, by way of which they would return, but to make their voyage longer by continuing beyond Egypt to the lands of the Far East.

Either because the countries were sufficiently well-known, however, or for some other motive, their itinerary was changed. Having arrived in sight of Egypt, they made an abrupt left turn, heading toward the waters of the Black Sea, through vast lands that were fairly densely inhabited, but furrowed in all direction by rivers, lakes and seas that were all connected, so deep and vast that they might have been taken for branches of the Atlantic Sea.

Until then they had scarcely paused on their route, in haste as they doubtless were to reach their goal. It was, however, five months since they had left Tehpuec when they entered the waters of the Black Sea, a vast sea of which we only know the extreme points today.

Until then their voyage had been untroubled. Sylax and Me-nu-tche had not noticed the passing of time, occupied as they were with philosophical and religious discussions, but Sylax had not yet made any progress in changing his friend's mind, and Me-nu-tche, although he had not convinced Sylax either, was enjoying himself naively and as a benevolent friend, because his arguments had not yielded any ground.

The Atlantean scientists, for their part, had not been wasting their time; they had collected along the way all the scientific evidence in search of which they had set out. They had done so calmly and confidently, the sea having been kinder to them than they had any right to expect. Even the Black Sea of such sad memory had not troubled them.

On leaving that sea which, while changing its name, led them gradually into unfamiliar territory, on waves that were all the more dangerous because they to were little known, they were obliged to advance circumspectly.

That prudence was fortunate for them because, in spite of a few difficulties and even sustaining some damage, which dogged their paces in those terrible northern seas strewn with more-or-less hostile peoples and tribes, the Atlanteans were able to congratulate themselves for having navigated for more than five whole months without having lost a single man or even run any serious danger.

Thus, they were advancing with confidence toward the unknown to which they had been looking forward so much, and which their scientific imagination filled with all the riches of the unexpected.

That boldness was not unfortunate for them, and toward the middle of the sixth month of their navigation they found themselves in the heart of Europe, facing a vast island toward which they were rowing hard. There, however, torrential rain, as frequently occurred in that epoch, caught them unawares and stopped them.

A frightful storm blew up both above and around them. Thunder burst forth in all directions; submarine rumbles were heard in the deepest waters; then mountains of water were suddenly hurled into the air, with horrible explosions, threatening to engulf the two unfortunate vessels at any moment, which were bobbing like floating leaves. Several boulders, brought up from the depths of the abyss by an invisible force that was nothing other than that of volcanoes, fell at the very feet of the navigators, who thought that their final hour had come.

The darkness was almost continuous, and the island was no longer in sight; perhaps it had been flooded, perhaps swallowed up in the volcanic abyss.

"My friend," said Sylax to Me-nu-tche, "God is punishing us for your incredulity."

"Forgive me for being the involuntary cause of your misfortune, my poor friend," replied the philosopher Me-nu-tche, "but I think it very bad that your God is punishing you for my sins, instead of extending mercy to me on account of your virtues."

"God's intentions are incomprehensible; let us worship them," said the Buddha, squeezing his friend's hand affectionately.

"If God's intentions are incomprehensible," Me-nu-tche retorted, smiling sadly at his friend, "why do you appear to want to comprehend them, in telling us that He intends to punish us? Why do you want the lightning to be unleashed arbitrarily from the hands of your God, volcanoes to open up beneath us like a fan, and God to move Heaven and earth vindictively to engulf an ant navigating on a wisp of straw? Why do you, a scholar, as everyone knows, not say to yourself: there are laws in nature that form and regulate storms, which make volcanoes burst forth, which inundate land and navigators-too bad for the unfortunates who find themselves in the path of those catastrophes?" And Me-nu-tche added: "I beg you, my friend to give up the impious habit of mistaking our appreciations for the will of God."

Sylax was about to reply when several voices cried: "Land! Land!"

That horrible storm had lasted a week. It had brought desolation to the island that was in view, destroying all of its crops and flattening almost all the habitations. The sea, for its part, had invaded the soil for a considerable distance and made horrible ravines in its coast.

It was the land of the Teutchs.[17]

---

[17] Author's note: "This island must be in the Rhine, near the mouth of the Lippe. Everyone knows that Teutchs is the original name of the Germans. In the second antiquity they were called Ker-mann, Wher-mann and finally Germans." The word that would nowadays be rendered Deutschland is rendered as Teutchsland in a small number of 18th and 19th century German sources.

IV. The Islands of the Teutchs

The sky had suddenly become serene again; the sea was calm, as if it had not just flown into a furious temper. The Atalantean voyagers, still very relieved by the idea that they had escaped catastrophe, were beginning to render thanks to Heaven when they saw a host of small boats coming toward them manned by a multitude of tall, strong, Herculean, half-naked men with pale skins, blue eyes and abundant red-tinted hair tied up in a topknot.

They were the Teutchs. The Atlanteans watched the boats approaching without anxiety, for nothing indicated that they were manned by enemies. In fact, the Teutchs did not look ferocious and their mores were hospitable, but shipwrecked victims were not guests so far as they were concerned: they were prey that their gods had sent them via storms. To rescue them from the waves and take them to their island was to them, in consequence, simply a matter of salvage to their own advantage.

Thus, they put all kinds of care into conducting that providential cargo of Atlanteans to a place of safety, and did so with perfect cordiality, even though the two large vessels were difficult to guide to the shore.

The Atlanteans marveled at that kindness, which they had not expected to find in a country so disconnected from the rest of the world, and they began blessing God for having directed them to a land where science would doubtless have much to harvest.

Their illusion did not last, however. It did not take them long to perceive that they were no longer human beings to the islanders but booty: slaves.

The pious Sylax was not disconcerted by this discovery; it matters little to him to whom he preached his doctrine; he had high hopes of convincing his listeners.

Me-nu-tche was not so easily consoled, for he could no longer see what advantage he was going to obtain from his voyage to Europe. The most obvious thing to him was that he was a prisoner, and also a slave.

Apart from the inhuman retention of considering any shipwreck victim as legitimately acquired wealth, however, the Teutchs were not people to be feared. They were neither savage nor cruel, and even though their civilization was essentially different from that of the Atlanteans, there was a certain wisdom and sensitivity in it.

It was considered a mark of civilization among them to be able to tie up their hair artistically on top of the head, to present the forms of bare limbs graciously, to shoot accurately at an enemy with a bow, and to sing in a loud and sonorous voice about the pleasures and dangers of the sea and incomprehensible and uncomprehended memories of the fatherland. Although they only researched in history what was happening around them, and in geography that of their island and the neighbors with whom they were often at war, and in astronomy that which their highly experienced eyes told them, they were, on the other hand, just in their social relationships, generous in regard to one another, habitually honest and full of deference for women.

That civilization surely had some merit.

In the epoch when the Atlanteans disembarked, their government was headed by leaders that historians call kings, doubtless for want of a more accurate term, because it would be difficult to classify the royalty of the

Teutchs, which was neither absolute, nor constitutional, nor democratic. It was scarcely more than a stewardship.

It was, at any rate, elective; it was always given to the bravest, the most learned or the most eloquent, and only for a year, with the proviso that the same steward-king could continue indefinitely so long as his services were acceptable.

There was no instance in the memory of the Teutchs, when the Atlanteans arrived, of any previous king having tried to render himself independent, omnipotent, or the proprietor of his fellow citizens to the point of administering them as he wished and bending them to his will.

At any rate, their power was not great; the military leaders were as powerful, and more so, and the united people were more powerful than anyone.

Everyone, moreover, held to his rights: the rights of any people that have not forgotten in dreams of egotistical ambition the principles of society, state and government. All public affairs were treated as comitias to which everyone came armed, not in order to fight and make force prevail over reason, but to applaud or criticize the proposals of the king by striking their weapons in a certain manner.

The king, therefore, never imposed any law or issued any decree, but made proposals, and the people, who were not a population of courtiers, gave their opinions without any hesitation or oratory precaution, which was always accepted without rancor and executed loyally, even by those opposed to it.

Everyone went into combat among the Teutchs, even old men, women and children. Their tactics were not a progressive science, but merely a tradition, a custom. It consisted entirely of courage. There were no studies or military exercises. There were, however, leaders, and leaders of great value.

It had remained in the memory of the Teutchs that in a remote era their island had been in great peril, assailed by a host of enemies of unknown origin.

A caravan of emigrants came from far away, from a land of which the entire world had forgotten the name, and had been received very hospitably some time before, on the orders of a divine oracle. Every man in that caravan was a hero; he paid for his hospitality by fighting so bravely and so successfully that the enemy host was dissipated and the island freed from them permanently.

Thanks were rendered to Heaven; the generous defenders were installed from that day on at the lead of the Teutchs' militia, with all the privileges of a noble corporation, uniquely charged with providing leaders for the protection of the country and wars undertaken abroad.

That corporation did not die with time; it prospered, grew and became, veritably, the unique force and glory of its adoptive country, without ever degenerating.

It was still brilliant when the Atlanteans arrived, by virtue of its position on the island and its courage, which had not degenerated relative to that of its ancestors. Its interests, moreover, did not differ from those of the rest of the Teutchs, with which it was perfectly identical, its primitive nationality having been almost forgotten—and, indeed, the blood of the two races had intermingled.

That corporation was known as the corporation of the Pah-ri-ziz.

Another corporation, no less important, was that of the Priests, whom the Teutchs called the Galls. Their functions consisted of rendering justice and practicing the ceremonies of religion during public meetings.

The great divinity of the Teutchs was the Night, so they counted their months and years not in days but in nights. They did not raise temples to her; they rendered their homage in the densest parts of their forests.

Those mores lasted a very long time, and we still discover them in part among the descendants of the Teutchs, the Germans,[18] in the second known antiquity. There would not have been anything alarming about them for the scholars of Atlantis had they not been reduced to slavery—but a slavery that was, in fact, quite mild.

Sylax found himself free enough to preach, and he did so courageously, even though he was preaching in a desert.

Me-nu-tche and the other scholars were solely occupied in conquering, by the graciousness and utility of the services they rendered, the esteem and affection of their masters, who were well able to appreciate them, and who all, in truth, while not forgetting their rights, responded to the favors with a grateful amity.

The Pah-ri-ziz above all, as well as the Galls, who were the most learned and the most benevolent men, were very devoted to them. One small event, quite simple and natural, but which was to have decisive consequences for everyone, rendered them brothers.

---

[18] Author's note: "See Tacitus." The reference is to Cornelius Tacitus' *De Origine et situ Germanotum* [On the Origin and Condition of the Germans], written at the end of the first century A.D. but lost and rediscovered in 1425. Mettais had no way of knowing that it would be adopted long after his death by the Nazis as a pillar of their sense of national identity, thus ruining its reputation.

Among the Teutchs, as among several other peoples of antiquity, it was customary, when a father wanted to marry off his daughter, to invite all the potentially acceptable suitors to a feast. The young woman would not attend the meal, but she would arrive at the end carrying a cup full of wine, which she would offer to the one she preferred.

Now, in those days, one of the Pah-ri-ziz chiefs, Lutetius, held that betrothal feast. He was Me-nu-tche's master. In his capacity as a slave, Me-nu-tche was to serve the guests and entertain them according to their wishes.

The meal passed as usual, and when it was finished, the chief's daughter, Lutecia, appeared. In accordance with a custom particular to the Teutchs, however, at that moment, before the young woman's choice was expressed, every guest had to sing a song adapted to the occasion. It was appropriate at a betrothal feast to sing about one's notable feats or those of one's ancestors, national or martial songs, ballads or ancient legends, but never anything frivolous.

The guests of the Pah-ri-ziz equipped themselves with all the enthusiasm of great desire, for each one was singing to impress the host's beautiful daughter.

The musical contest was always concluded by a song from the master of the feast, but Lutetius excused himself. Turning to Me-nu-tche, he said: "Slave, you have a fine voice; sing us, in order to replace the voice that I lack this evening, a song from your country.

Me-nu-tche was, in fact, a fine singer even in Atlantis; his song was bound to seem divine to the Teutchs. The impression it produced was, in fact, indescribable. He sang:

Uranus was a good king,
Who came down to earth.
*   To do what?*
To ask us the question
Why do you want a king?

That ballad, which had a lot of verses, was as old as Atlantis. It was a popular song from no one knew where, but which was evidently a song of governmental transition, probably the transformation of a monarchical government into a republican government.

The slave's voice had seduced all the guests, but the words, above all, had thrown them into a profound emotion, because they all knew the song, and they had all sung it many times in their life.

No one among the Pah-ri-ziz knew, any more than the Atlanteans did, where the song came from or who had written it, but the Pah-ri-ziz sang it as the national song of their ancestors—ancestors about whom they knew nothing. They had been in the land of the Teutchs for such a long time, perhaps many centuries, that the land in question was their only fatherland. All their history was there, all their projects and all their interests were there, but there was a tradition among them—and we already know that their corporation had not originated on the island—that their forefathers had once arrived there as refugees from their homeland. What homeland and in what era they did not know; they had only retained by way of history the fact that their ancestors had saved the island from its enemies, and Me-nu-tche's song.

But their history had just been revealed completely to their eyes. Their national song was the national song of Atlantis; therefore, Atlantis was their original homeland! Therefore, the Atlanteans were their brethren—and they had made them their slaves! Horror!

All the Pah-ri-ziz threw their arms around Me-nu-tche, shedding tears of joy. Lutecia presented him with the betrothal cup.

That news spread with lightning rapidity throughout the island. Instantly, the slavery of all the Atlanteans was ended; the law that rendered all castaways slaves appeared unjust, and was abolished that same day.

Joy was at its peak among the Atlantean scholars, who no longer saw their slavery as anything but a piquant episode to recount in the future. They conceived once again the pleasant hope of pursuing, even more fruitfully than before, the scientific results to which they had aspired. From that moment on the Teutchs became precious auxiliaries for them.

In fact, they found on the island all the assistance necessary to their expedition. Their project had not changed; it was still to explore that region of the seas, to go deeper and deeper into the lands of Europe, even though they had no certain notion of the route they ought to follow.

The Teutchs were quite incapable of informing them. They were only familiar with a few islands in the region, which they devastated from time to time, in order to prove their superiority over their neighbors. All the seas that lay beyond—and all the lands they contained, if any—were merely uncrossable regions so far as they were concerned, gulfs feared by the most skillful navigators or deserted lands populated exclusively by ferocious beasts.

The Atlanteans smiled at these lugubrious depictions; they only persisted more tenaciously in their voyage.

They departed, therefore, accompanied by a few bold Teutchs and a few adventurous Pah-ri-ziz. Lutecia did not want to be separated from her spouse, but she promised her father to come back as soon as possible. Me-nu-tche and the entire maritime caravan also promised, because they hoped to do so.

V. The Shipwreck

The first days of that navigation were very pleasant. They were employed in visiting the islands nearest to that of the Teutchs, especially the isle of the Sequans,[19] which was quite large, but diminished by a river that wound around it like a serpent, in such a way as to create an island within the island. The portion of land that was between the river and the sea was uninhabited and uninhabitable because of the continual inundations that kept it submerged for part of the year.

The studies to be made of that island were neither long nor difficult. The Sequans, like the other European peoples of that time, had no written history, nor any monuments other than the huts that served as their habitations and a few stones placed in a certain manner in order to have some significance in the narration of a memorable event.

---

[19] Author's note: "Sequan means serpent in the language of that people, as in that of the Gauls, who probably borrowed it from them. I apologize here for all these little notes, and hope that I shall not be accused of pedantry with regard to my subject. My intention is merely to prove the respect that I have for the truth, and that if I consent to group facts, perhaps arbitrarily, it is not purely for amusement or by virtue of eccentricity. My thinking is very serious and always respectful of the instruction of science." In fact, Sequani was a name given by Julius Caesar to one of the Gallic tribes living to the west of the Jura mountains. He also gave the name Sequana to the River Seine; although there seems to be no connection between the attributions, Mettais subsequently goes out of his way to contrive one.

These monuments, as can easily be imagined, were very fragile. The facts that they were intended to perpetuate could only weaken and be distorted as time passed, for tradition alone was their depository, and tradition, as everyone knows, always takes on the coloration of the epoch in which it arrives, the intelligence that receives and transmits it. What confidence can it inspire, in consequence, when it is found in a people where written history does not come to its aid?

The Atlantean scholars thought they had discovered, however, after extraordinary efforts of labor and imagination, that the small group of families of Sequania could well have emerged from the heart of Asia, as the Pah-ri-ziz had emerged from Atlantis and the Teutchs had emerged from the frontiers of India. But who had led them and the others here? How long had they been living in these islands? It was impossible to determine.

The mores of the Sequans offered nothing very particular to the Atlanteans, except for the simplicity of their legal code, which was enclosed in its entirety in a single question of judgment.

A judge was anyone to whom the accused and the accuser gave that title.

If your adversary had done to you what you have done to him, said the judge to the accused, what would you say?

The response of silence of the accused formed the judgment, which he never sought to falsify by subterfuge.

I do not know whether our costly and hypocritical civilization does any better than the Sequans. Their question was the corollary of the axiom that we recommend but never practice: Do not do to someone else what you would not want him to do to you.

After a few days of rest on the island of Sequania taken by the woman of the peaceful expedition, and a few days of futile preaching on the part of the Buddha Sylax, and geographical and astronomical studies to the advantage of the scholars, they embarked once again in order to take their research further into regions where they would henceforth find nothing but the unknown, the mysterious and the terrible, according to the Teutchs and the Pah-ri-ziz.

They had, indeed, scarcely put to sea when a number of ominous symptoms were manifest around them. A cold, moist and penetrating wind suddenly succeeded an air that was stifling but agreeable, in that it had never ceased to bring the two vessels the perfume of flowers from the nearby islands.

Sequania was lost in a thick fog that made it disappear completely from the voyagers' sight. The sky was covered with black, menacing clouds, traversed from time to time by fiery streaks, as a thunderstorm was in preparation. A few dull rumbles were, indeed, not long in becoming audible in the bosom of the clouds, probably reverberated by the profound echoes of the sea, for there too rumblings were heard—unless, Me-nu-tche thought, the latter rumbles were those of subterranean volcanoes.

An indefinable sentiment of unease gripped everyone. The voyagers huddled together, trembling as if at the moment of a catastrophe. The opinion was universal that they ought to go back to Sequania, but there was suddenly such an upheaval of the waters round them that the pilots were no longer masters of their vessels. Liquid mountains of a prodigious height, which appeared and disappeared by turns, drove them in spite of their efforts, without their being able to determine where they were going.

They had been struggling thus for several hours when they suddenly saw a column of water bearing down on them that seemed to them to rise up to the clouds, and which fell upon their vessels, gripping them as a giant might seize a wisp of straw, throwing them into the distance onto a forest of reefs, the points of which, sometimes sharp and sometimes broad, rose above sea level.[20]

The vessels were broken up; nothing more of them could be seen than a quantity of debris floating on the waters. Some of the victims of the shipwreck disappeared into the gulf, never to emerge again, while others clung on to a few pieces of floating debris, or onto the points of the reefs.

As if to insult them in such great misfortune the sea suddenly calmed down again.

At that moment, Me-nu-tche appeared, holding the unconscious Lutecia in one arm, pressed against his breast, while the other was wrapped around a wooden beam that dipped beneath the waves continually, to reappear thereafter.

Sylax, who could swim like a fish, had taken refuge on a protruding rock, around which he had already gathered a considerable number of victims, fixing them as best he could on the surrounding reefs, but his friend was not there; his eyes were searching for him everywhere when he perceived him struggling against exhaustion, on the point of being swallowed up. He leapt to-

---

[20] Author's note: "It is probable that this location was the present-day Switzerland. Scientists say, in fact, that in the first antiquity Switzerland, covered in water, formed a sea."

ward him, and was fortunate enough to bring him and his precious burden back to the precarious refuge where he was huddled.

The situation was critical, however; it was evident that it was impossible to remain there for long, so they set about seeking a means of escape. There was only one thing to do, if there was any possibility of salvation, and that was to construct a raft. There was no shortage of wreckage in the vicinity; the least exhausted and most agile immediately set to work. After hard labor and incredible difficulties, a miraculous deployment of energy and practical science, the raft finally appeared to be capable of taking to the sea.

In fact, it held together for ten days without breaking up, but, tossed about by the caprice of the currents and the waves, it drifted haphazardly over a sea in which they perceived the occasional island or scrap of land, only to see it recede every time they made an effort to get closer to it.

The castaways did not encounter anyone else, neither a ship nor a small boat; on the land they sometimes glimpsed in the distance no people ever appeared.

They had no oars and no tiller—and, what was more alarming, no food.

Finally, on the tenth day after the shipwreck, the raft ran aground on a deserted shore, in a land that none of them could name. It now only contained six passengers: Sylax, his friend Me-nu-tche, Lutecia and a young slave she had taken into her service, and two Buddhist nuns.

When they set foot on land, the first sentiment experienced by Sylax was gratitude to the God of the sea, who had preserved him and his friend; his first action was to kneel down on the edge of the perfidious waters to thank Him.

Me-nu-tche, for his part, although he was no less exhausted than his companions in misfortune, and probably as glad as Sylax to be safe and sound, immediately started searching for some edible plant or crustacean that he could bring back to the unfortunate castaways, who were dying of hunger. Perhaps he thanked God while collecting nourishment for everyone.

VI. Dream and Reality

In that epoch, continents were rare; to a greater or lesser extent, those we know today were under the sea; history and science tell us so.

There was nothing but islands almost everywhere.

The land on which the Atlantean castaways had run aground was one more island, and an island of no great extent, but which seemed isolated in the sea, for as far as the eye could see it only encountered the immensity of the waves.

It was deserted, although it presented a few traces of anterior habitation—but devastated, ruined habitations, as if they had been under the water, probably inundated by some invasion of the sea, perhaps some deluge that had carried the inhabitants away.

Sylax and Me-nu-tche had no doubt of that, knowing full well how frequent inundations and partial deluges were in the world, and how many countries had disappeared in consequence, while others had been born.

However unenviable a sojourn on that island seemed, they nevertheless found it at that moment to be a charming Elysium. They resigned themselves to installing themselves therein, and made arrangements to live there, temporarily at least, while awaiting a favorable opportunity to escape from the beneficent prison.

The awning of a few rocks served them as a retreat, the wild fruits of the island and the crustaceans that the sea yielded to them served as their nourishment for want of anything better.

Sylax and his friend were both scholars, educated in all subjects and very well versed in the theory of cultivating cereals. They therefore had no difficulty in finding the seeds of alimentary grains in the fields; courage and necessity immediately started them to work on the land.

When all those preparations had been made for the care of the body, Sylax naturally reverted to his preaching, and thought seriously once again about converting his friend, whose mind, it seemed to him, ought to be more accessible than before to the religious truths that would give him, he supposed, an immense consolation in the midst of the misfortunes that had recently overtaken them.

"My friend," he said to him one day, you're giving me a great deal of pain, for I see you marching resolutely over a terrain that will lead you straight to the abyss. You call yourself a philosopher, you're a true scholar, and yet you don't believe in God."

"Sylax, Sylax," replied Me-nu-tche, animatedly, "don't make me out to be more wicked than I am. I don't believe in God! But how can a man, at the sight of the brilliant spectacle of nature, not become ecstatic and seek the author of all the phenomena that surround him, and not recognize a God?

"I don't believe in God? Yes, I do believe—but what is that God? I've told you many times: it's the unknown God.[21] I seek Him, but you don't want me to seek

---

[21] One of the literary essays in calculated myth-transfiguration that Mettais would have had available to him when he wrote the present text was Edgar Quinet's *Merlin l'enchanteur* (1860; tr. as *The Enchanter Merlin*, ISBN 9781612273037), which also waxes lyrical on the subject of "the unknown God" whom Merlin prefers to all those specified by religious dogma.

Him. You tell me that you've found Him: good for you! But so many philosophers also say that they've found Him, and show Him to me in such various forms that I beg leave to doubt them all and continue searching.

"Sensitive and poetic souls have made a God as whimsical as themselves; philosophers and positive men have made a profound God, mystical in part, often material, and in any event incomprehensible.

"Where, then, is the true God? Are not all of them mistaken? The conclusion is not reckless, when we see how often the most expert scholars have erred in all times with regard to more graspable things, phenomena that we can touch with our fingers—the earth, for example, its formation, its composition, its form and its limits, its various transformations and the laws that regulate them.

"For our ancestors there was not one unique God; their Heaven was populated with an infinite number of gods. I believe that they made them themselves. Our modern civilization has found it more apt only to admit one God. Brahmanism only wants one, but in three persons. You, my friend only preach one, but also in several persons, with incoherent attributes, permit me to tell you, and with powerful passions based on ours. You give Him an essence that you don't understand, virtues that you don't understand, an existence of which you understand nothing, a will that is nothing other than your own imagination. Who, then, has told you all that?

"The Egyptians have a god other than yours. The Teutchs, among whom we have lived for some time— and, in sum, all the peoples who cover the Earth—have their own gods.

"What, then, my friend, is God? Is He not a king of stone or marble, who only speaks through the mouths of the fakirs who have built his altars?"

"Ingrate!" Sylax relied. "There is no God then."

"Have I said that, Sylax?" Me-nu-tche retorted, sharply. "Have I said that? God is! I affirm that, but I seek him, and in the meantime I have raised an altar in my heart to the unknown God! I don't want your God of all, as I've told you thousands of times, and I repeat to you firmly today, because you don't understand Him any better than I do, and, given that no one understands Him, everyone has made a God in his own fashion, in accordance with his own views, prejudices, interests and passions."

"What passions can I have, Me-nu-tche?" said the Buddha, sadly, "other than the desire to see you happy in the present and the future?"

"Oh, my friend, my friend," Me-nu-tche replied, embracing Sylax affectionately, "can I speak here for you? You talk about God as a scholar and a philanthropist, but your logic is faulty, your heart and mind have gone astray in the void of asceticism, and you want to summon the whole world to be happy. Poor friend, your fault is there—at least, I believe so. Well, I beg you, let me continue seeking; if I'm mistaken, perhaps I'll realize it someday."

Sylax shook his head, meaning that his friend's resolution was not that of a sage.

"A traveler," Me-un-tche said to him then, "one day finds on his route the magnificent ruins of an ancient city. Naturally, he wonders about the people who lived in it, and what evil befell them. He finds no one amid the ruins, but he takes shelter from a storm in the bosom of a magical monument, the remains of an enchanted castle.

He is anxious to go in quest of the master of the castle, to render him homage. If that master had written on the frontispiece: 'I am who am…traveler, rest, drink, eat, sleep and believe in me without worrying any longer about the master of the house; such is my will.' Oh, then I would obey that order—but that order alone.

"Everywhere that I have seen that order on the frontispiece of a palace, however, it is a human hand that has written it, in the name of the God it causes to speak. Alas, my friend, I am still looking on high, and have only ever heard voices calling to me from below."

Me-nu-tche was still talking, becoming more and more animated. Sylax tried more than once to interrupt in order to reply to him, but the intractable philosopher seemed to be in haste to finish, and to end the religious discussion once and for all, in the face of the necessities of the present life, and he implored his friend with a gesture to let him continue speaking.

"In conclusion," he said, "you have found God, you have surrounded Him with very scholarly attributes, it's true, and then you've created a religion, a doctrine, a morality, and you've damned all those who don't believe as you do. Well, my friend, I can say this to you: Why that religion? Why your dogma? Why your morality? Where have you got them from?

"In your morality, you want people to torment their bodies, annihilate their senses, bend their minds to an incomprehensible mysticism. Why, then, has God made those senses? Why has He given humans the power of reason? Was it so that people could make a virtue out of preventing the regular functioning of the being that God created? No, no, no! Leave me my belief, Sylax, my philosophy, my studies, and let's not talk about it any more. We have other things to do for the time being. Before thinking about tomorrow, let's think about today. In any case, to think about today is still to think about tomorrow."

Me-nu-tche's recommendations were futile; the Buddha could not give up his apostolic role like that, nor did he give it up. But the arguments became so sharp on the part of the incorrigible philosopher, his critiques were so cogent, his intelligence so brilliant and true throughout his polemic, that Sylax did not take long to perceive that, although he could not succeed in converting his friend, his friend was in the process of converting the two nuns. He therefore thought it prudent to reach an agreement with his friend not to make themselves apostles of any belief whatsoever.

It was agreed that the new inhabitants of the island would separate into two groups, as distant from one another as was necessary for the cultivation of the land, which was divided into two lots.

The two friends arranged a meeting place where they could argue at their ease every day.

That separation, which seemed painful to everyone, was nevertheless understood by everyone and accepted without opposition. Visits between the two groups were, in any case, not prohibited on either side. They softened the sadness of the separation somewhat, for they became frequent.

A time nevertheless arrived when the visits became rarer; then they finally stopped altogether, without the daily meetings of the two friends ceasing. That was the work of the Buddha.

Sylax, who still feared for the souls of his nuns, and who had made them expiate the sin of their indecision between his doctrine and Me-nu-tche's, gave them so many tasks to perform that the day was not long enough to complete them. Such, at least, was the excuse that the Buddha gave his friend.

And the days and the months went by in that fashion.

A day came when Me-nu-tche did not find his friend at the rendezvous—the rendezvous that he had never missed since the day of their separation. He was anxious about him, and without further ado he headed for his habitation at top speed. As he got close to it, he heard a few stifled cries, and then heart-rending screams.

He was only one bound away by then, and he burst like lightning into the little cavern that served the Buddha as a shelter. Dionah, one of his companions, was lying on a bed of dry moss; Sylax and Clito, the other nun, were beside her, lavishing cares and consolations upon her.

The unexpected arrival of Me-nu-tche took everyone by surprise; the cries ceased. Sylax lowered his head before his friend, without saying a word. One might have thought him a guilty man before his judge.

Me-nu-tche did not experience anything before the Buddha but a sentiment of amicable compassion; his heart was too noble to enjoy his adversary's defeat. He put his arms around him and embraced him with all the tenderness of a father forgiving his guilty and repentant son.

"Why lower your head before me, my friend," he said, "as if I were about to reproach you for having obeyed nature and God? Have I not said it to you? You've tried to stop a torrent, and it has dragged you away; you've tried to hold back the lightning, and it has knocked you down. What God has done is good, my worthy Sylax, and as you see, philosophy will always be in default when it tries to suppress is decrees..."

Me-nu-tche fell silent in order to hold out his hands to a little child who had entered the world by the way of pain, suffering and causing suffering, overwhelming his father and making his mother, who had unluckily been charged with a burden too heavy for her to bear, to turn red.

The course of the Buddha's ideas changed from that moment on. The voice of the family spoke more loudly in his heart than the sophisms of his mind. He modified his doctrine of celibacy, which he no longer imposed on his followers, but which, by virtue of a residue of habit, he advised them to adopt, without their being destined for a more brilliant throne in Heaven than others.

For himself, he openly renounced the perfection of chastity and took as wives the two women whom he had thus far taken for companions in his apostolate.

In the last days of his old age, the days when reason alone speaks to the soul, and the eye of intelligence sees without passion and without prejudice, he even modified the spirit of his religion, to the point of making an imperious precept of marriage, which remained in the laws of Atlantis.

The Buddha's marriage brought together once again the two families that had been separated by secret interests and intolerant thoughts. Everyone's happiness seemed greater for it.

That happiness soon became perfect.

VII. The Cradle of a Great People

It was a little over a year since the castaways had run aground on the island, and they had no idea how long the horrible sequestration would last that had taken them away from their families, their friends and all the hopes to which youth and a good social situation give rise.

They lived there in isolation, abandoned by the entire world, never seeing anything that could give them any hope of another future. They had no doubt that the desert had been inhabited one day, but it had been so completely forgotten by that time that no one came close to it from nearby or far away, and no one even seemed to suspect that it still existed. It had required the crazy expedition of a few extraordinary scholars to discover it, and it was scarcely probable that a similar desire would overtake others.

Sylax consoled himself for that in the bittersweetness of his fortunate sin; Me-nu-tche was mortally sad; and Lutecia continued to hope.

She was right, for one day, a number of pirogues were spotted, loaded with people, who were striving to reach the shore.

It was an expedition of Teutchs and Pah-ri-ziz; they were relatives and friends.

Despairing of seeing his daughter come back, as she had promised him, and convinced against all reason that she was in some danger from which he might be able to free her, Lutetius had decided set forth in search of her. To that effect, he had fitted out several pirogues, on which he had embarked the bravest of the Teutchs and the Pah-ri-ziz; then he had left, brandishing his mace and swearing to do battle even with the goddess of death in order to see his only child again.

The god of the seas had guided him generously, and the god of fathers had returned his dear Lutecia to him. He asked no more of God than that, and no more of the world.

The island where he landed was deserted, but it appeared to be as fecund as that of the Teutchs; he could create a retreat there as enviable as any other. Nothing, moreover, drew him back to his homeland; he did not regret either its riches or its honors. He wanted to be anywhere that the daughter might be whom he had lost among the Teutchs. He therefore resolved to settle there.

His project was agreed by everyone. It was, therefore, no longer a matter of living alone, isolated in the middle of uncrossable seas with sad memories of the shipwreck; it was a matter of creating a new fatherland, a society, and linking it with subsequent relationships to all the places where each of them had left memories.

One happiness never comes alone, says the wisdom of nations. A beaten path is soon frequented by everyone, says another.

While the Teutchs and the Pah-ri-ziz, joining the castaways on the island, took possession of the vast domain in the name of an incontestable right, and settled there, new guests arrived from various islands in the region, which no one knew and which had not been perceived until then.

Several days later, they saw more pirogues of emigrants prowling around them, which dared not land. They came from the direction of the isle of the Teutchs, notably from Sequania. They were friends; they were given the most amicable reception.

The colony thus became sizeable; it was necessary to think of organizing it, of dividing up the land, exploiting it advantageously, ameliorating it, and increasing cultivation as much as possible—in sum, rendering it habitable for everyone and prosperous.

For that, however, division was not sufficient; the leaders of the colony were wise, prudent and experienced men, and they understood that. They resolved to define everyone's rights and duties, in order that there could be no argument or misunderstanding in the relationships of the new associates, so that the necessary harmony and prosperity of the association would not cease to reign everywhere and in all things.

A clear and concise code was immediately drawn up by the most skillful, and then submitted to everyone, in order that anyone could offer observations thereon. Finally, a general assembly was held, and the code was discussed calmly and clearly, and definitively voted.

The name of the island, which everyone until then had designated at whim in accordance with their impressions, was fixed. To satisfy the memories of Sylax and his friend on the one hand, and those of Lutetius and his friends on the other, it was decided that the island would be called the Atlantis of the Pah-ri-ziz.

The Sequans called the arm of the sea that enveloped them the Sequanian Sea.

The few huts that had been built for a primary shelter, and which soon multiplied, firming the center of a government that did not lack a certain luster, took the name of Lutecia.

Lutetius was proclaimed the chief of the new state, with a council composed of Me-nu-Tche and nine other members. The chief in question was not a king, nor a sheikh, not an archon, nor a consul. The law alone and the people were all that. Lutetius was only charged with overseeing the observation of the law. Every time that it seemed to him to have been infringed, he referred the matter to the council, who called the delinquents to order. If there were difficulties in re-establishing the force of the law, the popular comitias were summoned, the Head of State and his council informed them, and the people judged.

No one had yet imagined having Heaven intervene in that business and accepting kings by divine right or kings as the saviors of nations. Nor had anyone judged it appropriate to create castes obtaining all their strength and credit from their gold, their privileged position or their dignities. Everyone collaborated to the same ends, everyone had the same rights and duties, accepted by everyone, and everything went well, because everyone was useful to the community, like the organs of the same body.

All the relationships between the citizens of the little nascent state seemed sufficiently well established for no one to complain very much.

Sylax, who had not ceased preaching, was named as the great Buddha. The scholars, and all the people with them, had thought and proclaimed, without the philosopher Me-nu-tse putting up any opposition, that it would be useful to preach a religious belief and manifest it publicly. Some thought it an essential social bond, others merely useful, but all of them thought it respectable.

Under this regime, which was modified from time to time in accordance with need, the Atlantis of the Pahri-ziz prospered. Its soil was ameliorated, a few changes in sea level sometimes adding a portion of land to the shore and sometimes a small island in the vicinity, with the result that a time came when the Atlantis found itself possessed of considerable territory and an imposing strength.

In sum, the Atlantis of the Pah-ri-ziz became, in time, a great country and a great people: one of the most civilized peoples of ancient times. Its history was brilliant and full of marvels.

It reigned for more than a thousand years.

I shall leave to others the care of recounting its splendors and the prodigies of its glory. For my part, I shall only take the eve of the catastrophe that bore it away, in order to recount a few more episodes—which will, however, sufficiently depict the decadence and the death-throes of a great nation.

PART TWO
THE ATLANTIS OF THE PAH-RI-ZIZ

I. How a Great People Falls

At its origin, as we have just seen, the Atlantis of the Pah-ri-ziz only thought of ensuring each of its members their daily bread and the labor necessary to achieve that objective.

It ought not to be congratulated for that, because that is merely what all peoples—those who associate themselves in order to contend more effectively with the vicissitudes of life—do at their commencement. One gives no thought, in those days, to causing the bird-lime of fortune, honors, distinctions and privileges to shine in the eyes of associates. The necessary and the useful are sufficient for everyone.

That is certainly not because it would have been very difficult for the founders of the new empire to take possession of favors and wealth, palaces and thrones, for themselves, their families and their friends, or even to obtain them with the apparent legitimacy of a general vote on the part of the little colony.

Lutetius, Me-nu-tche and Sylax were not novices in social and political life; they were perfectly well aware of the art of imposing on people—but they were, above all else, benevolent and honest men, and they did not abuse their ascendancy over their brethren, nor their ignorance, nor the embarrassment of their position.

Thus, they only decreed what was useful and good, only keeping for themselves just sufficient authority and supremacy to maintain good order and to guide the nascent State toward prosperity

The successive needs of different times sometimes modified their laws, but did not change them. Their laws were, moreover, regarded for a long time as sacred laws, for Lutetius, Sylax and Me-nu-tche, several centuries after the foundation of the Atlantis of the Pah-ri-ziz, were no longer what our history tells us, but individuals miraculously born to accomplish a divine mission.

Time had thus thrown its veil over the memory of the three friends, whom devotees had embellished with a highly sentimental legend that they recited with great religious faith—a faith worthy of all respect, at any rate, since it consoled them in their afflictions and rendered them happy.

Whatever happened, so long as that belief reigned, Atlantis was happy, as much, at least, as egotistical, versatile and envious human beings can be under the scepter of association. As I am not composing a pastoral but a philosophical history, I do not want to depict people other than they are, and the Atlanteans as perfect, biting into rocks of honey and slaking their thirst in streams of milk—but all in all, they were happy, I repeat, so long as they retained the code of Lutetius, and they retained it for a long time.

Under its influence, the Pah-ri-ziz prospered, and grew in a prodigious manner. Lutecia, their capital, acquired an unusual splendor; it even increased to the point of being a power in the land in its own right.

There came a day, however, when that growth of wealth and power overexcited the imagination of the

Atlanteans, who yielded to the love of gold, pleasure and enjoyments of every sort, and then to culpable ambition.

That ambition, the ambition of egotism and pride, finally burst forth among them; after several centuries of almost continuous peace, social and governmental tempests brought them once again to the brink of ruination, instead of bringing them the wealth that they had promised them.

In that remote era, in periods of revolution, they already had for watchwords the seductive devices employed today: progress, fraternity, public order. Alas, then as now, there was nothing in them. Such mottoes were merely the bait of fishermen, for they never produced anything in Atlantis but disorder and interested mutations. One saw them proclaimed, sometimes by ambitious despots, who, in the name of public good, took possession of the reins of empire for themselves and their descendants, thus creating hatreds and disastrous rivalries for the future, and sometimes by ambitious individuals of a different sort, who, not daring to offer themselves as heads of dynasties, represented themselves as liberators of a people that was not in jeopardy, thus slaking their avid cupidity and passion for domination.

In what epoch, however, did these symptoms of decadence commence? History does not say.

The Atlantis of the Pah-ri-ziz declined, in all probability, slowly and gradually, occasionally throwing off sparks of heroism, science and patriotic devotion. It fell little by little over centuries, until the day when it finally saw its supreme period arrive, two thousand three hundred and forty seven years before our era: the period when the heart of every Atlantean beat as on the eve of a strange and decisive event.

Now, in that year, the Atlantis of the Pah-ri-ziz was in great turmoil. A new evolutionary whirlwind had just carried away its government, and the revolution, embarrassed by its victory, did not cease making trials of administration that profoundly troubled the nation—the material interests of the nation, I ought to say, in the interests of clarity, for minds had already been troubled for a long time by evil passions, as many public as private.

There was no longer any question, in those days, of the paternal laws of the divine Lutetius. The benevolence and frankness that had dictated them had fallen into an even greater forgetfulness. At that time, no one any longer had anything but personal desires and aspirations, which were far from tending to social and political unity, the commonweal and the prosperity of the fatherland. There was no fatherland any longer; there was no longer anything but an association accepted for the sake of private interests, like a profitable exploitation, and nothing more.

Lutecian society, which arrogated the right of primacy in everything, set the tone for the rest of the country, and, in truth, the country gained no advantage from that, for the capital was even more corrupt in its principles than the nation. Its principles, it is true, had the aroma of a superior civilization; they were more refined and more polite, and also bolder and more cunning. Theft was good there, provided that it took on the soothing allures of good taste; murder was not a crime there, provided that it was committed with gloves on and presented itself under a borrowed name. Ignominy was, in sum, the order of high society, but in sentimental disguise.

Sentiment, among that people, had become the watchword of fine speech; it was everywhere, public law and private law. General opinion as nourished by its words and deeds; in sum, in the shadow of sentiment, everything was dormant, the law as well as the occasional good man. A sentimental expression legitimated all vices, excused all crimes, and honored all sins. Things had reached the point that an honest man, a man whose principles were uncompromised and undisguised, was shamed and vilified, and only presented himself to the law trembling, for fear of finding himself facing a skillful adversary who was able to evoke the necessary sentiment.

With principles so false, it ought to be understandable that it was very difficult for a moralist to unmask evil and the guilty—especially powerful guilty parties in whose interest it was to remain masked—so it was not permissible to tell the truth, as soon as it wounded someone. There were laws to stop indiscreet pens and voices; there was a public opinion that imposed silence.

The culpable and the cowardly, in high and low places, could thus prevaricate without fear, pillage, embezzle and abuse their credit in order to obtain enjoyments, to obtain gold. The law protected them; to speak of their misdeeds was treated as defamation.

And the strangest thing of all about that aberration of the people is that there had never been more talk of virtue, of benevolence, never so much boasting about one's merits and morality. Its statistics were all glorious. Its leaders were irreproachable in their disinterest, its magistrates admirable in their enlightenment, justice and devotion; its civilization was visibly growing, its population becoming increasingly perfect.

Poor people! Blind people! Could two of those panegyrists encounter one another without bursting into riotous laughter?

It is true to say, however, to be fair, that science had perhaps never risen so high as in those times; that in industry of the Atlanteans was prodigious then; that their civilization had all the most gracious and perfect forms; that the art of fine speaking was ravishing among them; in sum, that their knowledge and skill were so highly-developed and so subtle that with its aid, they could aspire to anything...

The government, for its part, was no longer a benevolent and conciliating father of a family but an acidic crucible of egotistic interests; its administrations were no more than factories of arbitrariness and petty tyrannies.

The arbitrary and the tyrannical had become, in the last times of that empire, so pestilential, so insupportable that several associations were formed, which became very important, to resist the encroachments and abuses of administrations large and small, in the hope of thus restricting them to their rights and duties. The means were good; they were legal; everyone understood that.

The sane individuals, in associating, had not wanted to paralyze the necessary operation of administrations, much less had they wanted to protest and conspire against the utility and good will of their creation and functioning; they had merely wanted to raise a dyke against the degeneration of the spirit of their institutions, to the malevolence of the vital hand that always moves machines of that sort. The vital hand is not always that of the master, that of the superior leader, or the responsible man who shines at the summit, but often that of a subaltern chief, or even sometimes an underling, one alone, who calls himself the administration, who speaks in the name of the administration, and attacks from within that fortress anything that threatens to breach it.

In order to resist that malevolent administration-man, whose perfidious hand strikes in the name of authority, in the name of a respectable principle, it was, in fact, necessary not to be alone with one's rights in facing him; something more was necessary: the word of an association and the weight of an association.

What harm could there be in that?

And yet, it is that association that malcontents have accused of the inopportune invasion of the latest revolution to turn the Atlantis of the Pah-ri-ziz upside down.

They had nothing to do with it, says one jovial critic of the times,[22] for those associations were made of up well-intentioned men, and well-intentioned men are not equipped to raise shields and wield weapons; it requires more energy than they have, and more enthusiasm.

Well-intentioned men always adapt, as well as they can, to the government to which they are subject. They know that they are a conquest, slaves to determination; they resign themselves, unable to do more with their pacific logic. Even if their bonds are sometimes too tight, a few cuts of the whip a little too sharp, tortures are sometimes too inquisitorial and cruel, they are scarcely roused. Even the most docile bird pecks the hand that chokes it, but the well-intentioned people of Atlantis would not, in the year two thousand three hundred and forty seven, have pecked anyone. Their cage was gilded, their chains were made of flowers, the code of ambition and despotism was sheltered by logic, the whiplashes were benevolent, the poisoned bread was cake, the mur-

---

[22] Mettais' political pamphlet, published not long before his return to literary work, was *Des Associations et des corporations en France* (1859)—a defense of what would be called trades or labor unions.

derer wore gloves and a smile on his lips and he only spoke to his victim politely and with an exceedingly touching respect.

Thus, concludes our malign critic of Atlantis, these well-intentioned people could not have taken up the sword—except, I confess to their honor, he adds, that they let it happen; they even expressed wishes for the combat, softly sounding the charge, and singing the victory loudly.

Then, they reflected...

It is a fact, let us say, seriously, that the last revolution in the Atlantis of the Pah-ri-ziz was not led by the protective associations; it is necessary to look further afield for the cause, in the murderous vices of the society of the day. Even the government and its voices had nothing to do with it; it would be wrong to accuse it, for what weight could it have had in a society so perverse?

What could have become, then, of such a people, a people that no longer had anything but the duties and rights of narrow and interested convention, outside of strict logic. What could have become of a people that no longer had any generosity, any disinterest except in maxims that it no longer practiced, any fatherland, any laws except laws that lent themselves to all kinds of arbitrary interpretation? What could have become of a people in whom there was no longer anything but privileges everywhere, privileges of birth and titles, privileges of gold and boudoirs, privileges of camaraderie, before which merit, good well and need always fail; a people of aristocrats who had written equality into the laws and were clever enough to prove that all Atlanteans were equal? What could have become of a people who no longer had any honest men but cowards?

History informs us cruelly, by showing us the condition of the Pah-ri-ziz Atlanteans in the year two thousand three hundred and forty-seven, the very year in which the first fires of their final revolution broke out.

In that year, the ruler was King Atrimachis IV.

King Atrimachis was a generous, great man with a just and impartial mind. He had reigned for ten years; he was only forty-five years old when he fell from the throne. He had succeeded his father, Evenor VII, an incapable man if ever there was one, who had succeeded one of his uncles, Gadirique I of sad memory, whose reign had made no small contribution to the collapse of the throne of his ancestors.

Evenor was good, mild and peaceful in his character. The story of a misfortune or a suffering never found him insensitive; he would have liked all Atlanteans to be as happy as him—but he was afflicted by an intellectual apathy that approached imbecility. He had no suspicion of the duties of a head of state, so he did not reign, and did not seek to reign. A throne, for him, was merely a comfortable seat in which he could sleep at his ease, without worrying about today or tomorrow.

Too unintelligent to understand people, he abandoned his authority to the ambitious, to the intriguers who governed in his name, who pillaged and drained the public treasury and sucked the sweat of laborers under the pretext of amelioration and progress.

Under Gadirique, by contrast, pillage had been conducted arrogantly and unceremoniously, in his name. His intelligence was superior, but debased by his ardor for material enjoyments. For him, royalty was simply a Land of Cockayne, an Eldorado where gold rolled along the streets, where pleasures flowed in the gutters. His luxurious palace overflowed by day with guests engaged in ignoble feasting, and by night with courtesans of repulsive lasciviousness.

His guests were his ministers.

His obliging nocturnal companions were pensioners of the State, which they devoured with the appetite of ogresses.

The people had ground their teeth at the sight of these costly ignominies, for the most precious of which they paid the expenses with their blood, but those ignominies had corrupted them.

Following the example of the court, the aristocracy had begun to live life at full tilt, the bourgeoisie had imitated the aristocracy, and the little people had followed the example of the bourgeoisie. The appetite for luxury and pleasures had become universal, and to satisfy it, no indelicacy was repugnant, and no penalty deterred anyone, provided that they thought themselves clever enough to skirt the abyss of the law without falling into it.

In the midst of all this family and public disorder, Atrimachis, the heir apparent, seemed to be forgotten. His father paid no attention to him except to wish that he might one day become as happy as himself. The young man therefore launched himself as he pleased into the life of the day, where he fortunately found more emptiness than he had expected, more disillusionment than real pleasure. His heart was, therefore, soon sated; his intelligence, however, was considerable and his will was good.

His errors only served for his instruction; his natural and curious intelligence easily grasped the falseness of the philosophy of grandeur, with the result that when the time came to mount the throne of his father, he was ready. He was sufficiently educated, and he promised the

Atlanteans a happiness that they had not known for a long time. But he could not provide all the riches and honors to satisfy everyone's tastes. He could only give them sage laws, labor and daily bread.

That was not the dream they had formulated. His good intentions foundered, therefore, against sloth and the love of luxury.

Too philosophical to reign in those days, too disgusted with the world to have the energy that might have saved him, he folded his arms and waited tranquilly for the final hour of his life or the final hour of his reign.

All his merit was, therefore, in being an honest man and devoting himself to private virtues, with which he did as much good as he could in his immediate surroundings. He did not believe that he was strong enough to do any more; public morality had arrived at a point of degradation so advanced that he dared not even try to raise its level. It was, in fact, bad, but everyone believed it to be good; the people thought that they were on the finest path to progress and high civilization. It would have been the glory of a great man to prove them wrong.

Meanwhile, everyone was suffering; as usual, no one was occupied with that malaise, but the government was blamed for it.

In any case, the situation was no longer tenable. What could be done about it? To push things to the extreme, to overthrow everything, would only be an exchange of miseries, the wisest people thought. They understood that the evil lay elsewhere, that Atrimachis would be difficult to replace, and that his government would only change its name.

It would have required a God to govern the Atlanteans, or angels to obey.

So the men of peace and good will, to acquit their conscience, contented themselves with merely asking for ameliorations, as if they were possible, while the restless men and the petty philosophers pushed with all their might for a revolution, regardless of the consequences.

For a long time, but most especially in those days, Lutecian society had been divided into castes, which became increasingly accentuated. The principled ones were that of titled individuals, the potentates of finance and the wealthy; that of Buddhists, who only recognized God as a master; the bourgeoisie; and finally the proletariat. There had always been a permanent antagonism between all these castes, which sometimes burst out in a formidable manner. If, in days of discontentment, they sometimes made alliances, it was only to tear one another apart afterwards, on the day of division.

Tossed about in the midst of them, the government had sometimes favored one and sometimes another, according to where it believed it could find the elements of success, but when the time came, it no longer found in the others anything but adversaries who were all the more redoubtable because they were more animated.

That state of affairs lasted a long time in the Atlantis of the Pah-ri-ziz, and was then effaced, giving birth to another kind of danger by giving birth to another kind of enemy—enemies all the more terrible because they based their claims on public rights, on the natural aspirations of the people, which they highlighted, and everyday grievances that were tangible to everyone.

Those enemies became ardent, political and proud, talking on an equal footing with the highly placed members of the governmental hierarchy, and people listened to them, sensing that they had strength—as, indeed, they had.

Those men did not form a distinct caste; they recruited support everywhere, but they had a historical past, a genealogy that went back a long way. It was found in all evolutionary epochs, in all social upheavals.

Among them there were good men who had a keen sense of their rights, natural human rights. There were also, unfortunately, ambitious men who had not yet found the prominent positions they coveted, men of restless character, unquiet and desirous minds who found themselves out of place in the sphere in which they lived. There were men that nothing ever satisfied, utopians, bunglers, arrogant petty tyrants. Finally, there were all the men in eternal opposition, men impossible in any society.

These people gave themselves the good name of democrats or republicans, and under that seductive name, which only ever speaks of rights, respectable because they are essentially true, and of generous projects, of civilization, rational progress, fraternal solidarity—a name that represents to humankind its reason for being, its social rationale, the primitive social contract without which association might never have taken place—under that name, those people had become an important power in the time of Atrimachis, for the majority of the country had united with them, as reminders of public interests in peril.

Even the king did not feel the courage to resist them to his own advantage, because he understood that they were right.

II. The God Chephren

The time was, therefore, ripe for a change of administration, but the respect that everyone had for the virtues of King Atrimachis, the recognition that was alive in all hearts for his good will and his constant efforts to spread wellbeing around him, delayed the catastrophe until his death.

That death occurred in the year two thousand three hundred and forty-seven, but it arrived too soon, because, in spite of all the muted conspiracies of the few and, in spite of the expressed desires of the many, no one was ready on the day of need. They were able to demolish, but they were not able to reconstruct, and the various pretentions of the pilots who took over the direction of the ship of state only contrived fruitless and perilous experiments.

The boldest and the less capable spoke loudly, so loudly that practical minds and men of good will drew away from them in order to avoid dangerous conflicts, perhaps more dangerous than the provisional administration that was installed, waiting for the appeasement of evil passions which they feared aggravating further by attempting to control them.

That retreat was a misfortune that everyone felt but no one admitted, for the Atlantis of the Pah-ri-ziz was abandoned from that day on to the utopists, the ambitious and the madmen who thought that a people could be guided like a flock of feeble and fearful children. The wisest people could, in consequence, see clearly that their country was running precipitately to its ruin. But what could they do? Nothing, except weep for the dying fatherland and say prayers for it.

Among those people there was then in Lutecia a considerable individual who was, before anything else, a good man. That was the philosopher—or, as he was called, the god—Chephren.

Chephren was still young, although he was known in Lutecia as "old Chephren." In the Atlantis of the Pah-ri-ziz, as in its maternal African Atlantis and a number of other antediluvian peoples, judging that old age had all the virtues of prudence and wisdom, and the knowledge that long experience gives, people often qualified as "old" anyone who possessed those virtues—hence the considerable number of years that were credited to several individuals of that epoch.

Now, Chephren was a very "old" man, because he had all those virtues to a supreme degree.

Profoundly possessed since childhood with a sense of human dignity, human rights and human duties, he had devoted all the force of his intelligence and all his studies to the philosophy of beautiful souls who saw nothing but the good to be done. No science was strange to him; he had studied them all, seeking the unknown and mysterious in all of them, the unknowns of human origin and human destiny. In order to devote himself to that task more easily, and not to be distracted by any other affection or any other duty, he had renounced the charms of the family.

If the life of the god Chephren had been one of continual study, however, he had not made that study from his fireside. No one, perhaps, traveled as widely in the world as him. Everywhere, he examined the various types of humankind, dissected their habits and their mores, comparing them with one another; he searched the remotest and least known nooks and crannies, the oldest and most obscure histories. He dug in the ground in all directions, descended into the deepest caverns, and scrutinized the most deserted rocks lost in the immensity of the seas.

And when he returned to his homeland, laden with the prodigious booty of his knowledge, he spread the fruits of his research everywhere with the prodigality of good taste that everyone knew to be his inclination, and recompensed him duly, for his reputation became immense.

He thought that it was time to profit from the ascendancy that he had to ameliorate public mores. He saw his principles held in such great esteem; people cited them everywhere; his veracity was highly praised, his justice lauded on all sides. People no longer approached him without talking about the god Chephren; many people no longer paid any attention to anything but his words, his deeds, and even his weaknesses—for he was not perfect—and took pride in imitating him in everything. People no longer swore except by the old god Chephren; that was the fashion.

Like any fashion, however, that one passed. It had been taken too far, too ardently for there not to be a passionate reaction against it.

The clear-sighted mind of Chephren, who could not discover beneath the civilization of the Atlanteans and in their mores anything but prejudices, errors and egotism—disguised vices, in sum—made the generous error of not sparing them, of attacking them, of preaching harsh truths to people who did not want to know them any longer, of criticizing the pleasant vices that they caressed lovingly, of saying to thieves: "Be disinterested!" and to assassins: "Protect your brethren!"

People did not take long to find it inconvenient and intolerable: a bizarre and ill-conceived philosophy. The boldest launched sarcasms at him that found favor with the public; he was no longer called anything but the prophet of doom, the god of tempests, or the old man of the mountain—because he never ceased representing civilization as a mountain that all peoples ought to climb, and he committed the crime of showing the people of Pah-ri-ziz heading down the slope of that mountain, at the bottom of which was the chasm in which they would be engulfed.

The most disciplined, the men of good company, who only ever insulted people politely and wittily, no longer called him anything but old Nholh-Chephren. Nholh, in the Atlantean language, was the equivalent of our word "recluse."[23] For them it was an epithet of derision, which referred to the forced retreat into which the forgetfulness of the world had thrown him.

Public opinion was too keenly stimulated with regard to the philosopher for the government, which was no wiser than public opinion, not to think it appropriate to intervene in the mater. It was bound to find Chephren's spoken and written preaching unhealthy; he was hauled before the bars of its tribunals, which would inevitably have condemned him but for the veto of King

---

[23] Author's note: "Noah, in the Hebrew language, similarly means something like 'recluse.' I leave it to the reader to decide whether the name and deeds of Noah have any analogy with the facts we are relating. It is permissible to wonder, when we know how many curious and sentimental legends born of perfectly natural and simple facts our forefathers have transmitted to us that have reached us through the ages with along all the marvels of their naïve beliefs."

Atrimachis, who held him in the highest esteem and loved him dearly, even though Chephren belonged to the breed of democrats. The king respected conviction everywhere, and he knew that an honest man of conviction has never been and never will be a danger to the adversary of his opinion.

The philosopher was thus not crushed by the courts, but he took it as a warning. He ceased his importunate preaching; he no longer wrote and he no longer spoke, shutting himself away in unapproachable retreat where he devoted himself to studies that absorbed all his time and all his faculties, seeking to resolve by strange experiments a problem that had been posed to the world for a long time, but had never been resolved.

That problem, which was grave, interesting, and an object of legitimate curiosity, which agitated the profound thinkers and, it is necessary to say in praise of the epoch, the masses of ordinary people, was this:

Where did humans come from? Had there been a first man? How had that first man come into being?

Opinions, of course, were fervently divided, and as with any insoluble question, or very nearly, the debate was very animated: affirmations and theories were infinitely various.

The belief emitted in the sacred books of Buddhism written by the divine Sylax more than a thousand years before that epoch was that God had created humans by a single act of will, as He had created all the other beings in the universe.

The sacred books maintained a prudent silence as to the epoch of that creation. Moreover, they did not advance that belief as an article of faith, but merely as a conventional belief—debatable, at any rate. The Buddhism of Sylax, as we have seen, was possessed of a polite tolerance. The influence of the philosopher Me-nu-tche is easily recognizable therein.

The field of combat therefore being open, everyone threw themselves into it head first.

Some who were devotees nevertheless, were convinced the God had made a statue of earth and then had animated it with the breath of his mouth.

That is a pretty invention, replied the adversaries of that belief, but provide us with proof. It is not sufficient to tell us what God could have done, what He wanted to do and that He did what you say. Were you there? Your assertion is insufficient. For our part, they added, we have another belief, and one that does not lack evidence. Follow our reasoning carefully...

Their reasoning it is necessary to admit was more scholarly, but it was not more convincing. In any case, it had multiple versions.

Some claimed that the first human had been entirely constituted by the combination of atoms, either hooked or at various angles, but at any rate sufficiently well-shaped to form the beautiful whole that we know, by virtue of a sympathetic aggregation.

Others found in the electricity of molecules enough intelligent forces to compose a human, provided that one went back to a sky and favorable conditions that were unknown, or no longer known.

Others claimed that there had once been in nature, at least in certain conditions unfortunately unspecifiable, fecund forces that had all the human generative properties, and that it would be useful to research.

Others, finally, based on the same theory, which they specified more categorically, affirmed that the opinion was true and that humans had been born from nothing—which is to say, from very little—by the spontaneous generation of some insects, an animate atom, which, improving under the influence of a special cause, had taken on increasingly perfect proportions in mounting the scale of generation, always under the influence of a special cause that they could not characterize, but which must exist in nature, or must at least have existed one day, perhaps only for one day, perhaps even one minute.

That question, to which we no longer attach much importance today, because we believe it to have been resolved, was taken very seriously by the antediluvian Atlanteans, either because it was of more recent provenance among them or because they had more reasons than us for not accepting a definitive solution.

It was to that question that the god Chephren attached himself most ardently in his retreat, where he devoted himself to experimentation that his adversaries and enemies turned to ridicule, calling him eccentric, bizarre, cabalistic—or even a maniac, according to some.

In any case, that mania rendered them an immense service, as we shall see.

The city of Lutecia was vast, extending over an immense plain strewn with mounds and rocks, which still retained all the imprints left therein by the erosion of the seawater under which they had been obliged to reside. The population was very large, and, as a great many houses were not very high because of the intensity of the heat, which was only tempered at certain times of day by sea breezes, one can imagine the vast expanse that they had to occupy.

All the private houses, and there were a great many, had only two stories, one of them hollowed out or built at the expense of the rocks and mounds, the other dominating that kind of basement in the form of tents made of textiles or animal hides, according to the wealth of the residents.

The tallest houses served as rental properties. They had four stories, ordinarily topped by a kind of belvedere in the form of a tent, similar in kind to those of private houses.

Lutecia extended further to the north than the south; to the south it was limited, in one part of its territory only, by a kind of desert of which no one made advantageous use and even seemed to be avoided. That terrain was stony, scored in all directions by sheer and deep crevices filled with stagnant and noisome water and filth of all kinds. It was also enveloped by broad ravines, sinuous and extreme, bristling with menacing rocks and hideous caverns, whose pestilential walls continually oozed green-tinted water.

The municipal administration had finally decided to fill in that inferno, from which fever and disease erupted from time to time. It had understood the necessity for a long time, but had always been stopped by an idea that had a certain respectability.

Tradition indicated that location as the retreat of the founder of the Atlantean religion, and a few passages in the sacred books revealed it as such. It was there that the spirit of God had come to take the Buddha Sylax and carry him to Heaven, from which he had returned a few days later to fetch the gods Me-nu-tche and Lutetius: a charming legend that, for those of us who know the history of the three friends, reveals to us in poetic terms that Sylax died first and did not take long to be joined in the tomb by his two friends.

For the Atlanteans, however, the Buddha and his associates had literally flown to the heavens, from which they would return one day to bring rewards to the faithful Pah-ri-ziz and convey them to a better life, while they would imprison miscreants in an unapproachable island from which they could never emerge, where they would be devoured by hideous and ferocious beasts that would make them suffer all the horrors of a cruel death without allowing them to die.

It is obvious that Me-nu-tche had not written that page of the sacred books, and that even the worthy Sylax had wanted to frighten the incorrigible and wicked, to whom one cannot show too many hideous images of remorse, even if one has to charge them with the darkest colors of the imagination. The imagination can never exaggerate the depiction of vice and the torments that are due to it.

Now, the philosopher Chephren offered to take responsibility for sanitizing that inferno on condition that the property in it would be assured to him, and also on the condition—imposed by the city—that the terrain would conserve its original appearance, to the extent that that could be reconciled with the objective to be attained.

The genius of the philosopher succeeded perfectly in his operations. A large bed of sufficient depths, without escarpments, was opened to the interior waters lurking in the filthy crevices. The crevices were filled in; the entire terrain conserved its ravines, which served it as both a boundary and a protection, giving passage to the interior waters and mingling its own with the stream that had been dug.[24]

He thus made himself a charming habitation, as useful for his studies as it was healthy for everyone. He

---

[24] Author's note: "The Atlantis of the Pah-ri-ziz being recognized as France and Lutecia as Paris, it is not improbable that Chephren's retreat occupied the territory of our Île de la Cité."

would have been able to obtain an immense profit from it if he had been a speculator.

He therefore installed himself there, resolved not to emerge again for any reason whatsoever, and to seek in the labor of his intelligence and the scientific booty that he had amassed over the years to forget the disillusionment that the ingratitude of his fellow citizens had caused him to experience.

It was in vain, however, that he sequestered himself from the world; the world followed him everywhere with its eyes and its sarcasms. The scientific installations that he built for his experiments were monitored maliciously.

He was of the opinion that sought to reproduce humans from nothing, to draw them out of oblivion—or, to put it better, to make a human with a substance that did not appear to have that destination, for Chephren was not an atheist. He thought that everything had a cause, that matter had not been created alone, that there was in addition a principle to which it would have been wrong to give a material and palpable name, but evident, nameless for him, and which had created humankind as well as everything else.

He thought, however, that the principle in question was not destroyed forever, that it was not impossible for it to create several times more a creature that it had already created at least once, and that it would be as well to research the conditions suitable for obtaining the same result himself.

That was his great preoccupation. The knowledge he had acquired, the environment in which he lived—which was very different from ours today—perhaps gave him the right to hope for a success that appears impossible to us, but which might not be in the future.

III. Chephren's Ark

The scientific occupations of the god Chephren were not alone in being lacerated by the mockery of his enemies and frivolous individuals; even his habitation received no mercy from them—not, of course, on account of the fine result of the salubriousness that he had brought about there and which no one could deny, but for various particularities of accommodation that could, in fact, seem rather singular at first glance.

The philosopher Chephren was, as we have said, a great observer, a great thinker and a great logician; he was an earnest man, seriously weighing up past and present facts in order to draw practical inductions therefrom whenever he could.

Now, science tells us and history does not allow us to ignore that in the oldest times of our knowledge, especially in antediluvian times, waters were widely expanded over the earth, to the point that we cannot say for sure whether there were any veritable continents. The regions called by that name are nothing but vast terrains, it is true, immense but furrowed in all directions by rivers, lakes and marshes, around which one always ends up encountering the sea.

Science also tells us, and history supports it with its authority, that in those remote times volcanic eruptions were frequent, and that immersions and emersions of islands, even large islands, were everyday events; inundations, either by torrential rains due to the vast extent of the seas, by the overflowing of rivers and lakes, or by sudden invasions of the sea, were frightful, burying entire countries, sometimes temporarily and sometimes permanently.

Everyone knows what the ancients report to us about a few inundations of which they retain a religious memory and which they converted into pious legends. They had been so devastating that they had created a word to designate them: the word Deluge.

The philosopher Chephren, who was not ignorant of anything and did not forget anything, had calculated that all the catastrophes of which his forefathers had transmitted the memory to him, and all those he had seen in his numerous and distant voyages, and all those of which he had palpable evidence close at hand, were bound to recur some day. The work that nature was doing on the coasts, the subterranean rumbles that his ear caught in all directions, the unusual changes in the level of the Sequanian Sea, and something whispering in the scientist's heart and mind, told him that the time was imminent, and he wanted to be ready for it.

As soon as he had completed the sanitization of the retreat that guaranteed the present for him, therefore, he thought about the future. That was not the least ridiculous thing for which he was reproached. People were able to do that when they had sufficiently frivolous minds to want to judge what they could not understand, so strange did his work appear, contrasting with normal habits.

The philosopher had pitched his habitation tent in the middle of his terrain, but beside that tent he constructed a large, solid vessel with different compartments. As soon as it was finished, he took up residence therein with the animals that he kept on his island for is experiments. He stored provisions of food therein, and all the objects indispensable for a long voyage.

It must be agreed that building such an ark in the middle of a field in order to live in it, and also fitting it out for a long and perilous voyage that was only a dream, was a fine subject of conversation for ill-intentioned neighbors, but the philosopher let them talk. He continued his work, continually renewing his food stories and taking personal care of the maintenance of his ark with all the attention of a castaway constructing his escape raft.

One evening, in the year two thousand three hundred and forty-eight, a year after the death of Atrimachis and the revolution of the Pah-ri-ziz,[25] he had just concluded the customary round he made to observe the transformations undergone by the various animals that he had placed in environments and conditions suitable to obtain the results for which he hoped, and he had gone back into his vessel in order to reflect there at his ease, when he suddenly found himself face to face with a stranger that he was not expecting.

"I'm Dr. Plunos," said the newcomer, bowing profoundly before the man he had come to visit.

"Welcome, Dr. Plunos," the philosopher relied, with a gentle smile, offering him a seat. "I'm happy to see you, for you too, I believe, are one of today's accursed."

"I am one of today's accursed," the doctor relied, "And I'm very honored by it, for I'm like you, and am cursed by the same people that curse you. Today is not a day of wisdom and moderation, which ought never to be forgotten by people who represent themselves as civilized and progressive."

---

[25] Mettais appears to have forgotten that the year 2348 B.C. was actually the year before 2347 B.C., not the year after.

The doctor smiled and continued: "It's true that they have the principles of civilization, they dream of its institutions, and they have their sacred books, outside of which there is no salvation—but look at what they make of those who are not of their petty church. You they curse because you preach moderation, conciliation, tolerance and effective fraternity in democracy; me they curse because I'm a skeptic who only believes in science, who only courts science, and who laughs at their politics and socialism as one laughs at sibylline oracles that say yes or no at the whim of interested parties."

The doctor went on: "Change humankind, my friend; render it good, just, disinterested, patriotic, and I shall be yours; if not, no. What does it matter to me, who wants nothing in the world but to live peacefully, whether ambitious and egotistical man at the head of the society into which hazard has cast me is called a sheikh, a king, a president or an archon? As long as he's a man, his fine language doesn't seduce me; I know that he'll act as a man—which is to say, in his own interests. So much the better if mine can adapt to that.

"But pardon me; I haven't come to see you in order to speak ill of my fellows but to learn from you the wisdom that people deny you, but which you nevertheless practice so well, it seems to me, and to discover the objective of your projects—if that would not be indiscreet."

"Pardon me, too, Doctor," the philosopher replied, "and be kind enough reply before anything else to my curiosity. I don't want to speak ill of my fellows either, but I've long been a stranger to the affairs of my nation, which is in great turmoil, I believe, and I'd like to learn from a man as competent as you to judge where their affairs stand. Are there still any royalists since the death of Atrimachis? What are they doing? What are the republicans doing?"

"The royalists are pitilessly proscribed; those who could have fled abroad; those who could not have been thrown into the sea with their hands and feet bound and an enormous stone tied around their neck, by order of the republicans.

"The republicans cannot agree among themselves how to found a sage and prosperous State; each one has his own petty system in his pocket, which he wants above all to prevail, and in order to succeed, persuasion not being sufficient, he employs violence. To that effect, each pretender has assembled disciples, aides and soldiers, and marches with his head held high, weapons at the ready and a warrant of proscription and death always in his hand, not only against the royalists, and not only against the dissidents, but against the suspect. The suspect are the people who do not rally quickly enough to his banner—with the result that I'm beginning to fear for myself.

"There are a few moderates among them, though: they only want to rob the rich, reduce genius to the level of stupidity, and equalize profits and fortunes in order to recruit devoted and incapable acolytes—in sum, to trouble a natural order that will assert itself some day in spite of them, and of which they are perhaps asking no more than to reduce the fortunate to their own level or to elevate themselves to theirs."

"So the camp is divided," said the philosopher Chephren, sadly.

"The camp is divided."

"The poor fools! To have such a beautiful throne in their hands, in democracy; such a beautiful code, in fraternity; and such a fine objective to attain, in progress, civilization and happiness; and to squander and dishonor all of that for the sake of petty ambition and reckless pride! Oh, my fatherland, my fatherland! But who are these men, then?"

"Orators, second-rate writers, clubmen—in sum, people of petty views from all classes, who think themselves important because they have a fluent pen, words to hand, and will find themselves devoid of status if they can't obtain an important position in the republic."

"Poor Atlantis of the Pah-ri-ziz!" exclaimed the philosopher. "You shall share the fate of thousands of peoples who have preceded us!" The god Chephren took on a prophetic tone: "To have so much sap, so much future, and only to live a thousand years! To be on the edge of the abyss and to argue over a preeminence of such short duration! To dance on a volcano instead of providing for one's safety and the safety of all!"

"Is that not your wisdom, philosopher Chephren?" said the doctor, in an interrogative tone, thus arriving at the purpose of his visit. "Is it not to provide for your safety that you've constructed an ark?"

"Yes—an ark that people laugh at; an ark that they'll soon envy me, I'm sure, for the time is near when the earth will undergo a frightful cataclysm, when the sea will race over the seas, and over humans, and lands will be engulfed in volcanoes that are already rumbling; and the man who is so proud today, who aspires to live in a palace and hold the scepter of a master in his hand will be happy to find a plank, some miserable piece of debris, in order to escape the fury of the waves...but let's leave it there; I'm a madman, I'm a Nholh. Talk to me about honest people; console me by telling me that there are men who honor our principles."

IV. Man and Beast

Dr. Plunos did not reply to the philosopher's question, and lowered his head.

"Atlas, however," Chephren went on, "the young Atlas who is so great today, and whom I've always admired since his sojourn in Sylacea, where he occupied such a minimal and precarious position, but in which he already showed so much wisdom and energy—isn't Atlas a rude jouster in the republican lists? In spite of the glory with which he has covered himself, in spite of the prosperity in which the republic has established him in recompense for his services, is he not still good, wise, a modest patriot and a true democrat? Does he not still open his window to listen to the plaints of those who are suffering, and keep his door ajar in order that those in need can open it when they will?

"And Nimrod, of whom there is so much talk, of whom so much good is said, the simple and generous man who is said to devote his life to the service of his friend Speos, when he could lead such a grandiose existence? And Speos, too? I beg you, Doctor, tell me all the good things that are said about those diamonds of democracy."

Dr. Plunos shook his head.

"No!" cried Chephren. "Those men are no longer just men! They too are ambitious, self-interested!"

"Have I said that, Philosopher?" the doctor retorted. "I would have been wrong, for in truth, nothing indicates that those men are not pure diamond. But I'm skeptical; I no longer believe in good; and if Sylax himself were to return to earth today, I would probably not believe in him."

"Too bad, Doctor! It's so good to believe in virtue. I believe in it myself, although I know it to be rare. Nothing accuses the men I esteem, does it?"

"No, nothing, and I would have been wrong to suspect them, for I see no reason why they should not be true in their principles and the glorious struggle they're sustaining. Atlas is young, but he's as wise as an old man; he uses the gifts of the fatherland with a charming modesty; he's disinterested to excess. Nimrod is his friend's steward, but that's out of devotion; everyone knows it and says so. Speos is rich, and his patriotic faith has no need to be animated by any other fire than that of conviction..."

"Thank you, Doctor Plunos," exclaimed the philosopher, enthusiastically. "God, principle of all things, principle of good, thank you! Thank you, illustrious prophets of the Atlantis of the Pah-ri-ziz, Sylax, Me-nutche and Lutetius, the divine founders and legislators of our empire, thank you, thank you!"

The philosopher Chephren was good and generous; he forgot the sarcasms that his compatriots heaped upon him, in order not to think of anything but wishing them well.

"Oh well," he said then, suddenly changing the tone of the conversation, but greatly relieved of an enormous weight that seemed to be crushing his heart, "you've seen the raft that I've prepared for myself for the day of the shipwreck; the disaster can come whenever it likes— I'm ready. But you haven't see anything of my home yet; you haven't seen my scientific experiments, my menagerie, in which I'm striving to effect transformations from one species to another. Come and see!"

Dr. Plunos was one of the great scholars of Atlantis. He knew about the possibility of transformations by virtue of observation, since there are animal species that are subject to continual metamorphoses; he knew it by virtue of the monstrosities that he had seen in certain species of superior animals—but neither he nor anyone of his acquaintance had ever obtained voluntary metamorphoses produced at the whim of science…and he was going to see them in the home of the philosopher Chephren!

"Patience," the philosopher said to him. "What you're going to see is very little, but I'll obtain more."

The doctor smiled; he understood Chephren's thinking. "You hope to be able to create a human."

"I hope so," the philosopher replied.

"You'll mold a statue and then animate it?" said the doctor, laughing in fits.

"No," Chephren retorted. "Only God can work that progeny."

"You'll combine cleverly electrified atoms," the implacable doctor went on, evidently mocking opinions that were not his own.

"No," said the philosopher. "I shan't create anything or combine any atoms, but I'll force the nature of a living being to develop in accordance with my will, in order one day to produce a human; I intend however, to keep a part of that secret."

Plunos shook his head. "I too," he said, "have tried like everyone else to create a human, and have not achieved anything—and I believe that one can only arrive at that conclusion. Perhaps we cannot create a human, because the generative human essence has disappeared, either because of the degeneration of the atmosphere or some other condition, or because it consisted one day of a powerful will that is no longer active. Anyway, it's nonetheless true that we can do nothing ourselves, and that it's prudent to admit that humans came from no one knows where, although we have no lack of theories on the subject. Personally, I think they're all full of extra-scientific boldness, illusions and errors, with which everyone has colored beliefs that are more religious than historic."

"You're mistaken, Dr. Plunos," Chephren replied, severely, "and you're not talking as a scientist. Although you've found nothing but despair in your research, you ought to wish that others might be more successful than you. Have you not seen anything in my home, then? You have seen, you have said—will you retract?"

"Oh, no," replied the doctor, with a hint of embarrassment in the face of his interlocutor's mercuriality. "What I meant to say is that, even supposing that you succeed in producing a human, as you say, by transformation—and, in truth, I'm tempted to take your word for it on the basis of what I've seen here—supposing that you succeed in developing all the limbs and all the organs of one of your experimental elements all the way to the human type, how will you animate him? Will he not be human in appearance only, while internally, the life—the soul, in sum—will be that of a brute? There, I believe, your power will stop; you'll only have an imperfect, hybrid being—a monster—because you won't be able to give him a soul."

The doctor seemed triumphant, because he was trying, like everyone else, to resolve the great problem of the creation of humankind, and he had had so little success that he would not be sorry not to be overtaken by anyone else.

"Does a brute have a soul, doctor?" asked the philosopher, with a sly smile, which indicated that he was asking a highly controversial question.

"A soul...a soul...," said the doctor, between his teeth.

"A beast is alive, however; it lives, as humans do," Chephren continued. "It dies, as humans do, it breathes, eats, digests as humans do. Because it does not speak their language, because it does not devote itself to their industry, their studies, their follies, their passions, their crimes, you say: it has no soul. And the Molochians, the Belphegorians and the Chananeans, a few of whose tribes only resemble humans in their configuration—all the savages, in sum—do they have a soul?

"Among us, maniacs, the hallucinated, madmen of every sort, every quality, every shade, cretins and idiots...do they have souls?

"Why, in that case, should beasts not have a soul, too? Don't deny it, Dr. Plunos—every animal has a soul; that soul has less perfected faculties, I don't deny, even less in some species than others. Of all the species we know, it's the human soul that appears to us to be the most perfect—absolutely, that is; relatively, every soul is perfectly adapted to the machine it has to animate.

"One more thing, and let's finish, my dear doctor, with the perfection of the soul. Tell me what the soul is, and I'll tell you whether a beast has one; tell me, in addition, why that soul is more or less perfect within the human species. Do you, personally, believe that it functions with the same perfection in all humans? Do you dare to say that there are not, in the scale of the human species, infinite gradations between the soul that functions with a rare perfection and the soul that is at the bottom rung of the intellectual level, approaching the relative perfection of the beast, of which it is not always in advance?

"Well, Doctor, what does all that imply? A material disposition that hinders the functioning of the soul in some, and leaves it free to operate in others. If, therefore, I succeed in giving human perfection to an imperfect being, I have no need to give it a soul; its own will develop more freely in its second state than in its first, to operate the new machine to which it finds itself adapted—the human, in sum...

"But forgive me, it's getting late, I'm keeping you too long," said the philosopher, who did not want to cut short the discussion of a question on which he had so much to say. "Until tomorrow, then, I beg you, Doctor! I invite you to follow with your own eyes the transformations I'm preparing. I have no pride; I'm hopeful, but if I fail, what does it matter? The game will begin again. If I don't find it, someone else will; for it will be found, you can be sure of that. Seek with perseverance and conviction, as Sylax says, and you shall find, for God has yielded all His knowledge to humans, but wants them to search for it."

Dr. Plunos shook philosopher Chephren's hand affectionately, saying to him: "I'll come back tomorrow, the day after and every day, since you've invited me." On the point of going out he stopped, and turned to the philosopher. "Thank you very much for your friendship," he said, "for it is friendship, not to fear surrendering your most precious secrets to me. Well, in return. I'll also give you mine, for I have one—and, more fortunate than you, I've very nearly found what I was looking for."

At this point Dr. Plunos lowered his voice. "Tomorrow," he said, "I'll give you my secret in detail, but tonight, know what it is. By means of cabalistic signs made powerful solely by my will, I can magnetize an object, or even a man. More willingly, however, I take a bracelet that I put around my arm, and then fall into an ecstasy. What surrounds me then becomes nothing to me; I no longer see and no longer hear anything but what I have resolved to see and hear in my ecstasy. My spirit transports itself anywhere, into the most distant places and the most impenetrable places; it reads the depths of hearts, it sees the past and the present; only the future is hidden from it; but I'm searching, and like you, I say: I shall find it.

"Well, in that ecstatic state, I've seen what no one, perhaps knows; I've seen an intimate history that will interest you, and which you will appreciate better than me, a poor scholar who only knows my books, while you have studied humans and their passions with a view to social wellbeing. The story—forgive me for having to cut it off at this point—is that of a few men that you hold in high esteem. I ask your forgiveness in advance if what I have to tell you is bad, if my science is indiscreet, and if my words take away illusions that are dear to you.

"Until tomorrow, then, philosopher Chephren! Confidence for confidence, secret for secret! Adieu!"

And Dr. Plunos retired, very pensive, but more preoccupied with what he had seen and heard in the philosopher's ark than what he had said himself and what he had to say.

The next day, he was on time at the rendezvous. He was awaited impatiently. Chephren was not jealous, but he was deeply impressed by the doctor's discovery, which he had not suspected, although he knew so many things and believed that he had studied everything. Perhaps he had, like many others, treated as dreams and ridiculous sortilege the mysteries of electricity and animal magnetism, which, in our day, still do not appear to be worthy of the study of a great thinker, and are willingly relegated to the level of the sibylline utterances of fortune-tellers.

Now, what he had disdained had yielded unexpected and prodigious results to a scientist as serious as he knew Plunos to be. He therefore felt very curious to converse again and to measure the success of his new friend, if he had been successful.

We shall gladly leave the two scientists to talk to one another about electricity, animal magnetism and occult science, but we shall retain for ourselves the story that Plunos had promised to tell.

I do not want, however, to tell it like him, with all his numerous and varied reflections, all its scholarly digressions, mingled with philosophical observations, which did not fail to multiply his exclamations of disappointment, sometimes of horror, and, above all, his questions.

The story, moreover, did not reach its denouement during the hour of conversation between the two friends, but the doctor followed all the twists and turns with a double interest—his own and that of the philosopher, whom he kept up to date until the end.

We shall not dispense with the end of Dr. Plunos' narration in order to return to our two scientists in the particular time and place. In any case, we shall not leave the Atlantis of the Pah-ri-ziz, and especially Lutecia.

PART THREE
THE ATLANTEAN REPUBLIC

I. The Orphans of the Dolmen

In the year 2347, at the end of the reign of Atrimachis IV, the small town of Sylacea[26] was greatly agitated. Its short distance from Lutecia, about thirty leagues, retained it under the influence of the troubles that were fomenting in the capital,

The town, however, was apparently tranquil; the magistrates sat in their tribunals without contest, the armed force functioned without opposition and the laws were executed there as in peacetime. But minds were troubled; people were complaining inside the houses; clubs had been established in cellars; agitators were moving around mysteriously in the evening and by night, going from door to door or into the fields to co-ordinate and organize a revolution. They were waiting for the signal to act, which was due to arrive, at any moment, from Lutecia.

It was an evening in the last days of summer; the sky was covered with hideously black clouds, and a gla-cial, whistling north wind had just got up, making the gaudy leaves of the tall palm trees bordering the road quiver noisily.

The carriage that maintained a direct service be-tween Lutecia and Sylacea suddenly appeared around a

---

[26] Author's note: "Probably Orléans."

bend in the road, scarcely grazing the road in its rapid flight, and then suddenly stopped, although it had not yet reached its destination.

A passenger got down and continued on foot, alone, toward the city. At the very edge of the suburb of Lutecia he stopped. He was hesitant; it appeared that he no longer knew where he was, and was searching his memory for forgotten indications. Perhaps the appearances of the suburb had changed, or perhaps a long absence had caused the traveler to forget its physiognomy.

It was difficult to say exactly how old the man was; he appeared to be about forty. Perhaps he was a just and good man, but in that case, his physiognomy was deceptive, for his eyebrows, strongly arched and inordinately long and bushy, which scarcely allowed this red and piercing eyes to be glimpsed in the depths of an impenetrable redoubt; his nose, long and hooked like the beak of a bird of prey; and his beard, red-tinted and unkempt, give him an intimidating expression of dissimulated harshness and mocking cunning.

The man's embarrassment seemed considerable, but he was about to go into the suburb anyway when he heard footsteps behind him.

He turned round, and saw a young woman, who seemed as anxious as he was, but for a different reason, for she was not searching but waiting. He went toward her.

"Are you from Sylacea?" he asked her.

"Yes, sir, I'm from Sylacea."

"Is this really the suburb of Lutecia?"

"Yes it is."

"That's strange; I don't recognize it at all. Has it changed a great deal, then?"

"No, sir," the young woman replied. "In the ten years I've been living here, it has changed very little."

"Yes, but since twenty years ago?"

"Twenty years ago, I don't know—I'm not that old."

The stranger reflected for a moment, then said: "Do you know in the suburb of Lutecia..."

He stopped suddenly at that point, on seeing a young man, toward whom the young woman turned abruptly and said: "I came to meet you, because I was anxious; you're so late coming back, and father isn't well."

"Pardon me, sir," said the stranger to the newcomer, "I understand that your presence is required elsewhere, and I don't want to keep you, but I wanted to ask this young woman, your sister or fiancée..."

"Both," replied the young man phlegmatically.

"I wanted to ask this young woman," the stranger repeated, not seeming to pay any heed to the singularity of that reply, "whether she knew in the suburb of Lutecia a peasant by the name of Ypsoer."

"We don't know him," the young man replied, in a curt voice, still walking.

The stranger bowed and was about to draw away when large raindrops began to fall amid thunderclaps that invited the little group to hasten their steps.

"Are you from this town, sir?" the young man said to him.

"No."

"Do you at least know someone who can give you shelter during the storm that is about to break violently, according to all the indications?"

"I don't know anyone."

"Would you care to accept our hospitality, then? It won't be very brilliant, but it will be given with a good heart."

"Thank you, young man. I'll come with you."

They hurried on, and it was just as well, for the clouds that had been threatening for some time immediately burst and released floods of hail—but they went into their dwelling at that moment.

It was a house of very simple appearance. As in other houses that nature did not permit to be hollowed out in some hill or rock, the ground floor was constructed of solid masonry and perfectly maintained. It was surmounted by a platform on which there was a tent with several compartments. A service stairway led from the ground floor to the tent, and another led directly to the platform from the outside.

The dwelling did not give the impression of fortune but of ease; the most exquisite neatness reigned there. Its population was only comprised of the two young people that we know and an old man, in the early phases of old age, normally strong and vigorous but presently lying in his bed, so ill that he was unable to recognize anyone.

The stranger greeted him without receiving any response; then, after having examined him with a profound gaze that doubtless did not reveal what he was looking for, he turned toward his hosts, to whom he addressed a few words of condolence. He retired hereafter to the room that had been allocated to him, where the young woman served him a light meal that he accepted with pleasure.

As she bowed to him in order to withdraw, he said: "Permit me, miss, to offer you once again the expression of the great chagrin I experience for the misfortune that is threatening you, and my profound sympathy for your poor father. I'm not a man of high position or great wealth, but if I can do anything, I place myself at your disposal."

"Thank you, sir," the young woman replied, in a tearful voice. "I haven't yet thought that I might need anything, so long as I was here. Today, though, you're right, I can't hide it from myself that our father is dying, and that from then on..."

The young woman could not conclude the thought, which the stranger understood perfectly. Sobs stifled her voice. She pulled herself together, however, and soon resumed the conversation.

"You see, sir," she said, then, "poor Song, who is so ill and whom Atlas and I call our father, isn't our father; he's our benefactor. He picked us up ten years ago by the side of the road where our parents had doubtless abandoned us. I say our parents, but that might be wrong, for I don't know whether the people we were with before were our parents."

"Have you always been in Sylacea?" asked the stranger, with a very particular interest.

"No, sir, we had come from far away, very far away, when Song took us into his home, but I was so young that I don't know where we came from, and when I talk about it to Atlas he seems not to know any more than I do about that."

"Atlas isn't your brother, then?"

"No, he's my fiancé. Our marriage has been delayed because of political affairs, which aren't going very well, he says—and he ought to know, because..."

The young woman stopped there and bit her lip until it bled, for she had perceived that she was about to betray a secret on which Atlas' liberty might depend, since the club-members of Sylacea, especially the ring-leaders, were hotly pursued by the police.

"Anyway," said the young woman, starting again, "We're not Song's children, and we aren't due to inherit anything from him when he dies. I think, in any case, that he has no wealth except what he earned by his labor. This house isn't his; it belongs to a rich lord in Lutecia, who also has a palace in Sylacea and vast lands in the vicinity of this suburb. Song cultivated that land, and we helped him."

"And what is that lord's name?"

"Lord Nirvana."

That name, which was perfectly familiar to him, made the stranger smile—and his smile was malevolent and mocking, for the name reminded of a cruel and un-expected disappointment.

"Lord Nirvana," the stranger repeated, in a reflec-tive tone. "The Lord Nirvana who has a pretty daughter of about your age?"

"Yes, Ormuzda," the young woman replied, with a stifled sigh that said more than her interlocutor could divine.

"Ormuzda," said the stranger, between his teeth, weighing his words, "who was betrothed in her cradle to the son of a rich man, nobly titled: one of the foremost in King Atrimachis' court—the illustrious and eminent Mo-Kie-Thi, whom secret difficulties once chased out of Atlantis, while his son died very fortunately, to enrich his heir…yes, I know that lord."

"Chemnis!" cried a voice suddenly, which came from the dying man's room, with a tone of despair that announced a catastrophe.

It was Atlas' voice, calling to the young woman. Song had rendered his last sigh. The stranger had no difficulty divining that accident, but he did not move. What, in fact, was the death of a man he did not know to him? He had better things to do than leave this room; he had to think before speaking.

He therefore leaned back in his chair, his legs crossed and his head supported by his left hand, while his right hand played mechanically on one of the arms of the chair. The numerous loose pleats of his large mantle, a kind of peplum in the fashion of the day, were hermetically sealed around him. He remained motionless like that for a long time, as if profoundly asleep. Then he got up and uttered a sigh from the utmost depths of his chest.

"In fact, it won't be so bad," he said, in response to some intimate thought, and heading for the small low and narrow window that let a little daylight and air into the room. "Of course," he continued, "It'd be very simple to run...after whom? Children that they don't know, and ought not to know. Thank you, my God for this encounter! These, I have under my hand, while the others...oh, to the devil with the others! Let someone else look for the undiscoverable Ypsoer. Until tomorrow—tomorrow, then! Let's spend the night up there; night, it's said, brings counsel."

The window was immediately reclosed, and the traveler went to bed, rubbing his hands with satisfaction. Then he went to sleep, with an infernal smile, while the most poignant desolation set in at Song's bedside.

Atlas and Chemnis had just lost their only friend, their only protector. Launched once again into the midst of the uncertain sea of life, they could no longer see a shore for which to head. The young woman had already forgotten the stranger's benevolent words, and Atlas no longer trusted anyone.

He was right. Who could he trust, at present? He looked into the past.

Chemnis had been right when she said that she knew nothing about her past. Atlas has said so in his turn; he too was ignorant of his past. He saw nothing at first but a family repudiating him, throwing him onto the rubbish-tip of the world like something filthy that might soil them. He could not see anything after that but a peasant depositing him one day at public mercy, in accordance with the prescription of the law, on the dolmen in the main square, at the foot of the statue of the Buddha Sylax. He did not even know who that peasant was; Song had not known either; everyone had forgotten his name.

It was Ypsoer.

Ypsoer was married, but had no child. He was not from Sylacea; he had arrived one day, fleeing the fields of his forefathers to search elsewhere for an ease he had not found at home.

He had hoped once in his new abode, because one evening, very late, his door opened mysteriously and an unknown and invisible hand had deposited a little child in his dwelling, without saying a word. It was a boy; it was Atlas.

A few years later, a similarly unknown and invisible hand deposited another child in the same hut—a little girl; that was Chemnis.

But no ease had come with them or after them. That was strange, because in those days the Pah-ri-ziz, who had no refuges open to abandoned children, usually got rid of them in public squares, but those who were introduced furtively into poor homes always brought with them unexpected favors, sometimes even fortune.

Ypsoer, having waited in vain for a few years, became restless, then set out again in search of wellbeing in another country...but shortly after his departure, two orphans were found on the dolmen of lost children.

It was from there that Song took them. It was to him that they owed the names that they bore, which he had given them, as was his right, and also the little happiness that they enjoyed before his death.

That was the whole of Atlas' past. What hope could he obtain from that?

All the past! There was also something else, much closer, which was nothing for a young man but a source of turbulence; but that, he only admitted and looked at secretly, even though it was the entire principle of his life.

We have said that Song was Lord Nirvana's tenant farmer. Lord Nirvana was a very important man in Sylacea; he had been its civil governor. Reckless and compromising expenditures had diminished his credit, and he was sacked from his post, but if he was less rich he was still wealthy; if he had incurred some disgrace at court, he still had great authority.

He had a daughter, Ormuzda, a little of whose unfortunate history we already know. She was beautiful, well-developed, although still almost a child. She promised to make a fine match for a great lord.

Atlas saw her; he saw her often, and poor Atlas loved her as he had never loved Chemnis.

What could he do about it? That was the worst part of his past, the past that he incriminated so much. He hid his love as much as he could, but Chemnis divined it.

Atlas had only one means of obtaining Ormuzda: to increase his own status to match hers, or reduce hers to match his; to cover his borrowed name with glory and become rich and powerful, or debase the name of Nirvana, decrease the power of his lordship and destroy his fortune.

Atlas had no aid to request of his past for that giant task, but he was able to find some hope in the democratic and social revolutions of the future. He therefore became a republican, and marched on that path with as much haste as he could.

But what a way he still had to travel to reach Ormuzda! He had covered so little on the day of Song's death and the arrival in his home of the mysterious stranger!

II. Servant and Master

Two days after Song's death, in the morning, a shower of fine and warm rain, such as one sometimes sees falling at the end of summer nights, had just watered the roads of Lutecia. The curtain of a tent moved aside gently near the middle of Dionah Street, the most beautiful street of the richest quarter of the capital. A pretty plump hand with gracefully slender fingers laden with diamonds supported the curtain; then a little slipper covered with rich embroideries appeared on the threshold; finally, a head extended very mysteriously outside and peered anxiously at the two sides of the street.

It was a woman's head, covered in an elegant morning coiffure, which obviously indicated fortune or coquetry—but the woman was too beautiful to be a coquette. She was no longer in the first flush of youth, however, in a country where people aged rapidly; she was certainly over thirty.

From time to time she listened to the interior of the apartment; then she returned all her attention to the outside, showing evidence of great impatience.

It was obvious that she was waiting for someone, and feared being caught.

"My God, it's him!" she said, letting the curtain of the tent fall back precipitately—for she had heard a noise inside the apartment.

Then, suddenly, she uttered a little cry, which might have been a cry of fright. She found herself confronted by a man, who bowed to her respectfully.

"It's me, Madame," he said, in a voice that strove to be gracious.

"You frightened me, appearing suddenly like that. You didn't knock."

"A thousand pardons, Madame, I did knock."

"No one replied to you," said the lady, with dignity.

"I saw that Madame was waiting for me."

"But if you'd found my husband here, or if he saw you in my apartment at this hour..."

"I know that Lord Speos is walking in Clito Square, smoking his opium pipe. I thought, in consequence, that there was no inconvenience in coming in to see Madame immediately, to give her the information I have."

The gracious wife of Lord Speos uttered a profound sigh then, as if her husband's absence had relaxed her lungs, which the fear of his presence had tightened.

Her phlegmatic visitor, who had come to bring her news, did not speak, however. He waited impassively for a question before recounting what he seemed to be proud of having learned. An indefinable expression of superiority, irony and perhaps challenge, seemed to reveal that secret sentiment. His mouth was slightly pursed. He let the fire of his gaze descend upon the poor woman, which appeared to make her ill at ease in the midst of the desire she had to interrogate her messenger.

One would not have thought that the man was merely a hired servant, and that the woman was the wife of the rich and powerful Lord Speos. It is true that Lord Speos himself bowed his head before him, growling, like a ferocious beast recognizing the hand of its master.

To understand that marvel, we need to go back a little and say a few words about a fundamental law of the Atlantis of the Pah-ri-ziz, which will explain better than any other narration the grave situation of our characters.

III. A Law of Marriage

If the Pah-ri-ziz Atlanteans were not always satisfied with all the laws of their country, which they turned upside-down from time to time with revolutions, only to recover them subsequently under other names, as is always the way, there were certain fundamental laws that they conserved with a religious respect.

They came in a direct line from the Buddha Sylax, Me-nu-tche and Lutetius, a divine trinity that they never separated, either in their invocations or the beneficent attributions that they derived from them.

The foremost of these laws was the one pertaining to marriage.

Now, that law permitted a young woman to marry at the age of fourteen; it ordered her to do so at twenty, on penalty of going into a convent and remaining cloistered there for five years. She was liberated again after that time, but always under the injunction of marriage, unless a panel of experts dispensed her of the obligation for reasons of health.

A young man was not permitted to exceed the age of twenty-two without entering into the bonds of matrimony without exposing himself to five years of expatriation. When that time was past, he could return, but only to obey the law.

Among the Pah-ri-ziz, the initiative of marriage was not, as among modern peoples, the sole privilege of young men. The first request was also accepted, on the part of both families, without any distinction.

A second article of the law specified that any young man who was in default of legal mores, if he were found to be guilty, would be expelled forever from the territory of Atlantis, unless he married within three months.

The young woman whose fault was recognized would be exposed in a small canoe, pushed out to sea with no oars and no sail—in sum, no means of steering—abandoned to the grace of God and the waves, forbidden ever to return to Atlantis if she survived, except to marry within a time designated by the law.

That entire law was severe, but it found a corrective in another article of the matrimonial code, which prescribed that spouses had to remarry every five years if they wanted to continue to live together. If they wanted to separate, they were free after that space of time—but separation was a stigma from which one did not recover easily.

Now, in the year two thousand three hundred and twenty-eight, there was in Lutecia a man of high intelligence, who had achieved wealth and honors by virtue of his own knowledge, firm determination and merit. He was the head of the militia. His name was Arimaspes.

Like all Atlanteans, Arimaspes had satisfied the prescriptions of the law with regard to marriage. Not long thereafter, however, he had lost his wife. He had then made the resolution to remain alone henceforth with his only child, his daughter Ludia. The love of his daughter and the memory of his wife were sufficient for him; he did not remarry, the law giving him that right.

Arimaspes had numerous friends, some who liked the man and doubtless others who only liked his credit. Frank and good, he delivered himself entirely to the pleasures of friendship and the familiarity of friends.

He was by no means suspicious of anyone's sentiments, and yet his daughter grew up and blossomed like a hothouse flower. She was beautiful, sensitive, inexperienced—as one is at that age—and unfortunately, too free beneath her father's tent. The poor father thought her still a child, but one day...

First, he perceived one day that his child was unusually thoughtful and sad, that she was ill; eventually, he perceived that she no longer had the innocence of a child.

Arimaspes did not blame his daughter; he only blamed himself. His despair was profound, and overwhelming for Ludia was not yet fourteen, and her seducer...her seducer was immensely rich, of very high status, of almost royal nobility—but what did that matter? Her seducer was married.

The law was there, inexorable; it applied to everyone. Ludia, his only daughter, his beloved daughter, his entire life, was to be cast adrift at sea, alone and with no hope of salvation.

Arimaspes wanted to elude the harshness of the law. To that effect he addressed himself to a man recommended to him by public opinion: a young man, it is true, but wise, good, religious above all, and yet somewhat needy, for he was devoid of parents, of any family—any admitted family, at least—and without any support to ensure his existence.

Where did he come from? Nobody knew. He was, it was said, like so many others among the Pah-ri-ziz, a child of hazard—the child of a seduction, one might have been able to say, but after all, who could tell? The young man was discreet, and did not say anything, if he knew himself. He was, in any case, wise beyond his years and revered by those who knew him as a young old man.

Lord Arimaspes heaped him with benefits, made him the most seductive promises and then confided his daughter to him, in order to hide her from everyone's gaze without arousing any suspicion.

That man and Ludia left one day, therefore, on a long journey, traveling far and wide until the day when the young woman brought a son into the world.

Arimaspes' secret but formal order was to make the child disappear at birth. The young mother divined that; she seduced her severe guardian by means of caresses, tears and promises. She consented to be separated from the child, never to see him again, provided that she knew that he was alive, and she also took responsibility for providing for all his needs.

It was arranged in accordance with her desire.

She therefore returned to Lutecia, happy and tranquil, her heart full of love for her son; but she found her father on his death-bed. The mortal threat that he saw continually hovering over the head of his beloved daughter had killed him. He died in his daughter's arms a few hours after her arrival.

Ludia remained alone, inconsolable for that great misfortune, but she was rich, honored, and uncontested in her virtue. She was therefore keenly sought in marriage; she passed the age of fourteen on her father's death.

She did not welcome any request; she wanted to wait. Everyone understood her filial discretion and praised it. They were mistaken, for it was the father of her child for whom she was waiting; it was him and him alone that she loved. He was married, it is true, and there was a stigma in marrying a man who divorced without a grave reason, but what did that matter to Ludia? She would accept the stigma, she would accept any ignominy, provided that she married her seducer. That seducer was Mo-kie-thi.

But Mok-kie-thi was no longer in Lutecia; he was not longer even in Atlantis. Unfortunately, the weakness of his heart had rendered him guilty of a crime in the eyes of the law, and of a crime punishable in such a terrible manner that he had been unable to bear the thought of the punishment that awaited his victim. He had fled before Ludia's fault became known—or, rather, he had gone on a long voyage with his wife, promising to return soon. Everything indicated that that was his intention, that his voyage would not be of long duration. He had a child—a very young child—and he had not taken the boy with him, fearing on his behalf the fatigues of a voyage in which he saw nothing but adventures and perils. He had entrusted him to a friend.

Mo-kie-thi had two intimate friends in Lutecia: two childhood friends, school friends, friends in social life—lifelong friends, in sum—whom he estimated to be equal in virtue, because they were both of proverbial probity. They were Lord Nirvana and Lord Speos.

An oath linked him to his friend Nirvana: an oath of betrothal. Nirvana had lost his wealth; Mo-kie-thi, who had enough for two, had thought it a good idea to recall fortune to his friend's home by a gracious means, and had betrothed his child in the cradle to Nirvana's similarly infant daughter.

Mo-kie-thi's son's refuge appeared, therefore, to be there, but Nirvana was indiscreet and the traveler feared his questions. He departed without seeing him; only a letter informed the other of his departure.

It was, therefore, to Speos that Mo-kie-thi addressed himself. "My friend," he said to him, on the eve of his departure, "I confide my son to you; let him be yours! I'm leaving for a long voyage, perhaps dangerous, but necessary. Don't ask me where I'm going, and you'll give me a great proof of friendship. Don't accuse me, either, of not trusting you, for the secret of the voyage isn't mine." Smiling, he added: "Look after my possessions, I beg you, for it's necessary to anticipate everything in life, and give that property to my son. You may keep them if—may Sylax, Me-nu-tche and Lutetius preserve us from that misfortune—my son should die. That's my testament."

At the same time, Mo-kie-thi gave his testament to his friend Speos, who shook his hand effusively, with a heart heavy with sighs.

Mo-kie-thi departed; he left Lutecia, and then Atlantis.

His son soon died.

The days, the months and even the years passed by, and the traveler did not return. Where was he? What had become of him? No one knew. He had perished in a shipwreck, some said, in a deluge, said others, in an encounter with brigands or wars in which he had taken part abroad, suggested others. The point on which there was no disagreement was that he had perished.

Meanwhile, Ludia reached the age of twenty; she married Lord Speos.

The man who held the young mother's secrets in his hands, the man who had saved her child, followed her there. Ludia Speos could not do without him; she had need of his services, and she had need of his silence.

He was, in any case, a precious man who always knew how to respond to the confidence that was placed in him, a man of genius who never flinched in any mission, no matter how delicate it was. He gave further proof of that in Lord Speos' house.

If the laws of marriage were severe in Atlantis, one could not say the same about its mores. Everyone only aspired to follow the caprices of his passion, especially the rich, because to the facility of pleasure that fortune gave them.

Lord Speos had coveted Ludia's hand for several years and had remained a widower in order to await the moment of a favorable decision. His love was immense, he said, and his heart desiccated by languor. One evening, however, a few days after his marriage to the woman after whom he had sighed so ardently, he received a mysterious visit from a young woman.

"Lord," she had said, throwing herself at his feet, "I'm doomed if you don't save me. I'll be thrown into a wretched canoe at the mercy of the waves."

"Lower your voice and get up, Basilea," said the lord, trembling that someone might see and hear the conversation. "I'll save you. What do you want, money?"

"No, lord."

"Yes, money—lots of money. Find a husband and I'll give him so much money that he'll take you as you are."

"The husband is found; I love him; I've always loved him, and I would never have betrayed him if I hadn't needed your protection to save my father's life when it was unjustly threatened."

"That's good, that's good," Speos replied, in a low voice. "How much does he want?"

"He doesn't want anything, lord, but he doesn't want to see my child, which is yours, in his bed or in his wife's arms. He'll forget my fault at that price: as soon as I give birth, I must give the child to you."

Speos made no reply. He smiled stupidly; then, nodding his head with determination, he said: "I accept,

Basilea. Marry, then, and when your child is born, let me know; I'll take care of it."

Ludia's confidant then became Speos' confidant. It was him who took charge of collecting the apocryphal child, and he carried out his mission with a skill that earned him numerous gratifications and his master's gratitude.

From that moment on his importance became immense; it never weakened for an instant. That was because he was perpetually necessary to the two spouses, as the guardian of their reputation, their honor and their life.

In the epoch about which we are speaking, that domestic tyranny had lasted fourteen years. The man's reign did not appear to be coming to an end soon, however, for he had just been employed again in the matter of a mysterious message, by means of which he was able to prepare very cleverly for new benefits and a new authority.

It was in the year two thousand three hundred and thirty-four that Lord Speos had married Ludia Arimaspes; in the year two thousand three hundred and forty-seven, no child had yet been born to them. Both of them naturally turned their gaze toward the past. In her past Ludia found a son that she had never seen, whom she wanted to see and bring close to her; for his part, Speos only wanted to recover his daughter, the daughter of Basilea.

The problem to be resolved, therefore, was this: to bring back into the bosom of the family a nameless child, and to leave it there without ruffling the sensibility of the spouse to whom it was irrelevant and without awakening anyone's suspicions.

The difficult was considerable, and worthy of occupying a profound genius. Each spouse entrusted it to the prudence of the usual confidant.

The confidant therefore set out with the promptitude of a man who has an easy solution in reserve, charged with two independent and equally secret messages. His right ear had Ludia's secret, his left ear that of Speos.

It was in the middle of that mission that we met him in the suburb of Sylacea, where we found him cutting the Gordian knot of his affair so briskly, by laying his hands on Atlas and Chemnis, even though he was quite convinced that they were not the two orphans desired...

That rare man was Nimrod, who passed for a simple and generous man, devoting his life to the interests of his friend Speos; he was the just and disinterested man with whom public opinion adorned with its most florid crowns.

Evidently, Nimrod was a clever man.

It was him for whom Ludia was waiting on the terrace of her house; it was him who had frightened her at that moment by his sudden appearance; it was him that she wanted to interrogate about his journey to Sylacea.

She did so, but what did she learn?

Nothing, for Nimrod lied in telling her that her son was handsome, but uncouth, like all children raised in small provincial towards; that he had thought that he ought to see to the development of his education in order to bring him closer to her more easily, and that he had plans in that regard; that in the meantime, he had placed him in a school not far from Lutecia, in the village of Me-nu-tche.

Ludia was so glad to hear this news that she poured the entire contents of her purse into Ninrod's hands, and

then, raising her eyes to the heavens, thanked the three
divine friends for the protection to which she had recommended her son in his cradle.

IV. The Me-nu-tcheans

Ludia's hopes were obliged to become somewhat dormant in the turbulent days that followed Nimrod's journey to Sylacea.

Atrimachis died; his worm-eaten throne collapsed; his only son was exiled; the Altlantean Republic was proclaimed, and seemed to want to build solid foundations in the midst of the enthusiasm of the early days.

But grave differences of opinion on behalf of the pretenders to the reins of power suddenly surged forth. Speos and Nimrod had not been slow to pose as glorious vanquishers of the past, nor were they slow to raise their voices in the midst of the republican conflict.

Petty domestic affairs were, therefore, postponed until tomorrow; the day was devoted to serious affairs of State. Nimrod was not sorry about that; Ludia moaned about it; and Lord Speos was more thoughtful than usual.

In those days, a riotous mob roamed the streets of the village of Me-nu-tche, where all the houses, their inhabitants trembling with anxiety, gave no sign of life—except one. One house in the village did not change its appearance; the windows remained open, as on fine and calm days; the coaching entrance never closed for a moment.

The seditious troop looked at it with an irritated gaze, circled its walls several times, measuring them with their menacing paces, but dared not go in.

That was the present habitation of Lord Nirvana, a modest habitation but which nevertheless enclosed an unreformed rich man, a noble of the old regime—in sum, a reactionary.

"Well, by Sylax!" said one of the boldest of the gang, finally, bravely extending a foot over the threshold of the coaching entrance, "What are we afraid of?"

And they all followed him, howling to give themselves more confidence, and hurtled into the middle of the courtyard. A robust young man with and energetic gaze came to meet them, with the sleeves of his smock rolled up like those of a laborer, and his trousers—or, at least, the garment that served the same function, although it seemed unusually wide—were retained at the waist by a strips of red cloth wound around his body.

"Well," he said, stopping in front of them, with his arms folded, his expression impassive and his thick hair thrown back from his head like a lion's mane, "what's new?"

"Nothing," said one of them, in a hoarse voice, "except the death of the tyrant, the flight of his cub and the reestablishment of the democratic and fraternal republic." Sniggering, he added: "Didn't you know?"

"Is that all?" responded the newcomer.

"No, that's just the beginning," retorted a mocking voice from the center of the group, "but it's enough, for the moment."

"Oh," replied the young man, "it's just that I thought, seeing you in this gang, that you'd come to tell me about yet another government—that of looters, subversives and people paid to terrify honest people and honest democracy."

That riposte provoked inarticulate and terrible cries that announced a tempest. No one, however, dared to budge yet, for the mass only had energy in its compact-

147

ness, and facing it was a redoubtable wrestler. They knew that.

"I thought you were courageous men," continued the intrepid interlocutor, "generous patriots on whom one could count for the glory and honor of democracy, for I know you all—but I fear that someone, an enemy of the fatherland, an enemy of order, perhaps a enemy of Nirvana, has deceived you by insinuating principles to you that are not good ones."

The tempest, which had been on the point of bursting, suddenly calmed down. The oratorical worker had scored a point. Everyone murmured words of approval, and the rabble-rouser with the hoarse voice, the leader of the mob, probably a hireling of the enemy of Nirvana of whom mention had just been made, lowered his head, blushing to the ears beneath the gazes of his followers, and hid himself at the back in order to avoid his adversary's searching gaze.

That adversary, whose energetic responses revealed a strong and profoundly inspired soul, still seemed to be young, although the broadness of his shoulders and the expression on his face indicated great vigor. He was only eighteen or nineteen years old. He was, however, one of the presidents of the Club of Me-nu-tche. It was Atlas.

Me-nu-tche, as we have said, was one of the numerous villages in the vicinity of Lutecia. As it was one of the nearest, it was also one of the most populous, with a very mixed and very active population. It had been one of the first to found a club in its bosom where the most exalted and influential men of the suburbs met, and from which emerged the boldest proposals, the most advanced wishes and the most impetuous projects.

Atlas' imposing stature, his proudly-held head, his sparkling eyes and his fluent although uncultivated

148

speech, his keenly progressive although unferocious opinions, and his often-good advice, always generous to the children of his caste, had put him in evidence from the first day, and had created an absolute empire for him among the clubmen, in spite of his precarious position and dependency in the employment of a supposed aristocrat.

The Club of the Me-nu-tcheans made a great deal of noise in the capital; its reputation became colossal in a very short space of time. Moderate men, who thought that it is always wise to march slowly along the social path, feared it more than all the rest. Even the provisional government sensed that it was a dangerous and powerful adversary. Everyone thought the same, with the result that those who wanted to arrive at their goal through the waves of the torment affiliated themselves to it, for it was evident to everyone that popularity could not be found more reliably elsewhere.

"How long has it been since you set foot in the club?" asked one of the most impetuous rioters, after a pause.

"Oh, by Sylax!" the criticized individual replied, humbly. "It's been nearly three days—but there's been a great deal of work to do here, and I have for a social principle, personally, that when a man is paid a wage from dawn till dusk, he ought to employ his arms from dawn till dusk."

"Yes, but it's been said that one of the leaders of the club ought not to miss a single meeting under any pretext, and you're going to be declared a bad Me-nu-tchean."

"Who would dare?" replied Atlas, in a dull voice, choked by a convulsive movement of the mouth that revealed a sharp indignation. "Who would dare? A coward, a liar—a man, in sum, who is unaware of the necessity of work and the sanctity of engagements."

Then he calmed down, lowered his head onto his breast and began to reflect profoundly. His pensive attitude gave new courage to his interlocutor, who had retired into the midst of his companions in order to speak with more assurance.

"It's also been said," he added, "that the servant and protector of an aristocrat can't be an honest Me-nu-tchean."

"Enough, fine orator, enough," Atlas replied, raising his head again, his face no longer glowing with indignation. "Tell me, do you believe that Speos is a pure democrat? Do you believe that Nimrod is a pure and generous democrat? Well, Speos, the illustrious Speos, is Nirvana's friend today, as he was yesterday, because that man is a loyal man who does not change the noble passions of his heart at the whim of the wind of public passion. Nimrod is also Nirvana's friend, and it was him who begged him, on the death of my adoptive father Song, to take me into his house in Me-nu-tche, in order to supervise the work on his lands. And I, who am under an obligation to him, who eat his bread, who sleep under his roof, to whom he provides a living—why should I hate him? Because he does not think like me?" He burst into laughter. "Oh, what a beautiful democracy!" His terrible eyes glaring, he added: "If I see him betray the republic, however, if I see him hindering the work of society, then I shall place myself before him in order to block his way."

Atlas softened his tone. "But enough talk," he said. "The misunderstanding is over; peace for all, and let's drink to the prosperity of the democratic and fraternal republic, and to the shame—or rather the appeasement—of its enemies."

The invitation did not need to be repeated. Atlas set himself at the head of the satisfied mob, and in the blink of an eye, the courtyard was deserted; no one any longer had any doubt abut the loyalty of the man who proposed to pay for an hour's joyous pastime. The atmosphere was, in any case, very hot; they drank a great deal, therefore, and dank until the state of bliss that encourages the most delicate confidences.

"Look, truly, I want to talk to you as a friend," said one of the drinkers, pouring himself the last drop of wine. "Believe me, leave your proud lord, your miserable so-called aristocrat…who'll be thrown into the sea within a fortnight, you'll see."

"Bah! They wouldn't dare," the host replied.

"Wouldn't dare, by Sylax! And why not?"

"Because I don't want it."

There was a moment's silence then, while everyone emptied his earthenware mug, in order not to have to reply to a determination so vigorously expressed.

"Listen friend," the same rioter—the one with the hoarse voice—went on, "what's said is said, and I won't hold it against you; but remember this, for you're my friend and I want to tell you everything: it's said that you're holding on to your Nirvana not because of his opinion, because, in the final count, perhaps yours can't reasonably be suspected, but because of his daughter, the beautiful Ormuzda, whom you love, it seems, ardently."

"So?"

"So…so…well, it's said that a handsome fop from Lutecia has more luck than you with her. So there."

The unfortunate lover did not reply. His expression became dark, and his unsteady hand seized the little jug that had just been emptied, and banged it on the table, as much out of anger as by way of a summons. He paid silently and started to leave the same way.

"Good night," he said, finally, shaking the hands of his friends as he went. To himself alone, he added: "Oh, if I were noble or powerful, perhaps she wouldn't disdain me."

He said that in a horribly grave voice. His eyebrows furrowed hideously, and the muscles of his arms twisted over his breast like irritated snakes.

"Aha!" said his friends, at the sound of the intoxicated voice. "We did well to have a little chat; he won't have any more to say on his own account. It's true, though, that he's a good lad."

Meanwhile, Atlas disappeared into Lord Nirvana's courtyard, while the drunken mob drew away, singing the ballad of Uranus:

Uranus was a good king,
Who came down to earth.
 To do what?
To ask us the question
Why do you want a king?

V. A Rival

Atlas and Chemnis had found a benevolent protector in Nimrod. Thanks to him, they had been able to take shelter from poverty in Lord Nirvana's small house in the village of Me-nu-tche.

They had not been residents there very long when the revolution of the Pah-ri-ziz burst forth, in which the clubman from Sylacea took a very active part, without worrying about his master's opinion. And he did well, because Nirvana only pampered him all the more. He was too well informed of public affairs not to see that he could no longer count on the past, and he had too much tact not to understand that in his servant there was all the amplitude of a man of the future. He was therefore careful to retain all his esteem, like a prudent man who puts a cloak over his garments on a stormy day.

Atlas did not abuse the unexpected favor of his master, but his secret hopes became all the firmer in consequence. The times, moreover, were in his favor. In days of political troubles, the great and the rich disguise themselves; they hide, and avoid one another. There was, therefore, a chance that Ormuzda would not be bothered by amorous pursuers. Perhaps, then, he would have time to create a position for himself fine enough to be inevitable.

Nirvana lived in the greatest solitude; even his only friend, Speos, barely knew the way to his village dwelling. Everything therefore went as desired. Atlas was far from fearing any rival, for the moment. And yet, he had one: a rival he had not divined, but whose name the insinuation of his friend the rabble-rouser had just hurled in his face like a thunderbolt.

That rival was, like him, a poor child of the people: a man lost in the crowd, one of the disinherited of society, a man without a family, devoid of relatives, a child of hazard, or rather of corruption, of which there were thousands in Atlantis, in spite—or perhaps because—of the severity of its laws.

He was Speos' secretary; his name was Hyperion.

By comparison with Atlas, who had a herculean vigor, Hyperion was frail, although well-proportioned in all his limbs; his face was not so expressive, but more seductive; his skull was less worthy of the eulogies of phrenology, but it was more gracious; it was easy to divine that the blood of the aristocracy ran in his veins.

Endowed with natural virtue, and a good mind, he had been able to profit from all the opportunities that hazard had offered him to develop his intelligence, and he was truly more perfect than one might expect of a young man abandoned to the cares of nature alone. He was almost the same age as Atlas.

Poor Atlas had believed, until then, that there was a vast abyss between himself and Ormuzda, the insignificant. In order to fill that abyss, he had launched himself into a giant task, only to discover, finally, that someone else, as insignificant as he was, had risen to the level of the young woman of his dreams, with a few petty perfections that he did not have.

A secret rage devoured his soul; he cursed his birth and his domesticity, which had not permitted him to increase his chances of success in time; he cursed Heaven and hazard for rendering him less gracious than Hyperion, and less lovable.

His thoughts became more audacious in consequence; a few ferocious words even slipped from his mouth, in thinking of the inequality of conditions, the pretensions of despotism, the shameful favoritism of his times and the great treason of the sinners of the aristocracy.

Love had rendered Atlas unhappy, and had caused him to suffer, but had not yet rendered him unjust. It had caused the scales to fall from his eyes; had rendered him scholarly, philosophical. A profound thinker, an ardent, determined citizen no longer seeing any but one thing: the sanctity of contracts, public or private, his rights and his duties: not the rights and duties of social convention, which varied from one country to another in accordance with governments, passions and the prejudices of the time—the century, the year or the hour—and which so often diminished men in the eyes of the just; but the rights of the being who ought to live happily and without obstacles beneath his feet other than those to which nature gives rise. Love, in brief, had made him into a great and good patriot. Let us not reproach him for it. What does the cause matter, when the result is so fine?

After leaving the tavern in Me-nu-tsche, Atlas went home precipitately, as we have seen, with his eyes ablaze and menace in his heart. He went straight to the garden where he seized his mattock violently, as if he wished to break it.

"They're right!" he cried, "and I'm just a fool for staying here, toiling away in the fields, hardening my hands for *her*, who disdains them, for getting sunburn, for *her*, who thinks me ugly, to protect aristocrats who scorn me. In these times of equality, can't I find something better to do?" He headed resolutely toward the exit from the house. "Yes, I have better things to do."

155

He found Chemnis there, who came to meet him.

"Is that you, Chemnis?" he said, hesitantly.

"It's me, your little sister," the young woman replied. "I saw you weeping, and I came to ask you why."

"I was thinking, Chemins," said Atlas, taking her hands and squeezing them affectionately, "that no one is more amiable than you, and that, if I were rich, you wouldn't remain at the mercy of others for long."

"Why were you thinking that, my friend? We're so comfortable here."

"Child," said Atlas, fixing Chemnis with his gleaming eyes, "you're content, as if this chance bread were yours, as if this noble domain would always be your home, as if all your days were going to be as beautiful."

"Oh, what do you expect, Atlas? I don't ask so much of the three divine friends. As long as I always see you by my side, I'll always be happy."

Atlas took Chemnis' hand and kissed it avidly, raising an angry gaze to the heavens.

"And to think that I can't love anyone but her!" he murmured. "Is the spirit of evil more powerful than God, then?"

Then he looked down at the young woman, his gaze softer and full of interest. He went back to his bedroom instead of continuing his route toward the exit.

Chemnis had guessed. Even though Atlas had not betrayed his secret thought and his secret torment by any word, she had read it in the depths of his heart.

She ran after her friend, therefore, to cheer up his somber thoughts a little, caught up with him and disappeared with him into the house.

An hour later, however, Atlas took the road to Lutecia.

Chemis stood on the threshold, weeping copiously. She followed him with her eyes for as long as she could.

"Oh, Sylax, Sylax, will he ever come back?" she cried, in the midst of her sobs. "Is it really true that he's only going to visit the generous Nimrod, our protector?"

VI. The Fire

The abrupt departure of Atlas, whose objective he suspected, was a thunderbolt for Lord Nirvana. He was not unaware that, in spite of the obscurity in which he lived, he had needed the officious intervention of his servant on more than one occasion.

Political affairs were not becoming any brighter; ambition and envy reigned everywhere, not advancing public stability. The provisional had not come to an end, and the provisional was by no means showing a smiling face to peaceful people.

Atlas, meanwhile, was walking sadly along the road to Lutecia. He was no longer thinking about the grandeurs of which he had dreamed, even though he was now running after them. He was no longer thinking about the future of Atlantis or his own; he was thinking about love, about Ormuzda, and he was desperate.

Before losing sight of the house he was fleeing, he looked back at it one last time, embracing it with a long and profound contemplation. Then, shaking his head proudly, he advanced resolutely toward the city.

He had only taken a few paces, however, when he stopped, utterly amazed. His feet did not advance, any more than they would have done if they had been buried in the ground. With his eyes he followed two riders who had just gone past and who had not noticed him, so rapid were the reindeer on which they were mounted.

His first impulse was to follow them, but he felt his legs totter beneath him. His face was pale and taut, his heart was beating violently. A new determination bore him in the direction of Lutecia, toward which he seemed to be running rather than walking. Then he stopped again, in great agitation, muttering unintelligible menaces, cursing his destiny. His gaze sought the two riders; they had disappeared.

A horrible grimace strayed over the young man's lips then; a horrible tempest was raging in his heart. Jealousy caused snakes to hiss in his ears, and the mockery of his riotous friends came to weigh with all its weight upon his memory.

He launched himself toward the village of Me-nutche, on the heels of Speos and Hyperion, whom he had recognized as the two riders.

He did not go back to Nirvana's house, however, but prowled around the vicinity all day, devoured by thousands of various and horrible thoughts.

When dusk fell, he went to the club, alone and silently, and crouched in a corner, as if he wanted to hide from all eyes. It was evident that habit had brought him there, but that a secret sentiment was driving him into the shadows now.

An orator with a hoarse voice, the rabble-rouser of the previous day, the malevolent counselor who had turned Atlas' heart upside-down and whom Atlas had accused of obeying malevolent orders—which was true—suddenly launched himself to the podium, where he delivered a violent diatribe against Atlas, the slave of an aristocrat, the disdained suitor of Nirvana's daughter.

At those words, Atlas, whom no one had noticed in his corner of the room, where he was keeping quiet, got to his feet as if he had received an electric shock, and leapt toward the tribune. His presence disconcerted the orator, who went pale, trembled and was gripped by a sudden weakness that caused his legs to totter.

That was because Atlas seemed frightful to behold. The flickering light that illuminated the room projected his shadow on the walls like that of a giant. It seemed that his hair was bristling on his head, and that his heart was rumbling like the dull and distant waves of a stormy sea; his features seemed hideously clenched, like the wrinkles of a tiger grimacing before tearing its prey apart.

"Citizens," he cried, standing up on tiptoe and threatening to descend with all the mass of his body on those surrounding him, "this man is a liar, a treacherous liar! I needed bread; I stretched out my head to take what the hand of an aristocrat offered me. Where is the evil? Where is the treason? Which of you would have wanted to feed me every day for doing nothing? Is it you, who are slandering me without knowing me? Is it you, whom the hand of some secret enemy is driving upon me like a ferocious beast on an unarmed enemy? Speak! Say so!"

And Atlas turned to his accuser, who made no reply, but who, having recovered from his initial surprise, sought to strike a pose as proud as the words he had hurled at the club, even though he did not feel bold enough to sustain them further.

Atlas then abandoned his mute enemy; he renewed his profession of faith, which everyone knew, but so emotively that several people suddenly got to their feet and left the room, utterly furious against the nobility whose provender they had supplied, against the former aristocrats, the powerful and the rich, the obstinate and incorrigible enemies of new things.

Atlas did not perceive the strange emotion that he had produced. Exhausted after the energy he had just expended, he let himself fall back into his seat and lowered his head as if under the weight of some overwhelming thought, and remained pensive for a long time.

Meanwhile, orators succeeded one another with frightful rapidity, spreading an entirely new bile around them. Animated by Atlas' fervor, they discoursed angrily about the affairs of the day, the ripping up of privileges, the innate equality of humans, the social contract and the future of fraternity and equality.

Night, however, was still advancing.

A strange noise was suddenly heard in the distance, vague, dull and uncertain, like the subterranean rumble of a volcano slowly building up to a terrible eruption.

The noise soon became more expressive, and then a few screams penetrated as far as the enclosure of the club, heart-rending cries that stirred all the Me-nutcheans in their seats.

Everyone got up spontaneously. Atlas was the first to launch himself over the threshold with a single bound, and then precipitated himself instinctively toward Lord Nirvana's house.

It was, in fact, there that the trouble was.

Thick smoke, speckled with streaks of fire, was emerging from the chimneys in great floods. The courtyard and its surroundings were enveloped by thick black clouds that were escaping from all the windows, which were cracking and breaking in the tongues of fire. It was a conflagration, and a serious one.

Atlas advanced resolutely, lending an attentive ear in order to seize a few screams emerging from inside the buildings. He heard nothing but a staccato sniggering emerging from the depths of the courtyard behind him. He ran in that direction, with fury in his heart and his eyes. He found himself in the presence of a small group of men who were rubbing their hands at the sight of the blaze and trying to stifle the expression of their infernal joy in order to listen to the sinister crepitations of the fire.

"Well, Citizen," said a hoarse voice that Atlas recognized perfectly, "that's how they'll all be grilled, your aristocrats."

"All! Wretch!" cried Atlas, seizing the arms of the ferocious jester and dragging him to a blazing window. "Save them, then! Save them, wretch!" He shoved the arsonist up against the window, where he almost suffocated.

"Poor fool," said the latter, straightening up. "You don't know everything. You don't know anything. There's someone in there," he added, in a low voice, "a great enemy of the fatherland, who's hiding with your Nirvana, and also your rival. You ought to kiss my hands."

Atlas did not hear that reply; a muffled groan from the interior had just reached them, and he launched himself through the window into the midst of the flames.

"By Me-nu-tche, I don't understand that democrat at all," said the incendiary, tranquilly rejoining his comrades, who were waiting for him at the back of the courtyard.

"He did, however, say that all the leftovers[27] should be killed," added another, as if to console the one who had just felt the force of Atlas' vigorous hand.

---

[27] The French *ci-devant*, which was used during the 1789 Revolution to refer to the resistant aristocrats who had been stripped of their privileges translates literally as "from before" or "former," but neither sounds right in English, nor does it carry the appropriate sarcastic scorn, so I have used "leftovers" instead.

"By Sylax, he said it!" retorted the raucous voice. "And citizen Nimrod said it too. Would we have set fire to that wolves' den otherwise?"

A few moments later a man emerged from the bosom of the blaze carrying two heavy burdens in his arms: two inert bodies. They were those of Ormuzda and Hyperion. He did not stop until he was outside the house, in the middle of a cultivated field.

He set Hyperion down, and then fled, carrying the young woman, with the rapidity of a wolf carrying off a lamb. Ormuzda's hair was loose, trailing on the ground, her head hanging down backwards, her eyes closed; her heart was no longer beating.

"Atlas! Atlas!" a young woman shouted to him, who was in his path—but Atlas did not hear anything; he paid no heed to Chemnis' voice.

Chemnis followed him with her eyes as best she could in the obscurity of the night, and then listened to the sound of his footsteps, which faded away in the distance.

When she could no longer hear anything, she returned to the burned house, and went back in, wiping away the large tears that were running down her cheeks, repairing the disorder of her garments, which she had torn with her fingernails in a fit of rage and jealousy.

VII. An Hour After the Conflagration

Lord Nirvana's residence had not burned completely. The tent on the platform, which was composed of wood and fabric, had suffered more than anything else. There was nothing left of it but a heap of ashes—but the basement, the house properly speaking, still had many sections that were intact, or nearly so.

The fire was out everywhere, and the crowd that had run to rescue the victims of the fire had ebbed away. The house had become as mute and dark as a tomb again.

Chemnis headed toward it by the gleam of a light that she could see through a window. That was where Nirvana was, with his wife and his dubious friend Speos, sitting face to face and maintaining a silence of desolation that they only interrupted from time to time with a few stifled sighs or exclamations of despair. They continually turned their eyes toward the door as if they were expecting someone whose arrival was not in doubt.

At the door, Chemnis bumped into a man who went back in precipitately without saying anything, and disappeared without her being able to recognize him in the darkness.

At the noise she made, Nirvana ran toward her, and stopped dead upon seeing that the young woman was alone and in the most profound desolation.

"My daughter! My daughter!" cried two voices, simultaneously.

"She's alive," Chemnis replied, in a tremulous voice.

"Oh, may the three divine friends be blessed!" they said.

The night, however, followed its course peacefully. The atmosphere spread the agreeable freshness of a beautiful summer night everywhere. Desolation was in the heart of everyone in Nirvana's house, but nothing had changed in nature, the calm of which seemed to be insulting the troubles of those who were suffering.

Some distance away, on the edge of a ditch dug around a little wood adjacent to the village of Me-nu-tche, Atlas was standing upright, immobile, his arms folded over his breast and his face turned toward the ditch. Ormuzda was there, half recumbent, so feeble was she still.

"I'm cold, Atlas," said the young woman, in a quavering voice.

Atlas took off his plebeian smock and laid it over her.

"Oh, I assure you that I'm very cold," Ormuzda repeated.

Atlas remained mute; he bent down toward the young woman, whom he took on his knees and warmed like a little child against his breast, with the aid of his muscular arms.

"You're very good, Atlas, but why don't you take me back to my father's house?"

"Because I haven't yet done enough to be loved by you," the clubman replied, in a dull voice.

Ormuzda made no reply.

"And him, *him*?" he went on. "What more has he done for you than me? Oh, if you loved me, if you only loved me a little, Ormuzda! But no. it's him that you love. Him, who wears a cloak like a rich man, him, a city fop, a fine lord reeking of perfumes to make one recoil at twenty paces, while I...I'm a bumpkin, a rustic, a wretch..."

"Oh! Who told you that, Atlas?"

"Who? Him...you...him, that handsome young fellow whose delicate lungs were suddenly paralyzed by the clouds of smoke, who fell down beside you, milady, while you were doubtless fleeing your mother's eyes for a delightful rendezvous."

"Atlas!"

"Oh, it's the chaste Sylax who has punished you, because you were doing wrong, milady."

A horrible grimace, which distorted Atlas' lips at that moment, indicated the cruel suspicion that was tearing his soul. Ormuzda, very emotional, put her fingers over the mouth of the man who was blaspheming against her virtue so harshly, and uttered a small cry of indignation.

"So you don't love me?" the young man retorted, following the train of his thoughts without paying any heed to the young woman's mute protest.

Ormuzda still made no reply.

"But do you think that I'm not worth as much as your Hyperion?" cried Atlas, who could no longer contain himself. "He's poor, like me, without a family, like me; but if you want, I'll become rich, laden with honors. Give the order! What do you want me to be? What treasure do you want me to lay at your feet? Come on, speak, speak then! Because it's for you that I'm made...oh, how do I know what I'm made for? I found under my hand a code that brought you nearer to me, laws that lifted me up to your level, and I embraced that code, and I blessed those laws, and that code and those laws will reign, understand that! And I'll be to you not a king, but whatever you wish: rich, powerful, honored, richer, more powerful, more honored than the greatest of aristocrats of times past…come on, milady, speak!"

Ormuzda was trembling with fear; she lowered her head and did not know what to say to the ardent man who was squeezing her knees in his arms and kissing the hem of her dress.

"You don't love me!" cried Atlas, "but I know a means to possess you, unless you want to be cast into the midst of the waves of the sea!"

Atlas' eyes were blazing at that moment. He had tightened his arms around the young woman, whom he was hugging like a madman; his breath mingled with hers, his heart was beating against her breast. Ormuzda was shedding a torrent of tears, imploring the pity of the furious Me-nu-tchean.

Atlas stood up suddenly.

"God forbid," he exclaimed, "that I only have a cadaver where I seek a soul! But I swear that I shall thwart all your amours! You'll never marry any other man than your servant Atlas!"

At the same time, he snatched back his smock, and left.

VIII. The First Symptoms of a Disaster

A few days later, two men were prowling around the burned house, searching for an open door through which to enter it. But all the doors and all the windows were shut. The fire-blackened shutters were barricaded; the coaching entrance did not open under the redoubtable blows of the two men. The house was mute.

"By Sylax!" said one of the two prowlers, in a chagrined tone. "Where's Nirvana, then?"

It was Lord Speos who said that.

"He's gone, my lord," replied Speos' companion, who was none other than Nimrod.

"Gone! Gone! Who told you that?"

"I've known for two days."

"And you didn't tell me! You've come with me all the way to Me-nu-tche, to visit a friend who'd told you about his imminent departure!"

"He didn't tell me, my lord," Nimrod replied. "I guessed. When I came here on your behalf two days ago, the day after the fire, to see Lord Nirvana, I had difficulty getting to see him. I told you that without your seeming to place any great confidence in what I said. I succeeded, however, not by making use of your name—that means had not succeeded, as I've already told you—but under the pretext of having important secrets to confide to him, which succeeded perfectly.

"I did indeed have a secret to reveal to him, but that secret was not a secret to him; I didn't know that. It was a fortuitous encounter that I'd had with one of his friends, on whom he was perhaps no longer counting. On going into his study, I perceived that friend, who was escaping through another door, doubtless in order not to find himself face to face with me."

"I had nothing more to say then, and I said nothing, but I had to learn something, and I did indeed learn it. I learned from a few hateful words emerging from Lord Nirvana's mouth that the fire in his house had been set by a traitor, a false friend: Lord Speos and his accomplices...me, no doubt," Nimrod added, with a little smile that said that Nirvana was not mistaken.

"Me!" cried Speos, sharply, drawing himself up to his full height and frowning.

"You, Master. Now, as Lord Nirvana despaired of the law at a time as little benevolent to the nobility, he made the decision to avenge himself on his old friend, hating him with all his soul and wishing all kinds of misfortune upon him."

"And...my daughter?" said Speos, hesitantly, his mind not quite following the thread of his servant's narration. "My daughter, whom you promised to enable me to meet one day in his house?"

"You've seen her, my lord."

"My daughter!" cried Speos, opening his eyes wide. "Is it Chemnis?"

"Yes, Chemnis, Ormuza's friend and companion."

"Well?"

"She's no longer there. He expelled her shamefully from his home, because she was your servant's protégée."

"And where is she?"

"I don't know yet, Master; I've been looking for her for two days."

"Oh, my friend, my friend!" said Speos, animatedly. "My daughter! We have to find my daughter!" Speos extended his hand toward the village of Me-nu-tche.

169

"Nirvana, I swear implacable hatred against you and all your family!"

"Oh, my lord," said Nimrod, with sly bonhomie, "my story has finally made an impression on you. The first words I said to you the other day found you very indifferent, though. If you had not seen this closed house with your own eyes, and its occupant, whom you called your friend, departed without any concern for you, you wouldn't have believed it."

"But it seems to me," said Speos, pulling at an ill-secured shutter, "that the house isn't empty. I thought I heard a noise inside."

"It is, in fact, the case that the house ought not to be entirely abandoned. I'd even wager, whatever anyone says, that Nirvana is hiding in Lutecia, and that the friend that I saw in his house the other day, whom I mentioned to you just now, is there in the house."

"But who is that friend, Nimrod?"

"Oh, you know him well, Master, you know him very well. You've mentioned him to me several times: he's an exile. I say an exile not because he's been banished from Atlantis since the day of our revolution, like all those of his caste, saving your respect, but because he's arrived in our midst so mysteriously that I have no doubt that he's strongly affiliated to the cause of the exiles, and that he's one of their envoys, who has probably come to see whether there's any means of organizing a counter-revolution here. So, he's a suspect individual. In truth, my lord, I don't know whether I ought to tell you his name, because the Me-nu-tcheans don't like those names."

At the same time, Nimrod looked at his master with an ironic smile, which his master did not see, for he had lowered his eyes and was thinking deeply.

"Come on, let's go," said Speos, finally, after a pause. "We have no need to scratch any longer at a door where we're not wanted."

They left, but the blow that Nimrod had delivered had struck home. Speos remained pensive for much of the journey, while Nimrod, for his part, was calculating profoundly all the benefits that his political skill was going to procure for him.

Lord Speos finally revived, full of kind attentions for his traveling companion. Nimrod was no longer an inconvenient tyrant so far as he was concerned, a gulf that he has incessantly obliged to fill with his fortune; he was an indispensable friend, an agent that he could not replace, a confidant who could read his heart like an open book. It seemed to him that Nimrod was the saving plank to which he had to cling in order to arrive safely in port.

Nomrod knew the human heart too well not to divine what Speos was thinking. He saw clearly at that moment what he had only understood imperfectly at first: that his master had finally realized the necessity of his entire intervention in his most secret affairs.

It was the memory of the exile that Nimrod had mentioned that had produced that prodigy. Speos was afraid of him. It was his evil genius. He had recognized that perfectly. On his own, however, he was incapable of extracting himself from that malign power. He sensed that, and Nimrod, who no longer had any doubt about it, had thought it appropriate to point out that necessity.

Such had been the objective of the journey to Me-nu-tche, which had not been a pleasure trip. Pleasure never entered into any of Nimrod's actions, unless it was the pleasure of doing evil.

Scarcely had he arrived home when Speos shut himself in his study on his own. Then he asked for Nimrod, who went to see him with a joy that he had a great deal of difficulty containing.

IX. Confidences

Nimrod was in Speos' study, beside his armchair. Speos had not yet seen him. All his attention was absorbed by reading a contract that was already old. He was reading the same page over and over, as if everything was contained therein. It would have been truer to say that he was not reading at all, although his eyes were scanning very attentively, apparently at least, all the lines of the contract. His mind was only seeing a single word within it: the word *restitution*.

In order to understand Speos' state of mind a little better, we need to go back a little.

We already know that Lord Speos had once accepted the deposit of the infant son and fortune of his friend Mo-kie-thi. Now, while Ludia's lover had fled Atlantis, directing his errant footsteps to distant lands and devoting himself to the strangest and most perilous adventures, when public rumor said that he had died, Lord Speos had been doing his best to struggle against adverse fortune.

Like all the great lords of that epoch who did not have enough millions and were searching everywhere to satisfy their luxurious caprices, he had sought them in gambling, and in the lottery of high finance: a terrible game that ruins or enriches a man of the yes or no of hazard; a game for the ambitious, a mortal game that a civilized society ought never to entertain.

Speos had the bad luck to win at first. He thought, in consequence, that he had discovered an inexhaustible mine. His needs became more demanding—but he soon began to lose.

Like all gamblers he thought then about reiterating the gains of the initial game. He lost again, but he did not stop playing, trying to return his fortune to its initial figure, promising himself that he would become wiser thereafter.

It was in vain, for his luck did not return; he doubled and tripled his stakes in vain in the perfidious frame of the lottery; everything sank into the abyss of the game. He lost his head then; he gambled his last resources, and lost them.

All those losses were so secret that no one suspected Speos' desperate situation. His household went on in the same way, his credit did not diminish. His borrowings had been immense, but the lenders, who thought that the loans securely guaranteed by the rich lord's wealth, were discreet.

Speos, who had made a bad bet in confiding the tranquility of his entire life to the hazards of gambling, did not make the second error of unfortunate gamblers who no longer want to exist after their treasures have been snatched away. He took a more graceful course, that of marriage: he married Ludia. Fortune therefore returned to his house, light and elegant, for she brought great credit with her.

It might have departed soon, however, because the debts were far from being paid. Speos, whose reputation for wisdom was still intact, was determined that his new wife should not know anything that might stain her husband's past. He therefore did not hasten to expend all of Ludia's fortune, hoping eventually to find a means of getting out of his embarrassing situation without a scandal. Thus he racked his brains incessantly in order to make them yield that difficult secret.

Heaven came to his aid. It was in those days, precisely, that Mo-kie-thi departed on his perilous voyages, instituting his friend as his sole heir in case of the death of his son. Now, his son soon died, as we already know, and the testament was subsequently accomplished in its entirety, for Mo-kie-thi did not come back.

Since the death of the son, however, Speos had eaten into it considerably, thus rendering definitive the temporary nature of his heritage.

Wealth, therefore, returned to his home, and, one might say, as quickly as it had fled. That was marvelous, in a time when Speos had such a great need of that fortunate hazard. Thus, there was no lack of talk about such a favorable death, especially on the part of Lord Nirvana, although no one knew as yet how very opportune it was.

There is no doubt that Nirvana would have protested vehemently against the appositeness of that inheritance, if the embarrassment of time had not stifled his voice. But he knew that Speos was entirely in tune with the times and that he was only a victim that would be sacrificed willingly, that the wisest thing to do was to stay carefully hidden. He therefore kept quiet, and everything remained as fortunate hazard had made it, each of the two friends keeping his secret to himself.

That entire order of facts and suspicions was sufficiently intimate for no one to know about it. Ludia was completely unaware of it, and Nimrod knew absolutely nothing.

It was perhaps the only secret of his master's that the latter did not know—but he was probably on the brink of knowing it, because that secret had been weighing horribly upon Speos' heart for an hour. Perhaps that was the object of the extraordinary preoccupation that veiled the presence of Nirmod, who was almost touching him, and was obliged to speak to announce his expected arrival.

"Master!" said Nimrod, placing himself directly in front of Speos.

"Oh, it's you, my friend," said Speos, getting to his feet precipitately and offering a chair to Nimrod, who said down without apologizing for that politeness, which he doubtless considered his due.

Speos sat down and remained silent, still holding his contract and seemingly too embarrassed to begin a conversation for which he was nevertheless mentally prepared.

Meanwhile, Nimrod waited patiently. He looked at the contract from the corner of his eye, and smiled casually at the sight of his master's embarrassment, which gave him high hopes for the interest of the occasion.

"My friend," said Speos, finally, without looking up at the man he could just as well have called his domestic demon, "I was rich before my marriage."

"I know, Master."

"But I suddenly became poor, ruined by gambling."

"Ah! It happens, my lord. In gambling, you might win. You lost. That's a misfortune, but not a crime."

"The loss of my fortune was not a crime, no, but it was an intolerable misfortune. Naturally, I had to think of means of repairing it; and I employed two, by taking a rich heiress in marriage and…" Speos lowered his voice: "…stealing a treasure that I had under my hand."

Lord Speos would have liked Nimrod to understand what he was saying, in order not to have to explain further. Either because Nimrod did not know enough about his master's antecedents to divine what he meant, however, or because he only wanted to reply in perfect knowledge of the facts, he looked at Speos with an astonished expression that demanded explanation.

"How, Master?" he asked.

Speos had to confess then. He recounted the precious deposit that his friend Mo-kie-thi had confided to him—but as he did not add anything more, Nimrod did not want to understand yet.

"And afterwards, Master?" he said.

"Afterwards…he died."

"That was a very slight misfortune, since you inherited as a consequence."

"But he didn't die," said Speos, in a muffled voice.

"Oh—too bad. What did you do with him, then, Master?" Nimrod went on, looking at his confidant with a malign smile.

"Well…well, I left him on the dolmen of lost children," Speos replied, resentful at having been forced to explain so overtly.

The fact that Lord Speos had just revealed was too serious for him not to demand an entire confidence. Nimrod already had an inkling of what was to be done, but he needed to know more. "Well, so what, Master?" he said, bringing his thick eyebrows down over the glair of his eyes, which was an expression of profound thought in him.

"What!" said Speos, sharply, still keeping his eyes lowered. "Don't you understand that I can't be the heir of a child who isn't dead?"

"Mo-kie-thie's child is well and truly dead, my lord. Who can prove his existence? You've doubtless taken appropriate measures to have his death legally certified; hence, he's dead. I don't think that the dolmen will ever throw him back into your path saying: 'Here he is!' Then

177

again, it was so long ago: sixteen, seventeen…perhaps eighteen years."

"If the son is dead, how do you know that the father is also dead, Nimrod?" said Speos, fixing his confidant with a knowing gaze, as if to say to him: *Remember the little house in Me-nu-tche.*

"Oh, as to that, you're right, my lord."

"So, I'm ruined; for Ludia's fortune, after being regularized, will be found not to be what it is supposed to be. Then again, I'm dishonored, for Mo-kie-thi's property is no longer intact. Part of it has paid my debts."

"Ruined…dishonored…," muttered Nimroad. "All that's not certain."

Nimrod stood up then and took hold of the contract that Speos had appeared to be reading so attentively when he arrived.

"Will Lord Speos give me a little of the contents of this scrap of paper," he said, "if I find a means of conserving the whole for him?"

"But that piece of paper is the contract of my heritage."

"I suspected as much, Master."

"Oh well! Yes, yes, Nimrod."

"Only a quarter."

"A quarter—so be it!"

"Are you sure, Master?"

"I swear on my honor!"

"Honor is a precious thing, and I esteem the honor of Lord Speos above the honor of the most honorable man in Atlantis—but will you, my lord, swear it in writing?"

Speos, who expected anything on the part of his despotic servant, did not think the moment appropriate for him to moralize about the insult of his request. He contented himself with making a slight grimace to signify his resentment, and started writing.

"There," he said, handing him the compromise he had just made.

"You're the legitimate heir of Lord Mo-kie-thi," said Nimrod, standing up and heading for the door of the study in order to leave.

Speos called him back. "One more word, Nimrod," he said. "I'm a man of honor; I'm not asking you to do anything base or to commit a crime in order to conserve my inheritance."

"Oh, my lord Master," Nimrod replied, "it's almost an insult to forbid me to commit a crime."

"That's true, in fact," Speos murmured, putting his hand on the contract as if someone might dispute its possession with him.

"Coward!" muttered Nimrod, as he went out. "He wants a man dead and doesn't have the courage to admit it. That's because he's also an honest man."

Nimrod closed the study door very softly, pressing to his heart the document of division that the Master had just signed.

X. The Demon of the Night

The next day, the entire village of Me-nu-tchi was in ecstasy before a horrible heap of ashes. Fire had broken out again during the night in Lord Nirvana's house, and had consumed everything that it had spared on the previous occasion.

There was no shortage of conjectures as to the cause of the blaze. One old lady thought that she alone knew the truth. She assured everyone that, at daybreak, she had seen the demon of fire escaping, all black and blazing, from the midst of the flames. Fear rendering her superstitious, she swore that she had recognized his two red horns and his scorpion's tail, which he had caused to whistle through the air as he flew off in the direction of Lutecia.

The said demon was none other than an unfortunate victim of the fire, who was incapable of flying like a malevolent angel and had quite simply fled along the road to Lutecia to avoid the peril that menaced him.

He was a man whose physiognomy indicated a frank and loyal character. A very singular bonhomie, but which did not lack dignity and energy, was imprinted on his entire person. His costume was very simple, similar to that of a worker, but that was undoubtedly a disguise, easily betrayed by the unknown individual's face and distinguished manners.

"After all," he said to himself, pausing in his precipitate flight, "Why be so fearful? What harm have I done? Who, then, is pursuing me? I'm hiding like a malefactor; it's really too ridiculous. Nirvana was trying to frighten me needlessly. Let's go, come what may!"

And the mysterious individual headed resolutely for a small isolated house painted red on all sides, displaying a large garland of oak-leaves above the door, announcing to everyone who knew how to read that one could get something to eat and drink there.

"Hey, my man!" said the traveler, striking the broad stone slab that served the wine-merchant as a counter, and putting on a detached expression, like that of a man accustomed to that sort of place in order not to belie his workman's costume. "Wine!"

"At your service," replied a fat man who was obliged to turn sideways to pass through a narrow door leading from his room to the counter.

"You're up very early, my lad," the fat merchant added, briskly pouring his measure into a small sandstone jug, in such a way as only to half-fill it, the rest disappearing into the hollow stone, where nothing was lost.

"By Sylax! If I'm up very early, my stout old fellow, I'm not the only one. That's understandable for a traveler like me, but you're at home, and already have your door open..."

"It's not entirely usual here, my old comrade," the merchant replied, sitting down facing his customer, in such a way that the latter was obliged to invite him to have a few drinks with him, which was not something that people did twice. "You're on the road very early," he added, when he had made himself comfortable, "but we've had a man who was on the road even before you, for it was scarcely two o'clock when he knocked on the door. As he was a friend, we emptied two jugs together. Then, as the sun was about to rise out there, I said to myself: Elasippe my friend, you won't go back to bed."

"I'm not sorry to have been preceded here by a traveler even earlier than myself," replied the dubious laborer, "for I needed a drink, and I wouldn't have dared wake you up."

"You'd have been wrong. Nimrod isn't so fussy. He arrived at an undue hour, it's true, but it doesn't matter—he came in all the same."

"Nimrod!" said the traveler, trying to remember something.

"The very same—do you know him? Ah, a good fellow, devilishly generous, always pays, always has a full purse. He's my friend. He's also a friend of Speos, a so-called, now one of our most illustrious Me-nu-tcheans."

"Oho! You're a friend of Speos," said the traveler, who became very thoughtful.

"As you say, Comrade," relied the wine merchant, smoothing his long moustache with satisfied fingers. "A good and honest patriot."

"I congratulate you, Citizen," said the stranger, who did not appear to pay much attention to the republican epithet that he applied to the fat wine-merchant, who nevertheless started.

"Citizen!" he exclaimed. "You're one of ours, aren't you, my lad? I'd already guessed. You're for the democratic and fraternal republic, such as it's in preparation in our glorious clubs. For myself, you see, when I don't scent good game, I don't reveal myself, but you have the odor of a good patriot. I'm truly sorry that Nimrod didn't run into you here. What a joy it would have been for him to make your acquaintance! He's one who likes nobles, by Sylax. If he got hold of them all, he'd gladly throw them into a furnace like the one he saw last night in Me-nu-tche. Did you see it? You came from that direction, I believe."

"Yes…yes, in fact, I did see it."

"By the three divine friends! That was well done—because, you see, it was the house of a noble, that one. I say this very quietly, but I wouldn't be astonished if it was a true patriot who did that fine work! And yet it's said—Nimrod said the same—that it was the work of nobles."

"What! Nobles who burn their own houses!"

"No doubt. It's a ruse, so that they can say afterwards that it was the democrats, in order to frighten the people who might, in the end, find themselves victim to a similar accident one day."

"Oh yes—that's true," replied the stranger, with an ironic and incredulous little smile.

"Anyway, I think that there soon won't be any need to roast the nobles, because they seem to me to have caught the scent of the straw and the firebrand already, and they're making themselves scarce. It's all the neighboring islands that are taking them in, and so much the better, because Nimrod tells me that our clubs have a law in their pocket, but a law…"

"Against the nobles?"

"Right, against the nobles…but a law that won't do me any harm, because my little house needs enlarging, since my business, thank God, isn't going too badly. There's a little plot of land nearby that would suit me very well, but it belongs to a leftover who's voyaging in the other world, or at least abroad."

"What's his name?"

"Mo-kie-thi. You don't know Mo-kie-thi? Everyone knows him. He's a rich man—very rich—who left Atlantis at least sixteen or seventeen years ago, perhaps more, for a voyage from which he's in no hurry to return. But what does it matter? Dead or alive, here or there..."

"Well?"

"The State will take his lands."

"Ah!"

"The law that Nimrod tells me that our club wants to obtain against the nobles is the law of confiscation: confiscation against the exiles, first, or the fugitives, and then confiscation against all the nobles, to the profit of the Republic."

"But is it really a republic that we'll have in the end? Because I can't see that anyone's in a hurry to found a stable government."

"It can't be long—we're on the right road. That's the first news I ask for every morning, myself, right away. But while waiting for our republic to be firmly based, and waiting for the laws to rid us of the nobility that has robbed us for such a long time, ours are taking care of them—for after all, we don't want to die of hunger, and it's the nobles who have all the money, all the wheat, and all the food. They've stolen three-quarters of the land from us; we have to take it back from them, and share it out as ought to have been done in the beginning. Then, everything will be better, even my little business—for, you see, the nobles don't drink and eat in my hostelry, and the workers, when they have the cash, have better things to spend it on. Isn't that right?"

"Oh! Yes..."

"That's right—and long live the Republic! Down...down with the aristocracy!" cried the excellent innkeeper, emptying his cup in a single draught.

The traveler smiled approvingly at his companion of the moment—but in truth, his smile was so sad and so constrained that it almost betrayed his most secret thoughts. The cheerful republican fixed him with two astonished eyes that demanded an explanation for his partner's silence, but the latter bent down, took his foot in his hand and made a horrible grimace that the inn-keeper appeared to understand.

"Damn!" he said. "Are you suffering, Comrade?"

"Yes, I'm suffering."

"Well, you can rest here as long as you like."

"On the contrary—the pain's telling me to march, and I'll be on my way."

He paid for the wine that his terrible companion had drunk, and left.

"Adieu, brother!" the wine-merchant called to him from the threshold. "And don't go past Master Elasippe's house, no matter what time it is, without go-ing in!"

The traveler nodded his head affirmatively while he drew away silently. That silence made the worthy Elasippe tremble horribly; he appeared somewhat lack-ing in courage away from the shelter of his counter.

The traveler, meanwhile, went on his way no less troubled than the man he had troubled so much. The innkeeper's sinister words were still ringing in his ears.

He had no difficulty convincing himself that his in-terlocutor was not one of those bold and dangerous indi-viduals to whom the secrets of a party have been confid-ed, but the man had an isolated house that might well be a meeting-place of revolutionaries, and if he could not lay claim to the honor of taking judicious account of what he had heard, he might well, at least, flatter himself on telling the truth.

Those reflections slowed down the traveler's pace. At present, he was far from having the firm resolution that had driven him into Elasippe's tavern, and the closer he came to Lutecia, the more he believed that a fatal event was imminent.

He found Nirvana's recommendations perfectly justified now, the latter having advised him to maintain a strict incognito until further notice, and he was inclined to obey them—but Nirvana had not foreseen the burning of his house and the imperative flight of his guest when making his recommendations.

He had, therefore, to make his own decisions now, and find a shelter on his own in the midst of the enemy camp—which redoubled all the terrors awakened by what the innkeeper Elasippe had said.

XI. Power and Poverty

The mysterious traveler finally went into the great city of Lutecia, which he feared so much. It was, however, calm; everything there inspired the greatest feeling of security. Even he, the accursed, the victim of the blaze whom everyone was pursuing, would be unnoticed in the crowd, he thought. Neither thieves, nor bailiffs, nor agents of the police were on his trail. No one would point the finger at him. Even so, the slightest noise made him tremble; he turned his head away abruptly at the slightest contact he made with the passers-by.

Evidently, he had been sternly warned about dangers that might only have been imaginary.

His anxiety calmed down somewhat, however, at the sight of the peace that reigned around him. He began considering the places around him more tranquilly, and the sight of the immense city where he had lived for such a long time.

He was in one of the most populous and most animated suburbs, the suburb of the Buddha. The place had lost much of its ancient physiognomy; anyone who had not seen it for ten years would certainly no longer have recognized it. He sought to recover half-forgotten memories; he wanted to get his bearings in order to direct his paces more reliably and eventually find the shelter he sought, but which was certainly not in that neighborhood of poverty, labor and misery.

At that moment, a few paces away from him, in one of the most miserable houses of the street where he was standing, on the third and top floor, a young woman was working with a vivacity full of courage. She was sitting next to a dilapidated small table, one which two places were set for a poor meal, and a few fruits. She was, in fact, poor; everything indicated the fact, including the furniture, the frugality of the meal, and the feverish activity with which the young woman was working, without wasting a single precious second.

At the noise of a familiar tread that she heard on the stairway, she ran to open the door.

It was Atlas.

He was sad, morose and consternated.

"Nothing yet," he said. "Nothing for me in this immense, rich, luxurious city of Lutecia, where there are people dying of indigestion while others are dying of hunger." He laughed bitterly. "Ha ha! For such a celebrated, glorious, important man, it's truly shameful. A poor fool who believed...what, then, did I believe? I thought that democracy was about to give me a good meal every day, a comfortable shelter and wealth. Yes, by Sylax! I thought that, whereas I don't even know now which way to turn, and whether I ought to be glad have the skillful fingers of my little Chemnis to give me something to eat today—me, a strong man full of vigor, but with no work, with no money and with no hope for tomorrow. Atlantis, I curse you! Heaven and earth, you're good for nothing! No, I'm mistaken—they're good for tormenting us. But what am I saying? It's humans who've rendered Heaven and earth futile. War against humans, then! Yes, war to the death!"

Atlas was beside himself, rage overflowing from his heat. Chemnis tried to calm him down with caresses. She had some slight success, and managed to sit him down at her little table, where she served the frugal nourishment she had prepared with a smile full of grace and encouragement.

"Don't give up hope, my friend," she said to him. "Heaven will be just to you, and the men you esteem will remember your merits. But have a little patience, and while waiting to be tranquil, be happy here. There's no lack of work for your little sister, and she'll never lack courage, as long as you wish her well."

"May your hand be blessed for the good it does!" said Atlas, with a tear in his eye, kissing Chemnis' hand. "Perhaps, one day, I'll be able to return a hundredfold the price of your courage and your generosity. For in the end, am I not on the right path? Can democracy be so ingrate for one of its combatants?"

Chemnis did not reply, and the most profound silence was then established around the little table, where the two diners ate with the best appetite they could. Atlas was pensive. Chemnis, understanding that he was painfully occupied with the thoughts that she suspected, dared not speak; she dared not oppose his dreams, hoping that they would be worn away of their own accord, for want of discussion. She was mistaken in her expectation, but she was right.

"It doesn't matter, Chemnis," Atlas suddenly said, doubtless afraid of seeing his inner fire go out by itself. "My heart is ulcerated because there's evil around us, and I can see where it is. It's not in the inequality of fortunes, but of favors, in bad divisions, in the egotistical divisions of a perverse society, in the social every-man-for-himself, in the forgetfulness of the rights of all, the abuse of everyone's duties, the meanness of a fraternity that speaks but doesn't act. I'll fight all that, I swear—and I'll fight it to the death."

Chemnis said nothing, but she darted a soothing glance at the young man, who did not see it, because his eyes and mind were elsewhere.

"Oh, the nobles, the nobles!" Atlas added, devouring his bread angrily. "What good is all that proud and egotistical aristocracy? Who sowed that bad grain in the field of a society of brothers?"

"Leave it be, my friend," said the swift voice of Chemnis, finally. "It's not you or anyone else who can change what has always been."

"That's true, sister," said Atlas, with a smile full of bitterness. "Yesterday it was the nobles who were the kings of Atlantis; today it's the rich; tomorrow it will be the clever—but there'll still be the great, the powerful, the favored and the unfortunate…like me." With the last despairing remark, he got up from the table.

At that moment, a strange noise, a great tumult, became audible in the street; inarticulate cries, and then patriotic songs, rose up to Atlas' little room. Atlas and Chemnis ran to the window and looked out.

The street was full of a compact crowd of men, women and children, who were following a banner carried by men who were affecting the utmost gravity.

It was a deputation of the Club of Me-nu-tcheans, going to the seat of government to present a petition. That petition was grave, and threatened a new revolution if it were sustained, for it demanded laws—the laws discussed in the clubs a few days before—and the laws were not those decreed by the present government.

"The imbeciles!" said Atlas, ill-humoredly, coming away from the window. "That's how they want to govern, with mobs?"

As he turned around he found himself face to face with a man who had just knocked on the door and come into the room at the same time. It was the innkeeper Elasippe's customer. His face was distraught; his clothes were in disorder, as if he had just been in a fight.

"Save me, sir!" he said, as he came in. "Save me from the savagery of those men!"

The savagery of which the newcomer was complaining was the brutality of a few strapping adolescents whom the procession of petitioners had excited, and who had thought it a good idea to take out the seething of their ill will on the back of the poor man, whose appearance had aggravated them.

"Who are you?" Atlas asked him.

"An exile sir," replied the newcomer, frankly and nobly, whose emotion had calmed down.

At that moment, someone knocked on the door. Atlas shoved the newcomer swiftly into a corner to hide him from indiscreet gazes and then went to open up. An unknown hand, which immediately disappeared, handed him a message.

That message was from Nimrod.

After having read it, Atlas went to dart a glance into the street, and then came back to the exile. "I won't ask you who you are, Sir Exile," he said, "and I don't want to know where you're going. The street is calm now; you can leave in complete safety."

The exile held out his hand, which Atlas shook willingly, and then he left.

A few moments later, Atlas went out in his turn.

XII. A Revenant

If agitation reigned in the wretched room of the Me-nu-tchean Atlas, it was no less great in the rich house of Lord Speos. Two men were conversing there in low voices, in a study.

One of them, Speos himself, had pale, contracted features. His eyes were almost continuously lowered toward the ground, as if in a profound reverie. The other, holding his head high, was smiling sardonically, only replying with a few brief and sententious remarks, which sometimes caused the Me-nu-tchean lord to stamp his feet with impatience, who would have preferred clear and precise advice in response to his question.

Long intervals of silence fell between them, during which each of them devoted himself to his own thoughts.

The sound of footsteps in the corridor leading to the study caused them both to turn toward the door, on which someone soon knocked.

"It's him!" they said, in unison, each darting a glance at the other, one painted with embarrassment, the other with hope.

At the same time, the door opened.

It was Atlas.

Atlas came in, clutching the note that he had just received from Nimrod.

"Welcome, Atlas," said Speos, in a hypocritical tone that the young man did not notice.

"Sit down," Nimrod said to him, offering him a chair and placing him between his master and himself.

"My dear friend," said Speos, "you probably know that some of our people have decided to present a petition—strongly supported, as you must be aware—to the effect of obtaining a definitive democratic government, which ought to provide the Pah-ri-ziz with progressive laws, with which you're familiar, since they emerge from our club. We would also like there to be at least one man in the council of that government on our side, purely in the interests of the proletariat. That man will be you. Would you like that, Atlas?"

"Me!" said Atlas, coming to his feet proudly and throwing back his luxuriant hair. "Me! Oh, then they wouldn't any longer say: that miserable peasant, that nameless child of the little people! I could finally be the equal of everyone. I'd be a man, a citizen. They wouldn't any longer kick me aside, like social refuse. Yes, yes, citizen, I'd like that—I'd like that very much!"

"It shall be," said Speos, darting a knowing look at Nimrod.

"On one condition, however," Nimrod added, looking at his master slyly.

"No, no, no conditions," said Speos.

"But after all," Nimrod went on, "Atlas has at least to support our laws, the laws of those who have put him in the council. He won't be speaking against his conscience; he'll be speaking on behalf of everyone in supporting the law of proscription, the law against the resistant aristocrats."

"I'll support it, I swear!" Atlas replied. "Oh yes, I swear it to support it with all my might!"

"You shall be in the council then," said Speos. "Everything has been prepared for that. May Me-nu-tche, our glorious patron, come to our aid! *Au revoir*, then, Atlas! Count on us, as we're counting on you. Justice will, therefore, finally be a verity among the Pah-ri-ziz."

Speos got up to shake Atlas' hand as he left. Nimrod escorted the future councilor to the exit door, while Speos rubbed his hands in glee; he was counting on a rude fighter in favor of his projects.

"You'll demand even more in the government council, Atlas," said Nimrod, as they were about to part. "You'll demand the division of lands—that's the true justice. Anyway, we'll discuss all that between ourselves, without saying anything to Speos, who still has a few scruples of caste..."

As he went back in, Nimrod said to himself; "What does it matter to me whether the law confiscates the wealth of resistant lords! What matters to me is that the law threatens to despoil Speos of the wealth he's stolen from the exile Mo-kie-thi, whose death is uncertain, but whose exile definite..."

When Nimrod went back into Speos' study, he said: "I said a few more words to him, for he might yet have scruples, that integral revolutionary."

He had scarcely pronounced those last words, when a man appeared on the threshold of the study, the sight of whom caused Lord Speos to recoil in fear and stammer: "Help me, Nimrod! It's *him!*"

Nimrod smiled, and did not appear to hear him. He left Speos alone with the newcomer.

The newcomer was the innkeeper Elasippe's customer, the exile who had obtained momentary shelter from Atlas. It was Lord Mo-kie-thi.

Mo-kie-thi extended his hand to Speos with an appearance of affection, which restored a little confidence to the frightened man's heart.

"Good day, my dear fellow!" he said.

"It's really you, then!" exclaimed Speos, in a halting voice.

"As you can see, full of life and health."

"It's truly prodigious, for in eighteen years...it has been eighteen years, I believe..."

"At least."

"In the eighteen years since you left, you've never given us any news—and in truth, I thought you were dead."

"I've noticed that—you've forced me to live on the enemy, forgetting the address of my correspondent bankers."

"You've done very well: a brave man, a soldier," said Speos, adopting a bantering tone and only responding to a part of his old friend's observation.

"Oh yes, you can joke," Mo-kie-thi retorted, "And I'm almost tempted to laugh myself, since the misery is past. It's true nonetheless that I've cursed you more than once for not having sent me a single pah-ri-ziz sou, while my property, thank God, hasn't been devastated and my houses haven't been burned. I left, as you know full well, enough to nourish myself out there, and my son here. My son! You haven't mentioned him..."

"Your son!" stammered Speos.

"He must he strong, tall, full of valor and chivalry," the visitor went on, confidently. "Oh, the blood of the Mo-kie-thi never fails. But where is he?"

"Your son!" said Speos again, with an embarrassment full of anxiety.

"Yes, by Sylax, my son! In truth, you're frightening me, Speos. Where is he, then?"

"He's dead."

"Dead! But that's impossible! I don't believe it."

"He died not long after your departure."

"No, no, no!" retorted Mo-kie-thi, vehemently. "He's not dead! I don't believe it, I tell you. He's alive, he's handsome, tall, strong, well-built—but you want to surprise me. How much gratitude I owe you, my friend, for all the care you've given him! Anyway, we'll talk about that later, because I know that you've experienced losses."

"Losses! Someone's misinformed you, Mo-kie-thi."

"So much the better, my dear fellow, so much the better if they've misinformed me. That error won't affect the extent of my gratitude in your regard."

Mo-kie-thi was speaking with so much confidence and such great bonhomie, that Speos was utterly confused.

"Oh, at any rate," Mo-Kie-thi went on, looking at his watch, "I'll leave you. You might need to go to the club at present."

"The club! Yes, I go there sometimes," Speos replied, in a sly tone that clearly revealed that he understood his friend's malicious intention.

"Oh, it's fashionable, I know," said Lord Mo-kie-thi. "Who doesn't go to the club? It's good form—I don't reproach you for it. Your club, however, doesn't seem to me to be handling things very well. Perhaps it's to the club that I owe the strict incognito in which I'm living."

"And which I advise you not to give up any time soon," the renegade Speos retorted, swiftly. "So I offer you, for greater safety, a refuge with me—the refuge of friendship."

"Bah! No need! I'm no longer afraid. At first, I allowed myself to be influenced by the advice of an excessive prudence, but now…oh! What about my son?" Mo-kie-thi added, reverting abruptly to that notion. "When and where shall I see him? For in truth, I'm impatient…the poor child!"

"As I told you, he died at least seventeen years ago."

"Seriously?" said Mo-kie-thi, looking at his friend incredulously. "My son is dead?"

"He's dead," replied Speos, sadly.

"Well," said Mo-kie-thi, in a quiet voice, "shall I tell you something? I thought you were a true friend, and I was mistaken."

Speos looked at his old friend stupidly, and made no reply.

"Yes," Mo-kie-thi continued, "I was mistaken. Either my son isn't dead, or you've killed him in order to take possession of my property, because you thought I had died too, in my distant travels, or in the fire in Me-nu-tche..." Fixing his piercing eyes on Speos' troubled eyes, he added: "You know—the fire in Nirvana's house at Me-nu-tche." After a momentary pause, he went on: "Yes, you've killed my son, doubtless with the hope of having his death forgotten one day, in the turbulence of the times, and perhaps also of having the father murdered. One sees that sometimes."

"Me! Ridiculous!" replied Speos, stupidly, not having the strength to adopt the tone of indignation appropriate to the crimes of which he was being accused.

"*Au revoir*, Speos," said Mo-kie-thi, bowing respectfully before his so-called friend. "Prepare your accounts without too much faith in the power of your club. Its voice isn't yet so loud that it can stifle the voice of the law of the land. *Au revoir*!"

And Mo-kie-thi left, leaving Speos paralyzed by a puerile fear.

"Nimrod! Nimrod!" he shouted, then.

Nimrod appeared in response to his master's voice, as the evil spirit, according to ancient legends, appears in response to the voice of a sorcerer.

"Did you see that man, Nimrod?" said Lord Speos.

"Yes, Master," Nimrod replied, coldly.

"Do you know who he is?"

"Of course."

"He wants his property."

"What! You're his heir."

"Give me other advice."

"It's necessary, my lord..."

"Enough! I want advice that will rid me of that man," said Speos, making a great effort, and turning his back on his servant.

"I'll get rid of him for you, Master."

"Good! But never mention it to me again."

Lord Speos went out. Nimrod did not follow him.

XIII. Memories and Projects

Nimrod went to knock very discreetly on the door of Ludia's room, which opened. He went in with as much precaution as he was received, as if both of them would be taking a great risk if they were found together.

"What do you want?" said Lord Speos' wife, who did not know what to think about the mystery with which Nimrod was coming to see her, and who was always afraid when she found herself alone with him.

"What do I want?" said Nimrod. "I want to talk to Ludia." Smiling, he added: "Tell Lady Speos, I beg you, to leave us alone."

"Well, speak!"

"Do you remember a terrible night some eighteen years ago, if not nineteen, or even more—I don't know exactly—when you were suffering so much, when your father was perhaps cursing you, but was certainly cursing the child that you had brought into the world and your seducer?"

"Well?" replied Ludia, trembling with anxiety and fright at that beginning.

"Don't worry, Lady Speos, I'm only talking to Ludia," said Nimrod, unemotionally. "Do you remember that, a few days later, I handed you a letter from…oh, my God, from your lover?" Nimrod's voice took on a malevolent inflection. "Your lover, who had left…"

"Get to the point!" snapped Ludia, quivering as much with indignation as impatience.

"You promised before me to be faithful to him, to wait for him, even though he'd left on a long voyage—because he swore to return."

"Well, then?" said Ludia, impatiently.

"As you were very young, as he was married, as your father cursed him and wished him dead..."

"Nimrod!" protested the poor woman in a muffled voice, going frightfully pale.

"You have waited."

Ludia lowered her head on to her bosom. Her arms fell convulsively to her sides, and she threw herself into a chair, her eyes haggard, her heart swollen and her lungs breathless.

Nimrod took a step toward her and continued, tranquilly: "Well, Madame, your father is dead; you have come of age; and your lover has come back without his wife."

"What did you say?" Ludia cried, vehemently, raising her eyes, full of anxiety, to look at her interlocutor.

"I said that Lord Mo-kie-thi has come back, and he believes you to be free, unless someone has told him otherwise."

"Ah!" said Ludia, with a profound sigh.

"Yes," said Nimrod, insouciantly. "But the strangest thing about all this, and perhaps the most troublesome, is that the pact that he made with his friend, now your husband..."

"What pact?" asked Ludia, who seemed to have lost her memory.

"Yes, you know very well. Mo-kie-thi had a son."

"Oh, yes, I know—but he died a long time ago."

"No, he didn't die."

"He's alive?"

"In truth, I don't know, but it might be better if he were dead."

"Enough! I understand. Oh, my God, my God! No, it's not true—he died long ago, I tell you."

"He didn't die, any more than his father—but he was singularly inconvenient, and the father is even more inconvenient now."

Lady Speos got up and launched herself at Nimrod as if moved by electricity. He seized her arms with an astonishing strength.

"Nimrod!" she cried, in a distraught voice, approaching her face to the impassive face of her torturer. "Nimrod!"

"It wasn't me who said that the child was dead, Madame. As for the father, it's to me that he's confided the case of sending him away…into exile."

"Into exile! To death, you mean! Oh, it won't be Nimrod, my good Nimrod, who does that." Ludia seized her servant's hand ardently and covered it with kisses.

"Yes and no," replied Nimrod, phlegmatically, not scorning the lady's expansive tenderness.

"Explain yourself," said Ludia, anxiously.

"No, if that's what you want."

"If that's what I want! But I don't want my husband to commit a crime."

"If I don't do it," Nimrod retorted, "your husband is doomed."

"Doomed? Why?"

"At any rate, he's doomed," said Nimrod.

"Oh, that can't be. I want to see Mo-kie-thi. I want to see him. Where is he?"

"Write a few words to him. I'll give them to him."

"Write! No!"

"Oh, just a few words. 'Come this evening'…or tomorrow evening, if you prefer… 'at such-and-such a time'…eleven, or midnight, perhaps, to be safer… 'I have to talk to you.' Sign it: 'Ludia.' I'll be watching, close at hand."

"And Speos? My intentions are pure, Nimrod, I swear by the three divine friends. But if Speos were to find out..."

"He won't know anything. Madame must be aware of my devotion to her."

Ludia started to write, while her perfidious servant, putting his hands together, raised his eyes to the heavens, as if to give thanks for the good fortune it had sent.

"Oh, by the way," he said, interrupting the lady. "I don't have any news of your son yet."

"Oh, I've given up asking," Ludia replied. "You've refused so many times to give me the information I want, and have humiliated my maternal love so many times, that I would never have dared to address any further questions to you on that subject."

"I am, however, still much occupied in his regard. I believe that it will soon be permitted to me, finally, to present him to you, as I'm desirous of so doing."

"Sylax by blessed!" said the poor mother, shivering with pleasure, and cheerfully sealing the letter, which she handed to Nimrod.

Nimrod took the letter, but did not move. The lady thought she understood. She opened a purse, from which she took out a handful of gold coins, which she held out to the avaricious messenger.

"Oh, that's not what I was waiting for, my lady," said Nimrod, extending his hand, "but I thought, because of your generosity, that I might as well reveal to you right away a little secret that you might be glad to know. Perhaps the time is right."

"Speak!"

"In fact, no—not yet," said Nimrod, after having reflected momentarily. "Let's be prudent and not try to do everything at once. First of all, Lord Mo-kie-thi!"

202

Nimrod left then, leaving the dagger of a new anxiety trembling in Ludia's heart.

XIV. The Hour of the Rendezvous

That same evening, Lord Speos' house was still giving signs of life at an hour when it was usually completely still.

It was midnight, and the porter had not yet gone to bed. The lamp set near the staircase to illuminate it until the masters went to bed was still yielding a feeble glow, whose flickering reflections formed thousands of phantoms along the walls.

Lord Speos was in his bedroom, sitting in a large armchair with his head in his hands and his elbows on a table. A pair of revolvers was before his eyes.

Nimrod and Hyperion were sitting a little way behind their master.

No one said a word; one might have thought them three cadavers.

Nimrod was sitting comfortably in a high-backed armchair, his arms folded, his legs outstretched and his head bowed over his breast, as if he were reflecting profoundly.

Hyperion's attitude was very similar, but a slight snore uttered from time to time that he was no longer meditating.

A small lamp, half extinct, illuminated the three human statues with its wan light.

In Ludia's room, by contrast, there was the greatest agitation. The lady was alone, but she was pacing back and forth, tormented by the idea of a crime. Suddenly, she ran to the door, convinced that someone had knocked on it—but there was no one there.

"No one!" she said. "I believe, in truth, that I'm going mad. My God, what shall I do? It's necessary, though, to save my husband. Anyway, I only have to say words to him to ask for mercy for Lord Speos. But what if Nimrod were to betray me? Oh, no, no—that's impossible. Mo-kie-thi will come secretly, in perfect safety for both of us...ah!"

She ran to the door, and opened it.

It was him: Lord Mo-kie-thi.

At that sight, the lady's heart ceased to beat. All her limbs remained motionless. There was a pause in her life. Then came memories, remorse, dread and hope. I do not believe that there was love any longer.

"You, my lord!" she said.

"Me, Madame; here at your orders. I'm listening."

"You mean to harm Speos," Ludia said, her face red and her eyes downcast.

"Me, Madame!"

"It's said that you want to render him responsible for your son's death."

"I don't know, Madame. I'll base that decision on information that will soon reach me."

"Without hatred, without remorse and without vengeance?" asked the lady, in voice that was weak and tremulous.

"Of course, milady. Why cite all those evil sentiments?"

"How do I know, my lord?"

"Is it because your son and mine, perhaps the only one that remain to me, will not have our name, thanks to you? Is it because Ludia Arimaspes has betrayed her oath? Is it because...?"

Ludia interrupted Mo-kie-thi with the impatient gestures she made, indicating that she wanted to speak.

"Forgive me, Madame," Mo-kie-thi continued. "I understand that I'm making myself a trifle ridiculous in reminding you, after sixteen years of absence, of words that might have been spoken in a moment of delirium. I'm still speaking like an amorous and credulous young man, whereas I'm no longer anything to you but an old man to be dismissed..."

Ludia, however, seemed to be suffering horribly. Every one of her interlocutor's words was a dagger-blow to her.

"Mo-kie-thi!" she said, finally. Stepping toward him and placing a convulsive hand on her shoulder.

"Madame," said the other, feeling an involuntary frisson run along all his limbs on contact with that hand, once so dear to him.

"Listen to me; I only merit pity."

"We'll see," said Mo-kie-thi, looking Ludia in the face, his eyes folded over his chest.

"When you left for your long voyage," the lady said, "it was as much, you ought to remember, out of personal fear as to defer to my pleas. I wanted you to shield your head from the resentments of my father. If you had other sentiments, they're unknown to me. But you were not the only one condemned in the eyes of Lord Arimaspes. As soon as he was born, they wanted to take him away from me to throw him into the sea. I saved his life, but at what price? Money, for one thing, and then on condition that I would not see him again, at least for many years—and, indeed, I haven't seen him."

"So what, Madame?" said Mo-kie-thi, coldly, affecting more insensitivity than he really had.

That memory of the past was not devoid of interest for him. The proof of that was that his face eased insensibly as Ludia spoke, and that he darted glances at her from time to time that testified to a great deal of anxiety and commiseration.

"My father died," he went on, in a tearful voice. "Poor father! I was free from then on, but you weren't here. I waited. I waited for you for a long time, and when my twentieth birthday was about to sound, you had not arrived. No one knew where you were. Your friends had had no news of you; it was said that you were dead."

"And then?" said Mo-kie-thi, emotionally, extending a hand to Ludia's arm, which he squeezed affectionately.

"Lord Speos asked for my hand; I accepted, in order to obey the law."

"Poor girl!" said Mo-kie-thi, drawing the lady closer to him.

"And I did well," Ludia added, "for Lord Speos was rich. My father's fortune, which I thought considerable, was burdened by debts, my husband told me, so that I found myself despoiled, and very glad to encounter the hospitality of a rich man. That, lord, is the extent of my crime."

"Your crime!" said Mo-kie-thi, drawing Ludia against his chest.

The lady extracted herself gently from that grip, and, moving a few paces away, she lowered her eyes and added: "And now I'm Lord Speos' wife."

"That's true," replied Mo-kie-thi, severely, "but you're also the mother of my son. Tell me about my son, Madame."

"Ask Nimrod what he did with him, my lord. I've been trying to find out for nineteen years, and haven't yet been able to succeed."

At that moment, someone knocked gently on the bedroom door. It was Nimrod, who had come fearfully to warn Lord Mo-kie-thi to leave as quickly as possible.

Mo-kie-thi darted an inquisitive glance at Ludia, who begged him, with her hands joined, to follow her servant's advice. He did not hesitate any longer, and escaped in haste.

An instant later, the sound of a revolver shot was heard, and then a muffled cry, and something like the sound of an inert mass falling down the stairs.

The lady ran out, breathlessly. She found herself face to face with her husband.

"He's dead, I think," said Speos, coldly, throwing his revolver down at the lady's feet.

"Who, my lord?" said Ludia, fearfully.

"Who? A thief, perhaps an assassin, whom I saw slipping swiftly along the corridor of our apartments."

"A thief!" cried the lady, in a distraught voice. "What if you were mistaken? What if it wasn't a thief?" Seizing her husband's arm wildly and feverishly, she added: "Have you killed him?"

"Let's go and see," replied Speos, calmly. At the same time, he took a small lamp from Nimrod's hands, which the perfidious servant had just brought, and they all went toward the victim.

The cadaver was lying on the stairs, head down, his feet still on the landing, with one hand clutching the banisters. Speos and Nimrod took hold of his clothing, while the lady, her eyes attentive and her ears pricked, waited in the most terrible anxiety for the result of the visit.

A trickle of blood was still escaping from the mouth of the victim, who uttered a prolonged gasp, which each of them felt in the depths of the heart, with various emotions.

Nimrod bent down to examine the face more closely, and uttered a stifled cry, looking at his master.

"Hyperion!" he exclaimed.

At the same time, the door to the street was heard to open and close, and the porter, half asleep, came up the stairs to put out the lamp that was still burning in the corridor.

XV. The Desert

A few leagues from Lutecia, to the north, in the year that we are talking about, there was a deserted valley, the soil of which was pitted at intervals with holes that were almost invariably filled with stagnant water: dangerous traps feared by everyone.

An arm of the sea had once extended there, it was said, which had partly disappeared, leaving nothing behind but bad memories. In the history of the country it was also said that the region had once, in a flourishing time, been extensively cultivated, very salubrious, nourishing a numerous and wealthy population; then, one day—no one knew in what epoch, which history mentioned vaguely, with countless and various suppositions—the soil had degenerated in order to become what was found in the year two thousand three hundred and forty-eight before our era: a place that was virtually uninhabitable.

The region formed a broad valley surrounded on all sides by mountains of volcanic appearance, for different craters that had opened at different times had not been completely filled in. Those mountains were extensively covered by forests, stunted on one slope—that of the valley—but more vibrant and lush on the others. On that side, the soil had a very different aspect. It was salubrious and fertile; life there was good and prosperous, so beautiful houses could be seen there: rich houses, and occasional manor houses.

By contrast, in the Valley of the Desert, thus warranting its name, life was so wretched and dangerous for everyone that it had gradually been abandoned, and the only habitations to be seen were a few hovels. There were, however, families native to the area that vegetated there as they always had, with no thought, for the most part, of seeking a better life elsewhere, so strong is human affection for the roof under which one is born.

The government paid no heed to those unfortunates whom it abandoned to their fates. If it did not give them any help, however, it did not torment them, perhaps considering them as people of the other world. It granted them the favor of not troubling their destinies.

The valley had another privilege, which was to be a place of refuge for those persecuted by society, for those proscribed by the government, which let them sleep in peace there, convinced as they were that their persecution would be abandoned, without any effort on its part, by virtue of the mephitic soil and without overmuch delay.

That murderous favor might have been a great favor in the year with which we are concerned.

One morning in that year, about six months after the gunshot in Lord Speos' house, the sun was radiant; the miasmatic fogs that covered the valley for much of the day had dissipated.

At the door of a rather neat cottage, suggestive of more careful care than the hands of the local inhabitants usually provided, a thin young man with a jaundiced and wrinkled face was sitting on a wooden stool. Everything about his pose and appearance indicated that he had been ill for a long time. His hands were resting on a staff and his chin on his hands. His clothing was not that of a peasant of the region.

Occasionally, at intervals, a young woman or an older one came out of the cottage as far as the threshold, where they exchanged a few words with the invalid and then went back inside. Their costume, simple as it was, was not peasant costume either.

"Well, Hyperion," said the young woman at one time, "do you like this sunshine?"

"The sun is doing me a great deal of good," the young man replied, with a smile in which there was more doubt than conviction—which the young woman noticed.

"You're not saying what you think, it seems to me," she said.

"Pardon me, Ormuzda, but I feel quite well. I even think that the sun in this ill-famed region is concealing its malevolence from me. Add to that, and most of all, your generous care, the tranquility and liberty that we enjoy here, and the hope we can entertain here, and what more could one want in order to emerge happily from a long illness? Then again, when one is in love..." Hyperion smiled.

"Yes, yes," replied the young woman, briskly, wanting to interrupt the expansion that she saw coming, "talk to us about your nineteen years and your love, as safeguards against malady!"

"Oh, they're not proof against a revolver, I admit, especially when one is imprudent, as you've said to me more than once. Imprudent! Oh, in truth, I merit that criticism, Can you imagine that I had spent a long, silent, bleak and sad night with Lord Speos and Nimrod. They both seemed absorbed in their thoughts, and were keeping themselves awake. I'd been struggling against tedium for a long time, against the drowsiness that was overtaking me; then, finally, I went to sleep.

"Painful dreams assailed me then; I saw myself pursued by horrible phantoms, by jailers, by murderers. In a moment of great fright I opened my eyes, I think, but I wasn't awake. I looked around. I was alone, or so it seemed.

"I wanted to flee then, so I went out precipitately and began slipping along the walls of the corridor without seeing anyone, although it seemed to me that I heard, some distance away, what I thought was an enemy. I fled more rapidly, but on the bottom step of the stairway I'd just come down, I was stopped by a gunshot, which was not aimed at me, since it was aimed at a burglar, according to some, or a perfectly honest man, according to others.

"When I woke up, I didn't know where I was; I was wounded, and Lord Speos was lavishing affectionate cares on me, full of regret, while the lady..."

"Oh, let's not talk about that," said Ormuzda, putting her hand over Hyperion's mouth.

"But that's another evidence I wanted to render of her good heart and her virtue, for she's innocent, I swear!" Hyperion retorted, ardently.

"Yes, the future will make everyone see that."

"The future!" said the young man, sadly, and then resumed with more confidence. "Oh yes, the future; it's our consoler, the world's great administrator of justice. That's the perspective that sustains me, which enables me to live and will cure me, for it gives me hope. The future will make me a useful man again, a citizen worthy of my Ormuzda. When shall we see your father, Ormuzda? Do you think that Lord Nirvana will accept my request?"

"Leave that aside," the young woman replied, trying to smile. "I have my secret in that regard. I'll reveal it to you when the time comes. In the meantime, I'll remind you that you've been forbidden to worry about anything at all, and especially not to talk so much. You've disobeyed orders: we aren't supposed to talk about love, politics, the past or the future."

Ormuzda went back into the cottage, wiping away a tear that Hyperion did not see.

There was, in fact, a great misfortune weighing upon her, and the young man knew nothing about it. Taken to that region before he had completely lost his reason, he did not know that Lord Nirvana was in prison, his property confiscated; that he was only left in peace because of his poor health; that he and his nurses were only undisturbed because they had sought refuge on the mortal soil; he did not know that a terrorist government reigned over Atlantis.

Lady Speos and Ormuzda took particular care not to allow anything to happen that might overexcite his imagination and endanger his life. His life had been so frail since the gunshot he had received in the chest, and his recovery was so uncertain that the sole concern of humanity of his guardians was to ease the last days of a dying man.

For himself, Hyperion hoped for something better: who has ever believed in imminent death at nineteen years of age? He was nurturing so many fine projects; his thoughts had become so beautiful in the presence of the woman he loved!

Scarcely had Ormuzda gone back into the cottage that Hyperion decided to follow her. He therefore got to his feet, awkwardly, with the aid of his staff.

At that moment, a peasant suddenly came round the corner of the little house and advanced toward him.

It was Ypsoer.

XVI. Ypsoer's Visit

"Good day, Sire Hyperion," said Ypsoer, approaching the young man very respectfully.

"Good day, neighbor," replied the invalid, by way of reply, standing still and leaning on his staff.

Ormuzda came out again. "Good day, sir," she said, with her customary affability.

Ypsoer bowed profoundly to the young woman. "Good day, my lady," he said, with some slight embarrassment, turning a little box around and around in his fingers, to which he wanted to attract attention.

"What have you got there?" asked the young woman, easily understanding the peasant's intention. She added: "A box! A pretty little box!" and extended her hand to take it.

"Pardon me, my lady, but it's not for you," said Ypsoer, smiling, as he presented the little box to the young woman.

"Oh? Who is it for, then?" Ormuzda replied, opening the box—from which she took a necklace of fine pearls, in amazement.

"It's for the good Lady Speos, who has rendered such great services to me and my wife...if she deigns to accept it." Ypsoer continued, in a mysterious tone: "I have, however, sworn that the necklace will never leave my hands."

"Why is that?" asked Hyperion, who understood that the fellow was only talking in order to be questioned.

"Because, you see, my lord," the peasant said, "a long time ago, that necklace was given to me...when I say given to me, that's not quite true, because it wasn't given to me. It was around the neck of a little boy, whom I called…but pardon me, the name doesn't matter, since everyone calls their children what they wish…and it was a good seventeen or eighteen years ago…any way, that necklace was around his neck."

The peasant made a gesture that implored extenuating circumstances for an action of dubious probity. "The little boy, oh, damn it…but the necklace, I kept it, because one never knows, and I said to myself: what if, one day, I were to run into the man who confided him to me? For the boy, I'll always be able to find him, for I've taken precautions for that, and the little girl too…oh, I didn't tell you that there was also a little girl, but she didn't have a beautiful necklace, only a little red ribbon from which a lead medallion was hanging, which I also have there."

"It's just that it's very fine, your necklace," said Ormuzda, who could not weary of admiring it.

"So much the better!" Ypsoer replied, going into the cottage after carefully closing the little box, in which he had replaced the necklace.

The two young people followed him. Ypsoer approached Ludia respectfully, very unsure as to the best means of getting her to accept his present. To that effect he took detours in which he alone could glimpse the path of which he was in search, remarking without rhyme or reason on the good weather, the quarrels of the neighborhood and curious anecdotes concerning the region.

"Have you heard the big news, my lady," he said, suddenly changing the subject again. "Our manor house…I say our because it's in our neighborhood…although it isn't, because it's on the other side of the mountain…anyway, it doesn't matter…what I mean is that our manor, which has been abandoned for months, has a new proprietor, who got it very cheap..."

"Really?" Ludia replied, with all the more interest because she was suspicious of the merit of the new owner, whom she did not know but could measure by the fact that he had obtained the property of an exile very cheap. She was quite familiar with the law of confiscation."

"Yes, and I've even seen him," said the peasant. "He's a big fellow with strong arms—stronger than mine—and a dark, hard face..."

"What's his name?"

"Ah! Well, I don't know...that's because, you see, I have no memory, I only recall one thing in my whole life..." Ypsoer looked at his listeners, whose attention encouraged his confidence. "Yes, I only recall one thing in my whole life. It was one evening...but it wasn't here, it was a long way from here...you see, I was born in this valley but I traveled a little to search for what I haven't found, and then, as they say...the swallow always returns to it's nest...I came back, and, well, one evening an invisible hand put a very small child into my hut..."

"Ah!" said Ludia, becoming more attentive.

"Yes, a little child who had a pretty necklace around his neck, so pretty..."

"Let me see!" said Ludia, sharply, reaching out as Ypsoer made as if to present the little box to her.

"Here it is," said Ypsoer, opening the box himself, and adding: "And if it's agreeable to you, my lady..."

Ludia turned the necklace over and over. Her eyes were shining with pleasure and hope, her face blossoming. She smiled blissfully. She took Ypsoer's hand and squeezed it convulsively as she drew him toward the door of the cottage.

"Who gave you this necklace?" she said to him, mysteriously. "Would you recognize him again?"

"Well, no…since I didn't see him."

"That's true," said Ludia.

"But I can tell you that it was sixteen or seventeen years ago, at least, if I remember correctly."

"Nineteen years," said Ludia, to herself, and added: "And the child who wore the necklace—would you recognize him?"

"Oh," said Ypsoer, smiling, "the child was so small, so small…however, my lady…" He went back into the room and headed toward Hyperion, whose arm he took. "I made a little mark on his arm…" So saying, the peasant casually lifted up the sleeve of Hyperion's mantle, in order to indicate the place where he had engraved the sign. Then he stopped in amazement, looking at Hyperion and Ludia.

"A mark like this," he added, finally, pointing with the tip of his finger at a small irregular cross that was imprinted on the young man's arm.

Hyperion could not help smiling at the amazement of the peasant, who was still dazedly contemplating the sign that he thought he recognized, while Lady Speos and Ormuzda stared at their invalid with an indefinable bewilderment, from which they were extracted by a sharp exclamation from the door of the cottage, which opened at that moment.

A vigorous young man with enormous shoulders was standing on the threshold. All eyes turned to him.

"My very humble respects to you, sir," Ypsoer said to the newcomer, bowing deeply toward him. To Ludia, he said, in a low voice: "That's the new owner of the manor."

"I've come to discuss very serious business with Lady Speos," said the visitor, in a severe voice. "There are so many people here that I'll come back another time, unless the lady consents to come to the manor, where we won't be disturbed, and where she'll find friends."

"Lady Speos will not go to the manor," said Hyperion, who was making an extraordinary effort to give his voice an intonation befitting the indignation that was rendering him furious.

"My lady will come," replied the importunate visitor, calmly, "because it's a matter of the life or death of someone who might be dear to her." Looking at Ormuzda, he added, emphatically: "As well as others..."

"Yes, my lord, I'll come," said Ludia, who seemed breathless. She looked determinedly at Hyperion and Ormuzda, who seemed consternated by the promise she had just made and added: "And I'll go alone," as she watched the lord of the manor draw away.

XVII. The Two Crosses

That same evening, Ludia left the little house on her own and climbed the mountain through the tall trees that separated the valley from the manor. Five o'clock had just chimed on the village's communal tower. The night was beginning to get dark beneath the thick fog of the marshes; the chill was sharp; the wind was whistling through the crowns of the oak trees, whose desiccated leaves were quivering in a magical manner.

Glacial and murderous winter was beginning to make its first assaults felt in the valley, which it exhausted like an unjust despot, leaving all the charms of a mild temperature to reign in neighboring regions.

The lady was impatiently awaited at the manor, where everything seemed to be silent. In a large drawing room with rich wall-hangings, decorated with precious furniture and filled with portraits of aristocratic families, there were three people who might have seemed out of place there.

One of them was admiring, distractedly, the luxury and elegance of the drawing room, which the former owner had left in a perfect state of conversation, perhaps out of generosity, but more likely having been taken by surprise. He was sprawled negligently in a large light-backed armchair, waiting for someone to speak to him.

The other two people formed a charming couple. There was a young man—Lady Speos' visitor—still pensive, and only relaxing slightly under the child-like caresses of a young woman who was striving almost in vain to cheer him up. He contrived a slight smile, but the smile was so distracted that it was easy to see that other thoughts were preying on his mind.

"Do you want anything else, Atlas?" asked the young woman, in a tender voice.

"No, nothing, Chemnis," the young man replied, "for I believe that you're going to be happy soon."

"Happy! But I always am, as long as you don't leave me... You're laughing at that, Nimrod?" she added, addressing the third person, whom she had seen smiling.

"No," Nimrod replied. "I'm only smiling—and I say that before anything else, Atlas has a duty to the fatherland, which has rewarded him generously for his devotion; he has a duty to the club that has given him a place on the great government council, in spite of his youth; and he has a duty to the future."

"Yes, I have a duty to the future," said the new lord of the manor, enthusiastically, suddenly becoming animated. Then he got up and went to the fireplace, on the mantelpiece of which he leaned, presenting his back to the fire, while Chemnis, whom he seemed to have dismissed, left the room in order not to witness a greater proof of indifference.

"What are you thinking about, then?" said Nirmod, who seemed to have been waiting until they were alone to make his reflections. "Honors? You have them. Riches? You no longer have any lack of them. Love? That little Chemnis loves you dearly. But you're thinking about Ormuzda, who didn't love you before and who detests you today, because you've put her father in prison on a charge of plotting against the security of the State."

"It's you who've done that," Atlas retorted, disdainfully.

"Me? No—I'm not powerful enough for that. I've advised, I've acted, I've undertaken commissions, I don't deny, but the essential word was pronounced by you."

"Well...," said Atlas, frowning.

"You've done well, by Sylax! But it's only partly succeeded. I would have liked his property to revert to you..."

"Never!" said Atlas, disdainfully.

"Or to me," Nimrod continued. "The State has kept it, unfortunately. I'm afraid that it will do the same with that of Mo-kie-thi, which I coveted. You recall Mo-kie-thi—that old friend of Speos whom you placed on the proscription list the other day, like his friend Nirvana, who is speaking out against my master, who refuses to recognize him in order to establish his identity—which establishment seems to me to be rather difficult, as there are only three people who would dare to testify against Speos: Nirvana, Ludia and me.

"After all, I can't see what Lord Speos has to gain. It's quite possible that if Mo-kie-thi isn't recognized, the State—which is hungry—will consider him proscribed, and confiscate his wealth. If, on the other hand, Mo-kie-thi is recognized, his wealth will revert to him by right, but only to pass, in spite of Speos, into the hands of the Republic—which, I believe, has a list of charges ready to launch against his culpability, which might well resemble Nirvana's. Oh, the Republic understands; it knows that those people never reform, no matter what they say."

"Well," said Atlas, finally emerging from the profundity of thought into which he had been plunged, "I wasn't thinking about any of that."

"Oh," said Nimrod. "What were you thinking about, then?"

"It seems to me that I've lived here before—in the Valley of the Desert, at least."

"Bah! I don't think so."

"Yes, when I was very young, with a peasant by the name of Ypsoer."

"What! Ypsoer!" said Nimrod, fixing Atlas with his lynx-like eyes.

"Ypsoer will tell us himself soon, for he's coming back."

"Ah! You'll want to be alone with him, then, and I'll leave you," Nimrod said, turning his head anxiously in the direction of the entrance door, where he had heard a sound, and slipping out of the room on the opposite side.

The door of the drawing room opened at the same time. It was Lady Speos. She came in with the assurance of a person who conserves a long superiority over the person she is visiting, but with the modesty of a woman who understands that it is necessary not to be arrogant in order to prevail.

"Please sit down, Madame," said Atlas, very affably, offering her the armchair of honor, "And let's get straight to the point. It appears, Madame, that you have appointed yourself the guardian of Lady Ormuzda?"

"Yes, my lord, since you have separated her from her father," Ludia replied, firmly.

"And your advice is graciously welcomed by her?"

"She is as submissive as a meek child; in any case, her life is so pure..."

"So pure! I believe it, Madame. However, she lives under the same roof as a young man whom she probably loves..." Atlas grimaced resentfully.

"Oh, my lord—a dying man..."

"Yes, but a young man."

"A young man from whom I cannot separate myself, my lord, for we owe, by way of reparation, at least as much care as the evil we have done...and then," the lady added, with great emotion, "I've adopted him as my son..."

"That's all very well," Atlas went on, sharply, "but the Lady Ormuzda..."

"Think, my lord! No father any longer..."

"But if he were returned to her..."

"May the three divine friends hear you!" Ludia exclaimed.

"On one condition, however," said Atlas, in a low voice, turning his head in order not to meet the eyes of Lady Speos, who was looking at him in bewilderment.

"What condition, if you please?"

"That of marrying a member of the present government," replied the Me-nu-tchean parvenu, severely, seeking to disguise the pettiness of his condition with the gravity of his voice.

"You, perhaps, my lord?" asked Ludia.

"Me, if you please, my lady."

"That's all right, Lord Atlas," said Ludia, getting up to leave. "Ormuzda will do that."

It was just in time, for Ypsoer, who had been kicking his heels for a quarter of an hour at the door, wondering whether he could go into the drawing room in the same fashion as he was accustomed to going into his neighbors' houses, had become impatient and opened the door at that very moment.

"Stay, my lady," said Atlas to Ludia, who was trying to leave. "It's late, at least in your valley; I only have

224

a few words to say to this man, and then I'll escort you down the mountain."

"Thank you, my lord, but I'm not afraid."

"Don't worry, my lady," said the peasant. "My lord needn't go to any trouble; I'll take you back myself."

Ludia hesitated, perhaps not entirely confident, in spite of what she said. In response to a further invitation, she decided to stay.

"Ypsoer," said Atlas to the peasant, "someone once entrusted a child to you."

"Two, my lord—a little boy and a little girl."

"What did you do with them?"

"My lord," Ypsoer replied, greatly embarrassed and lowering his head. "I could no longer feed them..."

"You abandoned them?"

"That's true, my lord, but..." Ypsoer turned to Ludia. "But I believe, my lord, that the little boy has been found."

"What!" said Atlas, with an anxiety suggesting that what the peasant had said had cast a disappointment into his heart.

"Yes, can you imagine, my lord, that a little while ago, in order to show my lady where I had put a sign on the arm of the child entrusted to me, I lifted up the sleeve of poor Lord Hyperion's mantle, just like this..." He also took hold of Atlas' sleeve, who lent himself readily to the demonstration, and lifted it to. "And there...damn!"

The word suddenly froze on Ypsoer's lips. He had found on Atlas' arm the same cross that he had seen on Hyperion's.

"That's strange!" exclaimed Ludia, getting up precipitately and seizing the Me-nu-tchean's arm avidly.

225

"I know one thing," the peasant said, then, "which is that I did what many others did—I made a cross, not knowing how do anything better. Not that I mean that my lord...but that really is my cross."

"And how long ago was this?" asked Atlas.

"Eighteen or nineteen years...perhaps eighteen...perhaps seventeen," he added, changing his mind, truing to please his listeners, who were looking at him with anxious eyes, whose aspirations he did not understand.

"Not nineteen?" asked Atlas.

"Damn! Perhaps, my lord...I'll ask my wife," Ypsoer replied, no longer knowing what to say.

Atlas greeted the peasant's uncertainty with a gesture of discontent that frightened the poor man, while Ludia lost herself in a void of hopes that she had thought filled in, but which she suddenly saw opening up in front of her once again.

She left, in consequence, full of discouragement, accompanied by Ypsoer, who was biting his fingernails at not having pronounced firmly the number nineteen, which seemed now agreeable to the new lord of the manor.

A moment later, Atlas looked up in order to ask further questions, but found himself alone. He had not heard his visitors' farewells. He fell into his armchair, as if exhausted, striking his forehead, grinding his teeth and cursing the fatality that weighed upon him.

Several times he had thought that he was on the point of discovering his birthplace; just now he had caressed that hope with delight, but it had just vanished again. It seemed to him, therefore, that he was destined to be the continual victim of cruel phantasmagorias directed by a power that laughed at his own.

For an ambitious man, however, Atlas' luck might have seemed excellent. To have departed from nothing in order to arrive at the height of grandeur—what more could he desire?

Nor did he desire anything—except for a little love on the part of Ormuzda. The favors of fortune were not those he had sought; it was not for his own sake that he wanted to find traces of his birthplace, but for the sake of that love.

Great things and great men often have an origin that is not the most pure. It is almost always personal interest, the stimulation of egotism, that raises a man out of his sphere and causes him to undertake striking deeds. But when the result is good, say men of conviction, what do the means matter?

Perhaps that equivocal maxim was the one that Atlas had adopted. At any rate, it presented nothing repulsive in his case, for, in spite of appearances, Atlas was not one of those grim and bloodthirsty democrats whose memory always causes tremors in all ages. A little ambition, quite natural at his age, and a great deal of love, had made him what we see.

For the harm that he did, one might reproach necessity more than him, and the blind force that continues indefinitely the initial impulsion given to a project whose twists and turns one has not always calculated. He was, in any case, no more guilty than the society that had made the privileged castes of which he was the victim, and no more than Ormudza, whom he loved and who did not love him. If he fought harshly against her, whose fault was that? If he was perhaps unjust, tyrannical, even—alas!—savage…he loved her so much...

To bring the young woman to him, to render her submissive to his will, he had thrown her father into a dungeon. Well, fatality! He had only succeeded in opening her arms to his rival, in rendering her the commensal and the maidservant of Hyperion.

What could he do, then? What he had done: soften her up, offer her the release of her father, and then his own hand, while showing his bride-to-be that he was not an unworthy man, that he had his birthplace, his name embellished by present power. Well, once again, fatality! That name, that birthplace on which he had put his finger, had just vanished like a deceptive will-o'-the-wisp.

He was, therefore, at bay; he was fidgeting with rage in his armchair, sometimes falling back into profound reveries that extended long into the night, in the midst of which he formed thousands of various projects.

The next day, Hyperion came to the manor house, supported on the arms of Lady Speos and Ormudza. His face was pale and drawn; his respiration was so weak and so precipitate that one would have thought he was about to expire.

When they arrived, Atlas, who was writing in his study, got up abruptly, and raised his head proudly, like a snake about to strike. Hyperion looked at him without arrogance, but without fear. Then, taking Ormudza by the hand, he led her toward the astonished clubman.

"My lord," he said, "here is my sister; if it is only up to me, be her husband and her protector, as you have promised to be her father's protector.

That speech was a thunderbolt for Atlas, who was far from expecting such a step. He no longer knew, in truth, whether he ought to rejoice in an event that placed his rival so high in his estimation. Accustomed to battling the vicissitudes of life, he found himself devoid of strength against its favors. He would certainly have preferred to have to knock down a rival than to owe him thanks for a unexpected benefit that he had sought by means of so many bad deeds...so many crimes, some might say—those who call the action criminal rather than the intention; those who take no account of innate human weakness and the innate fury of human passions.

Atlas was, therefore, deflated. He made no reply to Hyperion, but he extended his hand toward the young woman, who stood there motionless, her eyes lowered. He smiled bitterly.

Hyperion took a step toward him then, and shook his hand, saying: "What is said is said, my lord. It's up to you to obtain, not merely Ormuzda's hand but her heart."

He went out then with his companions, his heart full of tears, because he had just made a superhuman effort.

"Nimrod! Nimrod!" shouted Atlas, when he found himself alone, taking a deep breath into lungs that seemed violently oppressed.

But Nimrod, his adviser, did not respond. Atlas opened the door through which he had seen him go out when Hyperion arrived. Nimrod was not there; the only person there was Chemnis, prostrate before a statuette of the Buddha Sylax, pouring out a flood of tears.

That sight gripped his heart. He clenched his fists over his chest and cast a glance of malediction at the heavens...

Meanwhile, Nimrod was prowling around Ludia's cottage, waiting for an opportunity to speak to the lady in private. The opportunity eventually came.

Ludia shivered at the sight of him.

"Don't tremble, Madame," he said to her, smiling. "I've brought you some good news. I hope that in a fort-night, I'll be able to show you your son."

"I don't believe it, Nimrod," Ludia replied, coldly.

"In a fortnight, Madame," Nimrod repeated, emphasizing his words, "I will show you your son and reconcile you with my master, the lord. Adieu, Madame—rely on me!"

The lady was amazed. She did not know what meaning to attach to the words of her evil genius who had a habit of promising a good deed while preparing two evil ones.

In any case, Nimrod's assurance only served further to confuse her hopes and her quest.

XVIII. A Visit from Nimrod

A fortnight after that encounter, Lady Speos' little house was deserted. Ypsoer was its sole guardian; he came to open the door and windows from time to time to renew the air. Then, with his arms folded, his neck craning and his eyes fixed, he took up a station at a bend in the highway, as if he were expending someone to arrive by that route.

A similar monotony reigned on the other side of the mountain, in Atlas' manor house. Nothing was heard but the occasional sound of a door opening and closing again immediately. Sometimes, someone raised the curtain of a little high window overlooking the road that people coming from Lutecia had to follow in order to reach the village; then everything returned to complete immobility.

That was when Chemnis, left alone, fell back into her chair, hiding her face in her hands and making every effort to stifle her sobs.

One day, when she was in one of those crises of desolation, Ypsoer came into her room.

"Well, my lady, are you a little more content now?" he said to her, doubtless attributing the young woman's emotion to joy.

"Why would I be?"

"Because you've had news from Lutecia, about your brother."

"About my brother? From whom?"

"From whom? But from Nimrod, who arrived yesterday evening and only left this morning."

"Nimrod! Nimrod has come and gone again!" said the young woman, with an astonishment full of chagrin.

"Gone again...I don't know," Ypsoer replied, reproaching himself for his assumption. "I say that because I saw my neighbor Silene harnessing his two reindeer to his sleigh this morning to take Nimrod to the city...at least, that's what I thought..."

"And I haven't seen him!" the young woman exclaimed, in a heart-rending tone.

"You haven't seen him! Oh, well—but don't weep like that, my lady," the peasant said. "I can give you news myself. First of all, Nimrod came to the Desert yesterday; he came to our house. He asked me lots of questions about lost children, as if I weren't fearful of making reckless judgments. Anyway, he questioned me a great deal, about this and that, my travels, about Sylacea, where I lived for some time, about two charming children that I had there..." The peasant looked at Chemnis tenderly. "Then, he seemed content; he slapped his forehead with his hand, saying: 'That's it...I have them.' Then he went to the carriage-driver Silene and said: 'Take me to the city.' And he left."

Chemnis was still listening to Ypsoer, with all the more attention because she was expecting some news that would interest her—but there was none; there was nothing except Nimrod's clandestine journey, which she did not understand.

She waited with even more anxiety, therefore, for the return of Atlas, who had promised that he would not be away for long.

After leaving the Valley of the Desert, Nimrod had indeed, as he had told the peasant, gone directly to the city, but not to Lord Speos' house. He headed for a poor house in the poorest quarter of Lutecia, into which he entered as if he were familiar with it.

He went up at the first floor, opened a door very discreetly, which he closed in the same fashion, and carefully drew the curtains over the window, in such a fashion as to hide the light of a little lamp that was burning on the mantelpiece. It was dark.

"It's me, Mother," he said to an old woman who had stood up abruptly when he came in but was standing there open-mouthed, her neck taut, holding her breath, at the sight of her son's mysterious expression. She kept her eyes fixed on him, and her heart beat with all the anguish of anxiety, in expectation of what Nimrod was going to tell her.

"Sit down, Mother," he said, finally "and let's talk."

The old woman was, in fact, Nimrod's mother.

Nimrod, as we already know, was a lost child of the great city of the Pah-ri-ziz. Hazard, his skill, undoubtedly, and his boldness, most of all—which never failed in his conceptions—had made him what we see. Needless to say, however, that had not been without intimate conflicts, sometimes without remorse, always without regrets and without hatred—especially without hatred, for, more fortunate than others of his caste, he knew where he came from. His father was a member of the high aristocracy, rich and powerful, but his mother was only a humble daughter of the proletariat.

Neglectful, like all of those who only think of the pleasures of the moment, his father had abandoned him completely at the same time as he had abandoned his mother.

The young mother, for her part, was not neglectful; she never forgot; no more did her son.

Hence the horrible struggle that we have seen him maintain with so much obstinacy, which many people, obviously, would condemn, but which some might perhaps excuse, remembering that if one encountered many lost children like Nimrod in Atlantis, the depravity of mores was probably amended by the threat of the punishment of vengeance. For, we repeat once again, however strange the immorality of the Pah-ri-ziz might seem to us, the social crime for which we are reproaching them at present was so ordinary that it had become entirely commonplace, as a perfectly acceptable accident for people of good social standing.

"I thought you'd abandoned me, Nimrod," said the old woman, caressing her son's hands.

"Is there something you lack, Mother?"

"Oh, no! No...but I haven't seen you for years."

"Years! No—but it's been a long time, I know. But I didn't want to come to see you without bringing you some good news."

"Well?" said the old woman, widening her eyes, which shone with an unusual gleam.

"Well, Mother, it'll soon be finished," said Nimrod.

"Finished! Oh, divine Sylax, so much the better!" cried the old woman, standing up again abruptly. "That's been the dream of my whole life. But tell me, then, Nimrod, how this old woman of the poor people, who had neither money, nor status, nor power, has finally been able to avenge herself on the rich and the powerful? Tell me, son, for, you see, the poorer I am, the more I think that I ought to be rich; and the uglier I become, the more I think that I was once beautiful—and beautiful for one man in particular, who took advantage of my inexperience and good faith with lying promises; and the older I get, the more I think that my youth was not so very long ago, and that *he* alone made me old before my time. Well, speak, Nimrod—what have you done for me? What have you done for yourself, elder son of Speos, Lord Speos…? For you are his elder son, alas."

The old woman had become animated in a frightful manner as she hurled at her son a title he did not bear, although it ought to have belonged to him, and which decorated another. Nimrod did not smile, as he would once have done. He no longer had any energy for evil; evil was no longer anything to him but a profession to fulfill, since the woman who have given him everything asked it of him.

"What I've done, Mother," said Nimrod tranquilly, "is that eighteen years ago, I pricked their heart with a pin, to make them die. And that life, I confess to you, has wearied me, it has exhausted me; I want to enjoy the fruit of my labors at last. I only have two or three more blows to deliver, and then I can retire from business. I have an income—an aristocratic income; we'll be able to live henceforth like noble and powerful lords."

Nonchalantly, Nimrod continued: "It is, moreover, the balance-sheet of my position. The man who bears legally, and to my prejudice, the tile of Lord Speos is virtually ruined. His lawsuit against his old friend Mokie-thi, whom he refuses to recognize, will be settled, because I shall present myself as a witness. His wife will be dishonored in everyone's eyes, because she has a grown-up son whom I shall introduce to the husband and the whole of Lutecian society. For his part, the husband has a grown-up daughter, whom I shall introduce to the wife and all their friends. Lady Speos' son will be rejected by his fiancée; that's in progress; the lord's daughter, will lose her fiancé; that's settled. And thus, thanks to one another, they'll suffer unspeakable tor-

235

ments, which will outweigh those that the late Lord Speos caused Nimrod's mother to endure. Everything is ready, Mother; then, the future is ours!"

The old woman threw herself upon her son, hugged him in her arms and covered him with frantic kisses.

"That's it," she said. "I always knew that we'd get there in the end."

Nimrod opened the door again then, cautiously, and went out the same way. That night, he slept with all the calm of a good angel.

The next day, he went to Atlas with a clear expression. "Well," he said, "how's Speos?"

"He's triumphant. The fake Mo-kie-thi is unmasked; he's in prison."

"Bah! That's impossible. I know that man myself."

"You?"

"Yes, and it's necessary that you save him, Atlas. I've discovered something about him that will interest you greatly. Anyway, he really is the Lord Mo-kie-thi whose son was betrothed in his cradle to Ormudza Nirvana. The son isn't dead, I can assure you. I know where he is." He suddenly changed the subject: "What about Nirvana?"

"He's been promised his liberty; he'll have it, if he doesn't already."

"He must! It's necessary to thwart Speos. Speos is a great villain. Remember that, Atlas."

And he left abruptly, leaving the young man in an astonishment and perplexity that defied description.

XIX. The Day of the Deluge

Mid-November had arrived very quietly when Dr. Plunos retraced for the philosopher Chephren the various twists and turns of the strange story that he had seen in his ecstatic sleep. The evening of their final conversation, the doctor, who did not like going out in bad weather, had almost decided not to keep the appointment. However, as he had promised his friend, and as he was very desirous himself of revealing the exact extent of the virtue of the philosopher's diamonds of democracy, he—the skeptic who believed in virtue but not in virtuous men—took the risk.

Scarcely had he concluded the story of the meeting between Atlas and Nimrod than the philosopher rose to his feet, furious, waving his fist at someone he could not see, crying: "Infamous wretches! The infamous wretches!"

"Permit me to tell you, Philosopher Chephren," the doctor immediately replied, "That you're getting carried away at present, obedient to I don't know what zeal. To build one's fortune on the affairs of others is not an infamy but a skill. These men have been very clever, after all. Do you think that when they came into the world they were charged to pursue the wellbeing of others or their own? Their own, no? That's what they've done. Too bad if they've found obstacles in their passage, which they've broken through. God alone must provide for everyone, and to do that He often disrupts projects whose destruction is very sensible to their authors. What do you expect? It's no longer astonishing to me, Philosopher, that the Pah-ri-ziz have expelled you from their society. There's no means to live happily with that morality."

"Yes, but if my morality leads to wellbeing, to stability, to public prosperity, and if the morality of those men, on the contrary, leads the empire to its decadence, to its ruination... That's where it will lead, Doctor, and if it isn't God who takes care of that punishment, it will be humans themselves. Look around us, and see whether we're on the eve of our destruction."

"That's true, my friend," the doctor replied, this time gravely, "And I assure you that your belief is mine; but I also believe that our morality will be rejected so long as your diamonds are always in honor."

While making these reflections, Dr. Plunos was pacing back and forth in the compartment of the ark where they were, and his eyes often went to the window that looked outside. Night was falling rapidly, and the sky was so completely covered by thick clouds that it was threatening to be very dark.

"Pardon me, my friend," he said to the philosopher, "but I believe the weather's getting worse; I'll come back to see you tomorrow. In any case, I lack the definite information today to relate the end of our story."

"Oh, the weather isn't so bad yet," the philosopher replied, endeavoring to keep his friend with him, "although it's been threatening for several days. I can't let you go without your saying a few more words. What is Atlas doing in Lutecia?"

"Making preparations for his wedding, my friend."
"To Ormudza?"
"To Ormudza."
"And Hyperion?"

"The poor boy is in the Valley of the Desert, where he's dying in order to liberate Nirvana, the father of the woman he loves."

"Poor boy! And Chemnis?"

"She's still waiting for Atlas; she's hoping against all hope. Her own happiness is very dear to her, undoubtedly, but she isn't selfish, and that of Atlas is even dearer to her. If she can't become his wife, she'll nevertheless remain his sister; that's her hope…and then, who knows what the future holds? Who knows, after all, what the unexpected has in store?" The doctor suddenly became fearful. "But *au revoir*, Philosopher. The weather's getting worse. Thunder is rumbling; the storm's about to burst."

"No, not yet," Chephren replied, and added: "What about Nimrod? What is Nimrod doing to finish it, as he puts it?"

"Oh, who knows? I don't know yet. Perhaps I'll know tomorrow, and then I'll tell you, if you don't find out before I do."

"Evil angel!" Chephren exclaimed, meaning Nimrod, and holding on to the doctor's arm as he opened the door to leave. "And Speos? And Ludia?" he added, squeezing the arm tightly as it threatened to escape from his grip.

"Oh, as for them, I don't know what they're doing. I'll know this evening, for I owe them a visit—the husband at least—and I'll do that before going home. Tomorrow morning, I'll write a few words to you, if I don't come to see you at sunrise. But by Sylax, my friend, I beg you—can you hear those thunderclaps? We're going to have a rare storm."

"Perhaps a deluge," said Chephren, smiling.

"Ha ha! Who can tell?"

"Are you afraid?"

"No, since I'm in your ark," the doctor replied, caustically.

"But if we are indeed going to have a frightful tempest, floods and diluvian rainfall, wouldn't you do better to stay with me?"

"Aha! It's you who fears a deluge, Philosopher," the doctor said, turning to look at his friend.

"I don't know whether we're under threat," Chephren replied, seriously, "but if we look around, what do we see? What do we hear? Dull rumbling in the bed on the Sequanian Sea; more rumbling in the heart of the mountains, earthquakes—feeble as yet, but which might intensify; incredible seething in all the waters..."

Oh, all that's commonplace hereabouts."

"To this degree? No." The philosopher continued: "And extraordinary clouds in the sky, storms in preparation that threaten to be devastating. And that comet? That comet, which is visibly growing, taking giant strides toward us with every passing minute, so that if it continues, it will drown us all in the torrents of its tail within a matter of hours! Have not all deluges, as the most ancient histories tell us, as well as the history of our forefathers, commenced like that?"

"You'd frighten a man less skeptical than me, Philosopher," Plunos replied.

"I don't want to frighten you, my friend," Chephren retorted, "but I assure you that those are signs of the end of days for us."

"So I'm in haste to depart," said the doctor, darting a final glance outside. "I want to know the denouement of our story before the deluge arrives." He laughed, and shook his friend's hand. "So, *au revoir*!"

"No—adieu!"

"No, my friend, *au revoir!*"

"And if we don't see one another again?"

"Why? Because of the deluge?" said the doctor, smiling incredulously as he left.

"Who can tell?" said the philosopher, in his turn, going back into his ark, which he closed and made weather-tight with a very particular care.

It was the seventeenth of November.

On the morning of the next day, the eighteenth,[28] the philosopher did not receive a visit from the doctor, but he did get a brief letter send by him. The weather was too poor and offered too much threat of becoming a deluge, he wrote, underlining the last word, to risk going out, even to go to the ark of salvation.

He gave an account of the previous evening's visit to Lord Speos.

He had found Lady Ludia there, forming with her husband the most cheerful depiction of conjugal love. All hint of jealousy had disappeared; the presence of Mo-kie-thi in her room in the middle of the night had been adequately explained, and the nobleman, who loved his wife dearly, was trying to make her forget her exile with the most affectionate caresses.

The doctor had also learned there that Nirvana had been released and his daughter's marriage to Atlas had

---

[28] Author's note: "The celebrated English astronomer Whiston has calculated that the Deluge must have commenced on Friday 18 November in the year 2349 B.C. In order to conform with the opinion of Ussher, which is the best-known, if not the most accurate, I have imported a slight anachronism of one year into Whiston's estimate in making the year 2348." In fact, William Whiston asserted in 1696 that the comet of 1682, the periodicity of which he had calculated at 575 years, had cause the Biblical Deluge in the year 2346 B.C.

been conclusively decided. It was a guarantee of civic loyalty that Lord Nirvana owed the fatherland.

More than once, the philosopher Chephren interrupted his reading of the letter, short as it was, to dart anxious glances at the sky, from which water was pouring in torrents, as if to justify the apprehensions of Dr. Plunos, who was doubtless applauding himself inside his apartment for not having brought the news he had sent to his friend in person.

The news in question was unimportant, as is evident, but there had been considerable developments since the previous day, as events moved rapidly toward a denouement of which the doctor was probably unaware.

Since his release, Nirvana had taken up residence, with his daughter, in the house of his friend Speos, where he would remain until the marriage took place. That day had been fixed for the eighteenth of the month, as Dr. Plunos had written—the very day on which he was writing.

Early that morning, therefore, Atlas rigged himself out like a groom and presented himself at Ormudza's door, as was customary. The young woman was dressed in white, with a virginal crown on her head and tears in her eyes.

The young man stopped short at that sight, his feet glued to the doorstep. He lowered his head; then, taking a little flower from his cloak that he had attached there as a symbol of joy and hope, he dropped it at the young woman's feet.

"You're free, my lady," he said to her, a troubled and unsteady voice. "God forbid that I should want to make you shed tears to ensure my happiness." But he added: "And yet, the great prophet Sylax knows that everything that I have done until now was for you. For you, I became your father's servant; for you, I became a Me-nu-tchean, perhaps harsh and perhaps ferocious. For you, I wanted to become famous; I wanted to place you under and obligation to me in order that I might be generous to you. I know, lady, what you have made of me. What do you want of me? I'm not demanding, I'm begging."

The young woman looked at her father, who took his daughter's hand and placed it in the young man's.

"You're better than I thought, Atlas" Ormudza replied, with a smile mingled with large tears. "Who can tell? Perhaps I'll love you more one day, if the three divine friends will it!"

"Thank you, God!" said Atlas, raising his eyes to the heavens. "Can I ask more for the present?"

But his tongue suddenly froze and his legs became unsteady, while his fiancée, feeling faint, leaned heavily on her father's arm.

They had just seen Hyperion and Chemnis come in, whom no one expected—except for Nimrod, who had summoned them, and who appeared behind them, accompanied by Mo-kie-thi.

That appearance astounded everyone.

"My lords," said Nimrod, in a sarcastic voice, "You've all assembled here to celebrate a family fête. That fête, I wanted to render more complete by inviting those you had forgotten. First, know one thing: the government of the Me-nu-tcheans is over. Another, more progressive and, especially, more moral, was installed last night. It holds in its hands all the necessary force to be obeyed. Now, that government does not leave crimes unpunished, no matter how old they might be.

"It is a crime in our legislation, as you know, my lords, for a young woman to become a mother outside a legal contract; it's a crime to abandon one's children on dolmens in public places; it's a crime to kill or abandon other people's children on the dolmens in order to inherit their patrimonial wealth."

Nimrod's voice became thunderous, while all his listeners remained immobile, trembling under guilty memories. "Well, my lords, Ludia Arimaspes, now Lady Speos, brought into the world at the age of fourteen a son, whose father was Lord Mo-kie-thi; and her husband, Lord Speos has had since his marriage, and outside it, a child, in addition to stealing the wealth of his friend Mo-kie-thi, for which purpose he abandoned the son who had been confided to him.

"Here is Lucia's son." He pointed at Atlas. "This is Speos' child," he added, indicating Chemnis, "And this is the son of Mo-kie-thi." He pointed at Hyperion. "In the name of the law of the new government of the Atlantis of the Pah-ri-ziz," he went on, his ferocious eyes gleaming, "I arrest you all in order to take you before the tribunal by which you will be judged."

At the same time, the open doors and windows allowed the sight of an armed troop guarding all the exits from the house. It was, therefore, evident to everyone that Nimrod was telling the truth in representing himself as a representative of the new government.

When the initial emotion had passed, Atlas could only see one thing to do, above all, which was to defend himself and the threatened life of the family to which Nimrod had just attached him. His first movement, therefore, was to seize with his two Herculean arms the accuser who was standing before him, and hurl him into the street, where he fell into the arms of his satellites.

At the same time, the doors and windows closed as if by magic; everyone grabbed whatever weapon came to hand, and got ready to withstand a siege, no matter how disproportionate it might be.

A frightful clap of thunder rang out at that moment and caused the entire house to shake. It was followed by a continuous roll, which burst from the clouds from instant to instant, with raindrops so dense and so abundant that the daylight was darkened. There were strange noises, sinister whistlings in the tempests, extraordinary shocks, and then screams and moans were heard outside, coming from all directions.

All those frightful signs did not disconcert the besieged individuals, who closed their ears to the threats of the storm in order to hear nothing but Nimrod's threats. No one, however, attacked their fortress. They were astonished by that, but continued prudently to maintain an attentive and vigorous attitude. Then they perceived trickles of water penetrating into the ground-floor rooms on all sides, through the doors, which were not watertight.

Atlas ran up to the second floor in order to investigate. The house was not under siege by the armed force that had threatened it, but he saw, fearfully, that the streets had disappeared under a sheet of water that no longer permitted anything to be distinguished but the houses, which were gradually disappearing. A host of men, women and children, surprised some distance from their homes, were struggling ineffectively against the torrents in search of some shelter, but the habitations were all shut.

Meanwhile, the storm continued its rumblings and its racket, and the water was still rising.

The guests of the Speos house were soon unable to remain on the ground floor any longer. The water suddenly flooded in, breaking through the doors and windows. They went up to the second floor, and then on to the platform, where they found the frail shelter of the tent, which had only been constructed to provide shelter from overly ardent sunlight.

But the water followed them there; it soon threatened to invade the retreat they thought they had found from the inundation. From there they were able to see the cadavers of humans and animals floating all around them, along with infants' cribs, garments, items of furniture, the roofs of houses, and wooden beams ripped out of walls by the waters: debris of every sort, as well as a few unfortunates clinging with the ardor of desperation to fragments of wreckage, appearing and disappearing alternately before finally sinking into the immense gulf.

Nothing more of the anterior life was apparent anywhere, save for the summits of a few tall trees, the tips of his highest hills and the spires of a few public monuments.

The Speos house was one of the tallest in the city; it was apparent a long time after the disappearance of others, but the inundation, which was unceasing, threatened to engulf it imminently in its turn.

There was, however, a moment of hope. Either because some gulf had suddenly opened to carry water away, or some powerful dam had burst in order to let torrents flow away, the water finally stopped rising.

It was just in time, for it was already touching the platform of the Speos house, and everyone was looking at it in terror, calculating with anguish the minutes that they still had to live.

None of them, at that moment, was entertaining any bad memories, any desire for vengeance; was there even any love left in them? There was not only the love of life, but love for one another, forgiveness of the past;

there was an immense pity, which bound them all together. They formed a single group in the middle of the
platform, their arms linked together, in order to struggle,
if there were any means to do so, against the invasion of
the waves, or in order to die without being separated, if
they had to die.

That was a very minimal consolation, but it was
one, for in the union of the unfortunate there is always
the hope of the unexpected.

There was more than that, at that moment, among
Lord Speos' guests. The waters had stopped, they could
see that; that was hope; and the heavens, for their part,
began to smile. The sky became more serene; the rain,
without stopping completely, was falling like gentle
dew. Then, a ray of sunlight, still rather pale but full of
promise, became visible through the clouds.

All eyes turned gladly toward the heavens, thanking
God and praying for the mercy of life.

At that moment, only Mo-kie-thi's face went pale.
He had just seen, as he looked up at the sky, a star that
he feared more than any other, perhaps scientifically,
and perhaps instinctively, too: it was the comet, the pre-
dictive comet long held in Atlantis to precede great misfortunes. All Lutecia had been seeing it for several days,
but without trembling. The philosopher Chephren was
perhaps the only one to have talked about it as a threatening manifestation.

Mo-kie-thi was not a specialist scientist, but he had
some scientific knowledge, and at that moment, in the
critical situation in which he found himself, his science
was full of terror, for it seemed to him that the comet
was heading toward the Earth with an unspeakable rapidity, and that it was about to crash into it.

As if to confirm his fears, the clouds swelled up in the atmosphere at that moment, covering the sun completely, and a strange, indescribable noise was produced in the air. Then a sea of water suddenly collapsed on the city, which it swallowed in its entirety.

The tallest houses had disappeared; the hills and mountains were swallowed up; no vestige of land could any longer be seen; the sea was everywhere.

The comet-induced avalanche had created that sea in an instant: a turbulent and torrential sea. One might have thought that the sky had just opened all its cataracts, and emptied them at a stroke. But a few moments after that frightful fall, which had made the inundation turbulent all the way to its profoundest depths, there was a kind of calm on the surface of the waters.

Then, all the debris that the incredible downpour had driven into the gulf began to reappear again as flotsam: countless cadavers, the few unfortunates who had found a refuge thus far, and those who were disputing their lives with the fury of the waves with a tenacity worthy of a better future.

A little hope returned to the hearts of the castaways at that moment, for they suddenly perceived, afloat amid all the debris and all the cadavers, a vessel—one alone—which the waves were tossing about madly. It sometimes leaned over so far on its side that one might have thought that it was about to plunge into the watery gulf, but it suddenly righted itself, to recommence running the same dangers a moment later.

No one was steering that vessel. There was, however, someone inside it: a benevolent man, a hero of humankind—for, at the risk of causing it to sink, he had attached ropes all around the perimeter of his vessel, in order to serve for the salvation of swimmers, if there were any sufficiently powerful and sufficiently fortunate to grab hold of them.

There were some.

At the moment that the water that had just started licking the feet of the unfortunate group on the Speos house, at the moment when they all recovered a little hope, a sudden idea had flashed through Atlas' mind. With his robust hand, he had seized from amid all the debris within reach beams, uprooted trees and furniture, which he had attached to the platform, transforming it into a raft onto which he had roped, at the moment of greatest danger, Ludia, Ormuzda and Chemnis. The men were clinging to it as best they could.

It was a wisp of straw carrying ants on a stormy sea, but it was still a glimmer of hope, a few moments longer to live…and then, who can tell?

Unfortunately, the frail raft did not hold together for long; it was immediately swallowed up by the diluvian avalanche of the comet, but bobbed up again thereafter.

A few members of the poor family were already lacking; Hyperion had disappeared, and Speos was only hanging on to the branches of a tree with one hand—which lost its grip just as all the other hands reached out to grasp it.

It was at that moment that the ark of the philosopher Chephren appeared to the eyes of the castaways, for the fortunate waves were pushing it toward them. After extraordinary efforts recommended by prudence, and strange alternations of hope and dread, the philosopher was finally able to collect them. It was just in time, for they were dying of emotion and fatigue.

That frightful inundation, the immensity of which put it far above the flooding of a river or the sea, invaded the whole of Europe. It was our Deluge. It was probably the greatest inundation that has remained in the records of history, even though that of Ogyges frightened the memory of Attica and Boetia for a long time, and that of Deucalion, which, like Ogyges' and ours, has the honor of also bearing the title of deluge and is reputed to have completely depopulated Thessaly.

The Deluge lasted more than a month; in the meantime, the waters continued to grow, but with much less intensity in the latter days than the earlier ones. History records, and reason also tells us, that they required several months to decrease and finally to retreat to their respective beds, or to form new ones.

XX. The Day After the Deluge

The ark of the god Chephren was not very far from Lutecia; it stopped on a hill in the vicinity. When he got down from it, the philosopher raised his hands to the heavens to thank God for having inspired the precious idea of his ark. Perhaps he alone had had it, although he was not alone in knowing the information of history and science. But many had doubtless said, like poor Dr. Plunos: "What is done is done; let us live now, and let tomorrow come.

After emerging from the ark, the philosopher set out in search of Lutecia. Lutecia was no more. There was nothing on its soil by rubble, ruins and cadavers partly buried in the mud. A deathly silence reigned everywhere in the city that recently been so animated, so noisy, so tormented by the ardent passions of conspirators, rabble-rousers and revolutionaries, the plots of ambitious men and petty tyrants. Everyone—the great and the small, the rich and the poor—was now, underneath the water or lying in the mud, in the equality of death.

The philosopher wept for his homeland, for his enemies, so cruelly annihilated; he wept for that immense chaos, created by an immense misfortune.

There was no longer anyone alive in the Atlantis of the Pah-ri-ziz at that moment, nor in the whole of Europe, except the guests of Chephren's ark. There was only them to repopulate those vast regions, to reanimate Atlantis, to reconstitute its greatness, its wealth and its glory. They were as numerous, it is true, as those that the tempest had cast up a thousand years before to populate that island the first time, and create everything that had been annihilated.

Chephren knew that; his thoughts were magnified to the same extent. He considered himself in consequence as the savior of the name of the Pah-ri-ziz, as the leader of a creative colony whose mission was to resuscitate a people that had just died, and he prepared for the future by organizing the present seriously.

In the midst of the incredible chaos that the Deluge had made, the ark appeared to be the only habitable place in Lutecia. Everyone made the best of it while they waited for the soil to be cleansed, for the infection produced by the cadavers that were burned and by the stagnation of the waters, some of which disappeared of their own accord and others with assistance from laboring hands, to become harmless.

Families were then formed. The projected marriages of Atlas and Mo-kie-thi finally took place; the saddened Chemis decided to remain the sister of the man she had believed to be her fiancé, until the law of Sylax afflicted her, if the law of Sylax were to be retained. Chephren and Nirvana remained isolated, Nirvana regretting the past bitterly, the philosopher irritated by not seeing the transformations for which he had been preparing so long advance more rapidly.

One day, he renounced them, and on that day he opened the doors of his ark and released all the animals that he had collected into the midst of the fields and the waters. But it was not without a great chagrin that he took that resolution, for all his scientific dreams were broken then, in a single instant: all the illusions he had caressed for such a long time, and all the progress that he had already made; in sum, the fruits of all the works most dear to him.

In consequence, he found thereafter an immense void around him; his life languished, his energy ebbed away, his brightest hopes for the future were extinguished one by one. He was dying of idleness, retreat and ennui.

Every day he wandered on his own in the fields, over the hills, on the seashore and along the banks of a few rivers that the deluge had created. He liked, most of all, to go back to his old abode, on the land that he had sanitized with so much effort, in the heart of which he had formed his projects and seen them grow so promisingly, even though it was not as he had left it.

The deluge had made it into a gracious island by creating a beautiful river whose two parted arms embraced it in its entirety, coming together again at its two extremities and continuing their course into the distance. He called that river the Sequan, in memory of the Sequanian Sea that had almost bathed the walls of Lutecia before the recent inundation, but which had retreated several leagues.

The philosopher spent entire days there, sometimes gazing into the distance to see whether, by any chance, one of the animals that he had looked after for such a long time and then set free would finally offer him a head that he had longed to see, an arm that he had seen in the process of formation, or a leg that he had once seen almost perfected. Then he looked into the depths of the waters, in search of the same images—but he never saw anything but his own, and he sighed.

One morning, however, his heart quivered with pleasure. He arrived on the bank of the river, his eyes searching the distance as usual, when he thought he had perceived something unusual on the other bank: something half-buried in the mud and the reeds—an animate being, for it was moving. His anxiety became extreme; the ardor of his rowing was unparalleled. In a matter of seconds, he was on the other bank.

O prodigy! What he had seen was not a dream or a hallucination; there really was an animate being there: a human being. Not everyone had perished, then, under the waters of the deluge! But yes, he was sure of it; they had all perished, except for the guests of his ark.

The face of the being was beautiful, well-proportioned; hair, abundant but short, ornamented the head; the form was female. He held out his hand; she took it, pulled herself out of the mud and stood up in front of him. Her arms were perfect, except that one of her arms terminated in a flipper; her feet were supple, but the slender toes were linked together in the form of a fan, suggestive of some vestige of the limbs of a marine animal.

A suspicion suddenly passed through the philosopher's mind; he directed his gaze ardently toward the breast of the transformed being, where he recognized a symbol that he had once engraved.

He had succeeded, then! He had finally caused a creature to pass from one species to another; his secret was thus complete.

O Plunos! Plunos!

How he regretted, at that moment, the death of the unfortunate Dr. Plunos. How he regretted the destruction of Lutecia, its academicians, its scientists! He had discovered an immense secret, he had resolved a capital problem, he had found the secret of the creation of humans, and no one would know except for a few people who did not care.

But if it was written that the secret of the creation of humans would be revealed to the philosopher Chephren, it was also written that the secret would die with him.

XXI. The Last of the Pah-ri-ziz

A year after the philosopher Chephren's precious discovery, the whole of the little colony was strolling along the bank of the river Sequan one day. It had already increased by a few members, who were, it is true, only in the cradle. Even the god Chephren was a father twice over, and, grave as he was, he smiled lovingly at a spouse who was doubly dear to him because she was the work of his science.

Atlas, whose eyes were directed upriver, discussing joyfully with Ormuzda how far his gaze extended, suddenly perceived several black dots in the distance that were floating on the waves, soon increasing in such a way as to allow the deduction that they were advancing toward them.

The walkers were somewhat anxious at first; then curiosity gripped them, and then the desire to find themselves in the presence of the beings coming toward the, who were perhaps going to put an end to their isolation—for there was soon no more doubt that they were humans, traveling over the water by means of oars.

They were indeed humans, and humans in considerable numbers, manning boats made of tanned animal hides disposed over simple wickerwork frames, but solidly fitted.

The travelers approached the bank without frightening anyone, for they made no hostile demonstration. They were nearly naked, but around their loins they wore garments of animal hide or fabric, retained by a thong passed over one shoulder like a bandolier. All the visible parts of the body were tattooed with different symbols. Their hair was long and loose, ordinarily thrown backwards. They were armed with arrows and clubs, a few even had swords; each of them wore a long and narrow buckler on the left arm, to protect them in the event of combat.

They were obviously warriors, but in the midst of the warriors there were women and children. There were priests clad in long white robes, wearing crowns of oak-leaves on their heads and carrying bouquets of mistletoe. They called themselves Druids.

The Pah-ri-ziz had before their eyes an emigration of people who were evidently seeking in a corner of the globe where they had not been born a refuge because none was any longer to be found in their birthplace, or because their vagabond temperament prompted them to seek further afield.

Before any man had set foot on land, a druid advanced to the prow of a boat, raised his eyes to the heavens, and then, extending his bouquet of mistletoe toward the ruins of Lutecia, he said in a loud and inspired voice:

"In the name of Ogmius and Hesus, we, the glorious Galls,[29] have come from the extremities of the Orient into the places where our forefathers were, to take possession of their heritage. To you, sovereign Spirit, the first fruits of the blood of this people, whom we have just conquered, and who will be our slaves."

---

[29] Mettais has not forgotten that he had previous given the name Galls to the priests of the Teutchs; although his explanation of the coincidence is a trifle hasty, and certainly does not help to explain how certain key details of the destruction of the Atlantis of the Pah-ri-ziz appear to have reached the book of *Genesis*.

At the same moment, loud inarticulate cries resounded in all the boats. Hu, the great chief of the warriors, who was standing beside the priest, drew his bow, which he aimed toward the bank. That movement, which not all the members of the little colony saw, but which Ormudza observed, frightened the young woman, who threw herself in front of Atlas with one bound, and then fell dead in her husband's arms. A flint-tipped arrow had pierced her heart.

That death was the signal for a horrible carnage, for at that moment the traveling warriors leapt ashore. Atlas, as furious as a wounded lion, hurled himself upon them; he seized a club and massacred everyone that came within range of his blows until, overwhelmed by numbers, he fell, never to rise again.

Less vigorous than him, but as ardent in the attack, his companions fought desperately. But what could they do against that host? They were slaughtered.

The fall of Chephren drove his companion crazy. As impetuous as a tigress, she leapt into a boat that was about to land and made superhuman efforts to overturn it in the waters of the river. Unable to succeed and seized by the men—who, respectful of the blood of a woman, dared not strike her—she hurled herself into the river, dragging several of her enemies with her, and did not reappear.

No one any longer remained on the bank but Ludia and Chemnis, who were mad with terror, and the infants, whom the cruel visitors had not immolated. Of the Pahri-ziz, only the philosopher Chephren was not yet dead. He was lying on the ground. A Druid was by his side, bandaging his wound with a rare sentiment of pity. He had declared him to be his guest; no warrior dared any longer to touch him, for he was not an enemy from then on.

The Druid, who was a scholar, a desirous man, a seeker of the truth, believed that he had found in Chephren a man precious to the studies he was pursuing. It was at his instigation that the Galls had ventured so far. He knew from the traditions admitted by the Gallic tribes that lived on the shores of Asia that his forefathers had founded settlements in Europe. Where, he did not know, but he wanted to know, and he had drawn an entire tribe of his brethren in his wake.

The emigrants had not found in their passage the island of the Teutchs or Sequania, which perhaps might have retained them if the deluge had not carried them away. They had, therefore advanced all the way to the Atlantis of the Pah-ri-ziz, and, an unexpected joy, they had found that the land was fecund in scientific secrets, for which they still had one man to reveal to them.

Thus, the Druid had Chephren taken to his tent. There he gave him all the cares of his art; he lavished on him all the secrets of medical science that only the Druids practiced.

In spite of the sufferings he endured, and in spite of the hatred that he was obliged to bear toward that barbarian horde, he did not refuse to answer his protector's questions. He even appeared to obtain some relief from his troubles in talking about the past. He therefore told him everything he knew about the Atlantis of the Pah-ri-ziz, its modest and unfortunate origin, its successive and glorious growth, its grandeur and its decadence, its virtues and its faults, and then its final revolution, and finally its destruction by the waters of the deluge.

He even told him about the hopes of his philosophy, himself, the marvels of his ark, the happiness for which the little colony of the Pah-ri-ziz had still hoped, in the midst of the terrible catastrophe that had struck their fatherland, when the Galls descended upon them.[30] He was about to tell him about the miracle of the transformation of animal species when an incessant cough took him by surprise, and then fits of vomiting blood, in the midst of which he died.

The Druid was heart-broken; he wept bitterly for the loss of the friend he thought that he had made.

Meanwhile, the victors had drawn lots for Ludia and Chemnis, who were taken to the tents of their new masters, where they pierced their hearts with arrows in order to be free again.

The children remained orphans, but the Galls raised them with care, and they subsequently became the glory and honor of their adoptive fathers, who settled permanently in the Atlantis of the Pah-ri-ziz.

Their new fatherland then took from their name the name of Gallatchd, later to be known as Gaul.

---

[30] The information given to the Druid by Chephren must, in this account, have been the source of the information subsequently recorded by the Roman historian Ammianus Marcellinus regarding the fact that the population of Gaul in Caesar's time was partly indigenous and partly derived from emigrants from distant islands.

SF & FANTASY

Adolphe Alhaiza. *Cybele*

Alphonse Allais. *The Adventures of Captain Cap*

Henri Allorge. *The Great Cataclysm*

Guy d'Armen. *Doc Ardan: The City of Gold and Lepers*

G.-J. Arnaud. *The Ice Company*

Charles Asselineau. *The Double Life*

Henri Austruy. *The Eupantophone; The Olotelepan; The Petitpaon Era*

Cyprien Bérard. *The Vampire Lord Ruthwen*

S. Henry Berthoud. *Martyrs of Science*

Aloysius Bertrand. *Gaspard de la Nuit*

Richard Bessière. *The Gardens of the Apocalypse; The Masters of Silence*

Albert Bleunard. *Ever Smaller*

Félix Bodin. *The Novel of the Future*

Louis Boussenard. *Monsieur Synthesis*

Alphonse Brown. *City of Glass; The Conquest of the Air*

Emile Calvet. *In a Thousand Years*

André Caroff. *The Terror of Madame Atomos; Miss Atomos; The Return of Madame Atomos; The Mistake of Madame Atomos; The Monsters of Madame Atomos; The Revenge of Madame Atomos; The Resurrection of Madame Atomos; The Mark of Madame Atomos; The Spheres of Madame Atomos*

Félicien Champsaur. *The Human Arrow; Ouha, King of the Apes; Pharaoh's Wife*

Didier de Chousy. *Ignis*

Jules Clarétie. *Obsession*

Michel Corday. *The Eternal Flame*

André Couvreur. *The Necessary Evil*; *Caresco, Superman; The Exploits of Professor Tornada* (3 vols.)

Captain Danrit. *Undersea Odyssey*

C. I. Defontenay. *Star (Psi Cassiopeia)*

Charles Derennes. *The People of the Pole*

Georges Dodds (anthologist). *The Missing Link*

Charles Dodeman. *The Silent Bomb*

Harry Dickson. *The Heir of Dracula; Harry Dickson vs. The Spider*

Jules Dornay. *Lord Ruthven Begins*

Alfred Driou. *The Adventures of a Parisian Aeronaut*

Sâr Dubnotal *vs. Jack the Ripper*

Alexandre Dumas. *The Return of Lord Ruthven*

Renée Dunan. *Baal*

J.-C. Dunyach. *The Night Orchid; The Thieves of Silence*

Henri Duvernois. *The Man Who Found Himself*

Achille Eyraud. *Voyage to Venus*

Henri Falk. *The Age of Lead*

Paul Féval. *Anne of the Isles; Knightshade; Revenants; Vampire City; The Vampire Countess; The Wandering Jew's Daughter*

Paul Féval, *fils. Felifax, the Tiger-Man*

Charles de Fieux. *Lamékis*

Louis Forest. *Someone is Stealing Children in Paris*

Arnould Galopin. *Doctor Omega; Doctor Omega and the Shadowmen* (anthology)

Judith Gautier. *Isoline and the Serpent-Flower*

H. Gayar. *The Marvelous Adventures of Serge Myrandhal on Mars*

Léon Gozlan. *The Vampire of the Val-de-Grâce*

G.L. Gick. *Harry Dickson and the Werewolf of Rutherford Grange*

Edmond Haraucourt. *Illusions of Immortality*

Nathalie Henneberg. *The Green Gods*

V. Hugo, P. Foucher & P. Meurice. *The Hunchback of Notre-Dame*

Romain d'Huissier. *Hexagon: Dark Matter*

Jules Janin. *The Magnetized Corpse*

Michel Jeury. *Chronolysis*

Gustave Kahn. *The Tale of Gold and Silence*

Gérard Klein. *The Mote in Time's Eye*

Fernand Kolney. *Love in 5000 Years*

Paul Lacroix. *Danse Macabre*

Louis-Guillaume de La Follie. *The Unpretentious Philosopher*

Jean de La Hire. *Enter the Nyctalope; The Nyctalope on Mars; The Nyctalope vs. Lucifer; The Nyctalope Steps In; Night of the Nyctalope; Return of the Nyctalope; The Fiery Wheel*

Etienne-Léon de Lamothe-Langon. *The Virgin Vampire*

André Laurie. *Spiridon*

Gabriel de Lautrec. *The Vengeance of the Oval Portrait*

Alain le Drimeur. *The Future City*

Georges Le Faure & Henri de Graffigny. *The Extraordinary Adventures of a Russian Scientist Across the Solar System* (2 vols.)

Gustave Le Rouge. *The Mysterious Doctor Cornelius* (3 vols.); *The Vampires of Mars; The Dominion of the World* (w/Gustave Guitton) (4 vols.)

Jules Lermina. *Mysteryville; Panic in Paris; To-Ho and the Gold Destroyers; The Secret of Zippelius*
André Lichtenberger. *The Centaurs; The Children of the Crab*
Jean-Marc & Randy Lofficier. *Edgar Allan Poe on Mars; The Katrina Protocol; Pacifica; Robonocchio; Return of the Nyctalope;* (anthologists) *Tales of the Shadowmen 1-10*
Xavier Mauméjean. *The League of Heroes*
Joseph Méry. *The Tower of Destiny*
Hippolyte Mettais. *The Year 5865*
Louise Michel. *The Human Microbes; The New World*
Tony Moilin. *Paris in the Year 2000*
José Moselli. *Illa's End*
John-Antoine Nau. *Enemy Force*
Marie Nizet. *Captain Vampire*
C. Nodier, A. Beraud & Toussaint-Merle. *Frankenstein*
Henri de Parville. *An Inhabitant of the Planet Mars*
Gaston de Pawlowski. *Journey to the Land of the 4th Dimension*
Georges Pellerin. *The World in 2000 Years*
Ernest Pérochon. *The Frenetic People*
Pierre Pelot. *The Child Who Walked on the Sky*
J. Polidori, C. Nodier, E. Scribe. *Lord Ruthven the Vampire*
P.-A. Ponson du Terrail. *The Vampire and the Devil's Son; The Immortal Woman*
Edgar Quinet. *Ahasuerus; The Enchanter Merlin*
Henri de Régnier. *A Surfeit of Mirrors*
Maurice Renard. *The Blue Peril; Doctor Lerne; The Doctored Man; A Man Among the Microbes; The Master of Light*
Jean Richepin. *The Wing; The Crazy Corner*
Albert Robida. *The Adventures of Saturnin Farandoul; The Clock of the Centuries; Chalet in the Sky; The Electric Life*
J.-H. Rosny Aîné. *Helgvor of the Blue River; The Givreuse Enigma; The Mysterious Force; The Navigators of Space; Vamireh; The World of the Variants; The Young Vampire*
Marcel Rouff. *Journey to the Inverted World*
Han Ryner. *The Superhumans; The Human Ant*
Pierre de Selenes: *An Unknown World*
Angelo de Sorr. *The Vampires of London*
Brian Stableford. *The New Faust at the Tragicomique;The Empire of the Necromancers (The Shadow of Frankenstein; Frankenstein and the Vampire Countess; Frankenstein in London); Sherlock Holmes & The Vampires of Eternity; The Stones of Camelot; The Wayward*

Muse. (anthologist) *News from the Moon; The Germans on Venus; The Supreme Progress; The World Above the World; Nemoville; Investigations of the Future; The Conqueror of Death*
Jacques Spitz. *The Eye of Purgatory*
Kurt Steiner. *Ortog*
Eugène Thébault. *Radio-Terror*
C.-F. Tiphaigne de La Roche. *Amilec*
Louis Ulbach. *Prince Bonifacio*
Théo Varlet. *The Golden Rock. The Xenobiotic Invasion; The Castaways of Eros; Timeslip Troopers* (w/André Blandin); *The Martian Epic* (w/Octave Joncquel)
Paul Vibert. *The Mysterious Fluid*
Villiers de l'Isle-Adam. *The Scaffold; The Vampire Soul*
Philippe Ward. *Artahe*
Philippe Ward & Sylvie Miller. *The Song of Montségur*

MYSTERIES & THRILLERS

M. Allain & P. Souvestre. *The Daughter of Fantômas*
A. Anicet-Bourgeois, Lucien Dabril. *Rocambole*
A. Bernède. *Belphegor*; *Judex* (w/Louis Feuillade); *The Return of Judex* (w/Louis Feuillade); *The Shadow of Judex*
A. Bisson & G. Livet. *Nick Carter vs. Fantômas*
V. Darlay & H. de Gorsse. *Arsène Lupin vs. Sherlock Holmes: The Stage Play*
Séamas Duffy. *Sherlock Holmes in Paris*
Paul Féval. *Gentlemen of the Night; John Devil; The Black Coats ('Salem Street; The Invisible Weapon; The Parisian Jungle; The Companions of the Treasure; Heart of Steel; The Cadet Gang; The Sword-Swallower)*
Emile Gaboriau. *Monsieur Lecoq*
Goron & Emile Gautier. *Spawn of the Penitentiary*
Rick Lai. *Shadows of the Opera: Retribution in Blood; Sisters of the Shadows: The Curse of Cagliostro*
Steve Leadley. *Sherlock Holmes: The Circle of Blood*
Maurice Leblanc. *Arsène Lupin vs. Countess Cagliostro; Arsène Lupin vs. Sherlock Holmes (The Blonde Phantom; The Hollow Needle); The Many Faces of Arsène Lupin*
Gaston Leroux. *Chéri-Bibi; The Phantom of the Opera; Rouletabille & the Mystery of the Yellow Room; Rouletabille at Krupp's*
Richard Marsh. *The Complete Adventures of Judith Lee*

William Patrick Maynard. *The Terror of Fu Manchu; The Destiny of Fu Manchu*
Frank J. Morlock. *Sherlock Holmes: The Grand Horizontals; Sherlock Holmes vs Jack the Ripper*
Jean Petithuguenin. *The Adventures of Ethel King*
Antonin Reschal. *The Adventures of Miss Boston*
P. de Wattyne & Y. Walter. *Sherlock Holmes vs. Fantômas*
David White. *Fantômas in America*
Pierre Yrondy. *The Adventures of Thérèse Arnaud*

SCREENPLAYS

Mike Baron. *The Iron Triangle*
Emma Bull & Will Shetterly. *Nightspeeder; War for the Oaks*
Gerry Conway & Roy Thomas. *Doc Dynamo*
Steve Englehart. *Majorca*
James Hudnall. *The Devastator*
Jean-Marc & Randy Lofficier. *Royal Flush*
J.-M. & R. Lofficier & Marc Agapit. *Despair*
J.-M. & R. Lofficier & Joël Houssin. *City*
Andrew Paquette. *Peripheral Vision*
Robert L. Robinson, Jr. *Judex*
R. Thomas, J. Hendler & L. Sprague de Camp. *Rivers of Time*

NON-FICTION

Stephen R. Bissette. *Blur 1-5. Green Mountain Cinema 1; Teen Angels*
Win Scott Eckert. *Crossovers* (2 vols.)
Jean-Marc & Randy Lofficier. *Shadowmen* (2 vols.)
Randy Lofficier. *Over Here*

ART BOOKS

J.-M. Lofficier & D. Taylor. *Tongue Lash*
Jean-Pierre Normand. *Science Fiction Illustrations*
Raven Okeefe. *Raven's L'il Critters; Rave's Faves*
Randy Lofficier & Raven Okeefe. *If Your Possum Go Daylight...*
Daniele Serra. *Illusions*

HEXAGON COMICS

Franco Frescura & Luciano Bernasconi. *Wampus*
Franco Frescura & Giorgio Trevisan. *CLASH*
L. Bernasconi, J.-M. Lofficier & Juan Roncagliolo. *Phenix*
Claude Legrand, J.-M. Lofficier & L. Bernasconi. *Kabur*
Franco Oneta. *Zembla*
L. Buffolente, Lofficier & J.-J. Dzialowski. *Strangers: Homicron*
Danilo Grossi. *Strangers: Jaydee*
Claude Legrand & Luciano Bernasconi. *Strangers: Starlock*
Thierry Mornet & Juan Roncagliolo. *Guardian of the Republic*
J.-M. Lofficier, M. Garcia, F. Blanco & J. Pima. *Strangers in a Strange Land*

www.ingramcontent.com/pod-product-compliance
Lightning Source LLC
Chambersburg PA
CBHW060345030726
47497CB00003B/603